Wordland 8

TIME WE LEFT

W o r d l a n d 8

TIME WE LEFT

Edited by

Terry Grimwood

theEXAGGERATEDpress

https://exaggeratedpress.weebly.com/

TIME WE LEFT

Edited by Terry Grimwood

ISBN: 978-1-71693-272-4

theEXAGGERATEDpress

http://exaggeratedpress.weebly.com/

ACKNOWLEDGEMENTS

LAIKA | Sarah Doyle
Previously published on *Keats-Shelley Association's* website
It was a runner-up in the 2019 Keats-Shelley Poetry Prize

THE OLD NEIGHBOURHOODS ON MARS | J. J. Steinfeld
Previously published in
Wicked Words Quarterly (UK)
Mars: Poetry and Fiction from the Red Planet (Atlantean Publishing, UK)
Polar Borealis Magazine (Canada)

THE GRIEF ENGINE | Terry Grimwood
Previously published in *Ghost Highways* ed Trevor Denyer (Midnight Street)

PETRICHOR | Mike Adamson
One of the author's *Tales of the Middle Stars*
Silver-level Honourable Mention in the *Writers of the Future* contest 2016

THE LAST TRANSPORT | Frank Coffman
Previously published in
Apex
Abyss

SYMPHONY | Douglas Smith
Previously published in *Prairie Fire Magazine* in 1999.
Second place in *Prairie Fire's* Science Fiction contest to commemorate A. E. van Vogt,
Canada's Aurora Award finalist.

Contents

TALKING ABOUT MY GENERATION STARSHIP

Allen Ashley

It certainly is time we left (this world today) as poor Gaia may not be able to sustain us for much longer. Looking beyond a Moon base, a Martian settlement and maybe an outpost on Titan, we're going to have to head off for the so-called "Goldilocks" planets of any nearby star systems. For the sake of argument, let's say up to twenty to twenty-five lightyears away counts as nearby.

First off, are those planets actually there? NASA and various world scientists have used spectroscopic analysis, and variations in light projection from named suns, to blithely assure us that there is a plethora of worlds out there. Almost every week, MSN carries a story about some "newly discovered" planetary system just awaiting us tourists to travel some trillions of miles to land in paradise on the evidence of a narrow reading of light waves. Well, excuse me while I keep my sense of wonder in check and my feet on terra firma. The thing is: I've seen Mars, Jupiter and Venus in the night sky; I've seen Saturn and its rings through a telescope; and, in the grand old schoolboy joke tradition, I've seen pictures of Uranus. No such wholly convincing, incontrovertible proof of this nature exists for these far-flung gems; we will have to take the scientific contentions on faith.

So, let's allow that there are some Earth-like planets out there with copious water, oxygen, nutrient-rich soil and other necessities. How do we get there?

The easiest route would be to find a wormhole through space-time or to invent a faster than light drive or instantaneous matter transmitter or any other transportation method or portal that would see us reach Aldebaran as easily and swiftly as St Albans. As science fiction writers, we often have a little shorthand catch-all device to get characters to places quickly and not hold up the plot. *Star Trek* uses warp factor and beam me up, beam me down. In my stories, I occasionally slip in references to a "Blink drive". The trouble is: we hear occasional guff about quantum physics and we may be quite concerned about the real purpose of the Large Hadron Collider, but FTL (Faster than Light) travel or matter transmission still seem a very long way off, if you'll excuse the pun.

Which leaves us with the generation starship. The basic premise is that it may take so long to reach a distant star that the arrivistes will be the descendants of those brave souls who set off from Earth in the first place. These contrivances were famously first used as plot locations in Brian Aldiss' *Non-Stop* and Robert Heinlein's *Universe*. A generation starship also crops up in the *Star Trek* episode *For The World Is Hollow And I Have Seen The Sky*. In all three of these scenarios, there are key characters who believe that what they see and experience is their world; they don't realise they are actually living inside a giant, human-created metal starship.

That's just one of the psychological and emotional issues these brave homo sapiens dandelion seeds might face. Another is what might be termed "Mutiny on the Space Bounty". A rebellion, a change of course or reconfiguration of the mission, a civil war on board the "New Discovery". Crimes. Murder. Hoarding of supplies. Termination of any occupants journeying in deep freeze. A refusal by one generation to hand over the reins to the next generation; or a refusal by the younger generation to take on the task, the burden being passed to them.

Sarah Doyle has a tale about going to a riverboat disco. All fine for the first hour or two but when your boat is not going to dock until midnight or later, the sense of imprisonment becomes palpable. Let me off. Please. Now imagine that experience magnified many-fold. You've got no choice but to spend the next ten, twenty, fifty years… the rest of your life with these twerps.

Just to underline: Sarah and I did a seven-day cruise a few years ago. Some of the people we got on well with; others we were happy to wave goodbye to at the end of the holiday. No such option on a starship. Or just think: you are stuck on a works outing or training day with your colleagues forever.

Of course, there's always the deep sleep option. But that brings its own problems. Apart from the fact that we haven't yet perfected viable suspended animation, there's the issue of muscle atrophy in space. Very much a case of if you don't use it, you'll lose it. All those videos of Major Tim Peake and his pals on the International Space Station doing daily workouts so that they don't simply waste away. Tough to do press-ups, sit-ups, cycling or hard jogs when you're fast asleep.

I've given some thought to the question of fuel. This may not be the biggest stumbling block. Let's say you set off from the Moon or an orbiting station: the thrust needed to achieve escape velocity shouldn't be that onerous. And once you're on your way, you should be able to keep going, barring bashes with asteroids, as there is no air resistance to stifle your progress. It's the empty void of space, after all. You will need to keep some propellant in the tank to slow down and stop once you reach Arcturus.

This is all assuming, of course, that the metals comprising the ship's hull are strong enough to withstand speeds of several thousand miles an hour, moving up to maybe a quarter or half that of light speed. I'm reminded of something that is attributed to 1960s astronaut John Glenn. I'm paraphrasing but he remarked that there he was orbiting Earth in this tiny Gemini capsule in the knowledge that every single component that got him there and that was keeping him alive had been made by companies who pitched in with the lowest bid.

Will cost-cutting and efficiency savings and our outsourcing culture scupper our brave star children on their voyage to truly new worlds?

But there's another uncomfortable issue that our crew and passengers will have to face, which is that everything they need to eat or drink will have to already be on board when they set off. You might hear some talk of hydroponics and growing your own food as you wend your way to Proxima Centauri. With rapidly diminishing and disappearing sunlight?

No, the key word is: recycle. And recycle again and again. In a human-sized model of how some physicists believe the universe works at a molecular level – that all energy is conserved, that nothing is ever wasted or exhausted – every urination, every defecation will have to be treated and reused in some manner so that our explorers can eat and drink during the voyage. And if somebody snuffs it – likely to happen on such a long trip – they will have to go in the compost bin because every molecule counts. There's a common scientific aphorism that we are drinking the same water as the dinosaurs did, that every glass we imbibe has been drunk eight times previously. But the distance between us and the dinosaurs means we can compartmentalise and not think too deeply about it: I'm drinking Buxton mineral water not Brachiosaurus wee-wee. On board the starship, though, there's no getting away from where your H2O has been before and where it will end up next.

The same with the air that you breathe, too. Sting was obviously quite prescient in singing, "Every breath you take."

On the other hand, we might get all Green and New Eden project about this and see our starship as a model for sustainability. It's certainly the case that if you haven't got it on board at the time you set off, you really will have to do without it for the duration of the voyage. No Jupiter Gap Motorway Service Station available to call in at and restock on grub, booze, bedding, etc.

Something else occurred to me as a potential concern and it is about the calibre of the occupants of the New Discovery starship. Not just the range of skills that might be needed across the crew or amongst any cryogenically frozen future landing party. Firstly, this will not be an equal opportunities or quota mission. Disabilities or "challenged" states or congenital conditions and inheritable ailments will rule you out of the astral touchdown team. I'm not going to argue the rights and wrongs of this. It's likely that a lot of people who aren't quite up to it physically / mentally / psychologically / emotionally will be quietly weeded out during the regular astronaut training. I'm OK with that – I've no desire to sit in that pod that whizzes round with nausea and dizziness inducing centrifugal speed. But what I really wanted to say is this: the early astronauts were all military and air force guys. Trained. Tough already. It made sense – watch *The Right Stuff* and see Chuck Jaeger pushing at the limits of speed through the stratosphere as a precursor to the Mercury and Gemini missions. But let's consider: who would be the cohort for a proper generation starship? One that sets off into space with the knowledge that all the original occupants will die long before landfall, that it will be their great-grandchildren or further down the line who will live to be the first human settlers… if all goes well. What kind of person signs up for a trip during which you know for certain that you are going to die? Nutters. Martyrs. Over-inflated, self-sacrificial do-gooders. Those who hope to be remembered and later worshipped as some sort of demi-god…? We are on this voyage to Arcturus and we follow the law of our first Captain Calvert for that is how it has always been and always shall be…

And I haven't even mentioned the possibility that we will get there and find indigenous species or even hominids already with their feet firmly planted on our dream orbs. Meaning the colonists from Earth will convey more than one meaning of the word…

So, given the rich possibilities of this theme – the voyage to a destination perhaps many centuries hence with the likelihood of all sorts of social and societal problems being played out on the passenger deck, it's perhaps surprising that there isn't more generational starship literature cluttering up the straining SF shelves. Maybe you'll be inspired now to write some.

Time We Left (This World Today) appears as a key track on Hawkwind's album *Space Ritual* – although I prefer the version on the precursor album *Doremi Fasol Latido*. The concept of Hawkwind's *Space Ritual* was the thoughts, dreams and experiences of a group of astronauts heading off on a lengthy voyage through deep space. Or maybe it was just an extended aural LSD trip by a bunch of Notting Hill stoners.

Choose your fellow pioneers carefully. Hold tight, the countdown has begun.

LAIKA

Sarah Doyle

Moscow street-mutt, unloved
stray. Eleven pounds of bone,
of pelt, of tail. Who can weigh
the heart of dog? What dials
or instruments may measure
loyalty; the desire, hard-wired,
to obey? Dogs have no gods,
know only to worship the hand
that feeds. There is no canine
word for *pray*. Brave little
cosmonaut, faithful to a fault;
caught and collared, Earth no
more than a distant ball with
which you cannot play. How
the words that sent you on
your way crackle through
the ragged dishes of your ears,
a comet's tail of breaking
syllables that even now leave
their trail: *Laika, in. Laika, lay.*
Good girl, Laika. Wait. Stay.

Note

Laika: 1957 Soviet space dog, one of the first animals in space and the first to orbit Earth, she died from overheating. Laika's craft, *Sputnik 2*, and her remains, disintegrated on re-entering Earth's atmosphere.

YOU CAN TELL IT'S REAL BECAUSE IT LOOKS SO FAKE

Sophie Essex

After Elon Musk on CBS News 6th February 2018

I had this image
    the most exciting thing I've ever seen

literally ! 300 miles an hour

incredible
spectacular   pretty fun

    ROCKET
    EPIC
    SURREAL
    IMAGERY
    SURREAL
    TESLA

I'm tripping balls here

    basically   a thousand things

imagine: faith architecture codename

    basically   I'll try

basically impossible
basically CGI

    amazing

consider   expendability

no atmospheric occlusion

a normal car
cruising ridiculous

literally, the absurdity of that

look closely tiny spaceman
crazy things can come true

I didn't think this would work

honestly,
I didn't think

SPACE OPERA

David Rix

This one is for Quentin and Jasmin.

Many years ago, through an oblique process, Quentin seeded the beach in my head. And Jasmin always liked the name Ola!

WATER MIRROR

It was when the wave machine broke down that the dream was complete. Then the pool lay as smooth as a polished crystal – a surface so pure that she could see a whole universe of stars in there. Not flat though. It had taken a while to get used to a water body in which the surface curved gently upwards away from her, but now it just added to the dreamlike feeling of the scene. The calmest lake in history, the calmest swimming pool in the small hours, the miraculous curved mirror of a telescope … the comparisons came and went as she leaned in wonder over the balcony, staring down into the vast main hall of the InterSpace Hotel.

Down was to stare outwards, yet left was also down. Inwards was upwards, yet right was as upwards-looking as you could ever be. Everything about this place was as a dream. Overhead, a vaulted metal ceiling built like a spinal column and ribcage, yet thinner and wispier than anything on earth – hiding the rest of the station. Below her, the lounge and the pool – the pool mostly clear-bottomed and below that, nothing. Dive down to stare out at a horizon of turning stars. On either side of the hall, vast windows several storeys high – and outside, more nothing. Right, above, was the void. Left, below, a vast blue circle marked with the familiar shapes of the continents and coastlines. A bloated Europe disappearing over the horizon and out of sight. The view spun with disturbing speed as this place spun – inputting an energy that her body denied. She was the turning wheel yet the only forces she could feel pointed entirely elsewhere.

This was a low orbit, but she was still a long way from home – if indeed home it was. And, extraordinary though the view was, for her, it came with a sense of bleakness. Terror.

The strangest part was that the disk didn't look any different now. It was still blue – and brown – and green. It wasn't black. It wasn't a scorched wasteland. Occasionally, if she looked very, very carefully, something would intrude. Some disruption of the regular precision of the city streets. Something like a smudge or scuff-mark. The only visual hint of something wrong in what was now an utterly silent world.

*

After a while, she turned away, breaking eye-contact with the dream below, beyond, outside. She snapped her laptop shut with a sigh – there was little point to writing now save for scribbled journal entries that, who knows, might never be seen by another human eye.

A staircase took her down through two storeys of similar rooms and out into the main hall, the pool climbing away from her like a gleaming wave. She was pretty sure by this time that the entire vast orbiting complex was deserted and had been since all but one of the escape pods had vanished about a week ago, leaving her behind. Maybe the staff and scientists had landed safely below, but in the more dreamlike places of her mind, she found herself starting to wonder whether there were any other humans left in the universe. And if not, maybe this space hotel was a good place to be. A tomb with a view for the last living watcher of a now dead species.

She passed the silent bar – a short but varied row of drinks, not in heavy bottles but in foil pouches installed in dispensers that did their best to preserve a certain sophistication. She passed the restaurant, all faux-leather chairs and gleaming tables. Then an open space filled with loungers. All seemingly luxurious yet tacky and paradoxically feeling of low value. There was a subversion becoming apparent in all this – a basic contradiction. Maybe light-weight could never feel truly luxurious, yet light-weight was all you could get up here. Heavy wood or metal could almost wear dirt and age with pride, but the wispy feathers of plastic, sheet aluminium or foil were instantly negated by it. And one of the great constants of life was that there was always dirt.

And then she ran down the last few steps onto the beach – soft sand beneath her feet, it, too, a strange mid-point between luxurious and dirty. It was smooth – every so often in the 24-hour cycle, the little sand bots would be trundling around, ordering and cleaning, sifting and levelling. With no tides here to wash it, however, it still gave that feeling of being contaminated. Dusty. A speckling of alien colours among the sand grains – tiny fragments of rubbish beyond the ability of the cleaners to catch and leaving a slight oily-sticky feeling on her skin.

She ignored that though and broke into a run for the last few yards down to the water's edge. Close-up, it only looked more unreal. Water shouldn't curve. That was one of the great fundamentals of life, even now. She changed direction and sprinted along the very edge, her feet alternately kicking up splashes and sand. For all the dramatic size of this hall, it was still quite compact in design and a few yards took her to the edge where the beach was framed and built up with a cascade of faux-rocks that echoed slightly underfoot. A half-hidden staircase was built into them and she continued up it to where a diving board leaned out over deeper water and quickly dragged off her clothes. This was water where the sand phased out into the clear floor and an abyss of stars opened up. Below, beyond. Horizon. To her left, down, a vast expanse of blue like a wall peppered with clouds. It never failed to make her skin thrill to stand here and, with a few short paces and a jump, to dive into the sky.

There was a crash as though she had fallen through glass. A massive fracture that exploded the entire surface into shards. The impact on her body felt as violent as glass as well, but after a few confused moments, surfacing with a shrill breath, she realised that this was because of the chill. It was several degrees colder than she expected. The heating must be down as well. She allowed herself a moment of unease. If anything in this place was starting to break down, that could be very bad indeed.

It was not so cold as to be unpleasant, however, and she lay there floating on her back, getting used to it, watching the swinging darkness of space, the disk of the earth … letting time pass. There was something delicious about that, at least. Time – it had changed fundamentally in the last week.

And then the sun returned. It came and went quickly here as everything spun, but this time it found the edge of the great wall of windows at just the right moment. The glass here, if glass it was, protected her from much of the glare but it was still a blaze of glory. The rays shot across the room, hit the curved water surface and blazed, flashes and ripples of light on every surface. They played over the metal ribs and spine overhead, they danced on the clear floor below her, painting the Earth's horizon with a hot aurora.

At that point, staring up, down and then out at the old planet again, she was overwhelmed by a longing for wind on her skin – the cool movement of air. This mirror in which she was swimming was extraordinary but until now, she had never realised just how oppressive total calm could be.

Blog – Ghost Hotel

Day 16

I should have been home from this orbiting fun palace by now if everything had gone normally. The shuttle never arrived to collect me, of course, but nothing I can do about that. I am quite happy really – or so I tell myself. All my life, a part of me pined for isolation. For freedom from watching eyes, even as I stood up on stage before an ocean of them. Even as I drank them into me, let them eye-fuck me and feeling the euphoria flow through me as I sang. I sometimes retreated into electronic albums but was always drawn back to the stage eventually – as one might retreat from sex because of your own fear, only to be drawn back again by the sheer imperative. But now – what? Now I am not sure if there is anybody left in the world, let alone up here. The silence is terrifying. And quests for isolation always seem to prove delusional eventually – when you find it. What is isolation without the fantasy of someone to cut through it?

This hotel has always been a ghost house. The shuttle brought me up here alone, entirely automated. I was strapped into my seat as though for surgery or kinky sex – sat there as the vehicle shook, as g-forces blasted me. "Yes, I'm fine," I said through the video link, trying to smile up at the various cameras watching me, recording me. At least five of them – oh the price of fame. "Yes – absolutely fine," as I felt the disorienting gravity of space – as the shuttle docked with a muted bump – as the door opened to the welcoming yet grave greeting of … our friend dressed in a bottle-green waistcoat and trim black trousers. I sat sprawled in my seat for several seconds, just staring at him and blinking, feeling my hair floating in the air around me, making my scalp tingle and sending goosebumps all over my body.

But our friend is long gone of course – buggered off and left me here, as far as I can tell. Now I am cooking my own food and the hotel is stark. Empty. Silent.

I learned that silence can oh so easily get more silent. Isolation oh so easily more isolated.

And at night I am dreaming far too many dreams …

DANCE

Being completely alone came with a delirious sense of freedom. Freedom from a constant background pressure. Instructions. Notices. Orders. Commitments. Necessities. Even people staring. Judging. Thinking about you. It wasn't until that, like a champagne bottle shaken for decades, had finally been released that she fully realised what it meant. And now, she didn't walk the corridors, she danced along them, yelling aloud, speaking the first things on her tongue. She could run around naked or covered with paint. She could laugh and cry, break things and make things. In that sense at least, it was beautiful.

The corridor curved upwards but without any slope, following the circle of the space station. Even with cargo in hand – a large industrial fan and a bulging backpack – she could still dance here with greater strides than anything back on earth. She had never figured out the scientific details of how this artificial gravity worked, beyond the basics that the whole wheel-like structure spun around its central hub, leading to an outward pressure that felt a little like downward. Artificial gravity was a comfortable-sounding term – it suggested that everything would feel more or less normal. However, during the basic training, they had warned her about how alien the forces acting on her body would actually be – and they had been right. The first few days had mostly been spent lying in bed wishing for oblivion with every new dry heave. Even the slightest movement would induce waves of dizziness and disorientation, and an act as simple as standing up or bending over would be enough to drop her into a curled whimpering heap on the floor. Her body weight seemed to change in different ways depending on the direction she was walking or where she happened to be. Movement always came with the feeling of strange forces trying to sweep her into the air or drop her to her knees. The closest comparison she could find to it was walking in a smoothly accelerating or decelerating train, with no outside references that made sense – but even that barely came close. The problem was that the scale of even this substantial space hotel and science station was so small that the artificial gravity would change significantly in the distance between her head and her feet, something humans definitely hadn't evolved to deal with. Which effectively meant that even a quick reach downward would be equivalent to lurching miles on earth.

No wonder this place didn't see many visitors. You needed to be both impossibly rich and very tough or determined to take it in your stride.

She had eventually found her feet though, like the legendary sea legs back down on earth. The strangeness of it never went away, but her body's ability to cope improved. And now she found herself quite enjoying it, at least most of the time. It was like living in a permanent dream. And now, several storeys away from the edge, her weight had dropped and the direction of her dance was making her lighter still. At the centre of this thing, in the complex science facility, weight dropped to zero. She remembered it vaguely from arrival. One day, she would have to find that place again.

"As we gather to commend our brothers … sisters … whatever … to the gods and to commit their bodies to the elements," she chanted, a slightly hysterical smile on her lips, "to the wind and water, but first to the fire. And last to the earth. Let us express in song and prayer our common faith in … in the end of all things. The death of all glories … nothing in nothing … blank on blank … kapow!"

Around here, the sparse glitz and glamour of the hotel had given way to something more like a new but badly maintained tube station back home in London. A world of metal – cramped, dusty, grimy and heavy. This was not the place for paying guests – this part of the building had been created for staff and scientists – the machinery and computers that controlled the resort and its accompanying science work. This was a place of mystery, yet she still felt more at home here than further towards the outside.

She reached a hatch and climbed down to the next level – or, more accurately, climbed outwards, and even this small change ended her dance simply because her rucksack and the industrial fan she had found were feeling so much heavier. She hung onto a handrail for a moment, her head swimming again, eyes screwed tightly shut. A cold sweat on her skin. Sometimes, it was so hard to be active around here.

One thing she had learned early on was not to overestimate what she could carry. Just because she could lift it here did not mean she could still lift it when she got it closer to the outside of the craft. More than one odd item of furniture or equipment had been left abandoned in one of the corridors simply because dragging it the final distance had proved too much.

She opened her eyes again and continued, pacing down the corridor, fan bumping lightly behind her. Get used to it, she thought. Who knows. Maybe this will be your 'ground' for the rest of your life.

"Our true home is in heaven," she sang, half under her breath, though with a considerably slower rhythm now. "Among the stars. And here I am. You put me up here … but nobody is coming from heaven to save us. Never was. Never will. And the stars burn cold …"

By the time she stumbled into her room, she was towing the rucksack along the ground and she dumped it on the floor with a grunt of relief. The large fan joined it and she plugged it in and switched on. It was almost three feet across and it blew a mini-hurricane, scattering any loose papers around. But the feel of the wind against her skin again after so many days of stasis was pure bliss and she crashed on the bed, breathing heavily and letting it ripple her clothes.

She still thought of this as 'her' room, though no doubt she could have any room she liked now, even one of the really swanky ones. Who was going to tell her otherwise in a deserted hotel in a deserted space station orbiting a seemingly deserted planet? She was used to this place though. She had already made her mark on it a bit and felt no impetus to move. This room had felt like a thing of wonder at first – such luxury and softness. The whole put together with a clean modern simplicity – gentle hanging fabrics, carved wood, metal, a soft carpet on the floor that her bare feet loved, and a gigantic double bed with a mattress that cradled her like a cloud. There was also a huge mirror on the wall behind the bed that wouldn't have fitted into a single one of the rooms she lived in back home. How they had got all this up here, she had no idea, but no doubt it wasn't as solid as it looked. These fittings would have opened up like an umbrella or unrolled or something, as everything here did.

The wonder hadn't lasted, though. Soon enough, the room and the whole hotel had started to feel a little sickly. A little inhuman. It was luxurious, but there was nothing here. No books. No art. Nothing really human. She had taken some steps to remedy that though. Several cans of emulsion paint had been found and dragged up here – and the pristine walls were now disrupted spectacularly with some huge painted shapes and slogans. Dance yourself to death, one said. Life is not an opera. Is anybody out there? Why am I here? And, of course, her performer's name of Cinnamon Thorns. They were no doubt futile and pointless, but doing something with her hands and disrupting this cloying luxury both felt positive. No doubt she could paint them out again one day and replace them with something more philosophically profound.

If only there had been some spraypaint. Then she would have been in her element. Mentally at least, it would have brought her back to the grungy streets of East London, their brown brickwork and stupefying metal siding coming to life with colours under her hands.

There was a large window by her bed, looking out into blackness – no great disk of earth on this side. She'd initially been disappointed, but now she felt nothing but relief. She didn't want to look down any more than she could help. She didn't want to see the scars – especially the one in the centre of London. Sometimes the sun was visible, sometimes the moon – but she preferred it when they were gone and there was nothing but the endless dusting of stars. She could stare out at them and find a kind of comfort in their sheer otherness and distance. They had always called to people – reminding those that wanted to listen that there were larger things – unimaginably larger things – than anything human beings did to themselves. And now they spoke of a universe where the seeming vanishing of humanity barely even mattered.

In the hub, there were escape pods that would take her back down – one at least remaining. The training and safety notices had explained it all in great detail. But right now, there seemed no impetus to use them. With no idea what she would find back home, this station was starting to feel the safest place in the whole universe. Even if she was alone.

And again, Cinnamon smiled to herself as she lay in bed, the fan-wind fluttering her clothes.

Blog 2 - Opera

Day 14

… I think it was. Nothing is in order

So, InterSpace Corporation, you who organised all this, you who thought I might achieve something for you in these End Times ... I guess my contract is in ruins now. I was always going to be as subversive as I possibly could. I'd have done the advertising you wanted me to do, but definitely on my own terms. Now I can't publish anything even if I wanted to and all I can do is blather.

Internet connection cannot be established.

I sometimes wish I could have been an opera singer, instead of whatever the hell I was – one who wandered off into the wilderness and left post-punk behind after it became populated by idiots. I suppose the two are not so different if you can look beyond, well ... almost everything. Modern opera sometimes has the sharpness of needles – an angry rebellious political rage as strong as any punk lyrics. And yet, as long as I have been performing, I have felt a sense of the transitory in the act – as the feeling grew in the world that we as a species had doomed ourselves. That the chaos and self-destruction were basically inescapable.

Performing in the moment thus became the most profound thing of all and long-breathed development, vast art forms, careers etc. started to seem false. What's the point of any of those in a world that is going downwards, not upwards? So yes, I sang for my friends, for my fans, for the counterculture crowds, as though every concert was my last. You can't do opera like that. At least ... I don't think so.

But anyway, now, up here, I am only left feeling the futility of art even more. Sooner or later, everything we do is surrounded by a great void. You emerge within it, maybe as a small glowing spark, then you fade away again. The storms of humanity and the vastness of the universe both conspiring to drown out our small magics. The great substrate to all that we do is the power and horror of what people are capable of as a mass of frightened, confused entities desperately embracing darkness because the light blinds them, while simultaneously rejecting the earth for dreamland. Me sitting up here alone barely seems to have changed anything. This space hotel is no different to standing on stage in east London before a thousand eyes. My last blog post was wrong. I was as isolated then as I am now. Being eye-fucked is no different at heart to being fucked by a void.

So thank you InterSpace, for spending millions on moving me a few miles and changing almost nothing.

Still – nice to have the vacuum of space between me and Earth for a bit, I'll say that. I don't miss it very much.

OLA

"Hello?" she tried. "Ground control … or whatever the fuck you are called? This is the InterSpace Hotel. Is anybody there? Do you hear me?"

As always, silence.

She sighed, her hand shaking slightly. "Fuck it." A pause. "There must be someone still alive," she said. "I know the internet is dead but this link seems to be working. Is anyone else listening in? What are you doing down there? You take the opportunity to destroy everything that the bombs didn't?"

Still silence. Always silence. What that meant, she wasn't sure. This was the small communications office – better than her laptop or the control panel in her room but still quite limited. She had a vague memory that the internet and phone operated by remotely controlling computers in the InterSpace ground control through a satellite link rather than any kind of direct connection. There must be more than that here, however. Somewhere there was a much more sophisticated communications centre, but until she could figure out where it was and how to make it work, this was all she had.

"Ah well. Just to let you know that I'm still here … for however long the supplies last. Or until something breaks down. And I guess that's fine. Maybe when I can no longer go on living I'll just bust a hole in the side – then space will freeze-dry me. And who knows – a few centuries down the line, if anyone ever comes up here again … they'll find me, a wizened piece of girl-jerky. And … I guess that's fine. You really fucked up this time, humanity. And if anyone down there is still alive and hearing this, then all I can say is I hope you die."

That last word came out a bit louder than she intended and she froze in silence for a moment, staring at the computer screen. Then she closed the program with a grunt and took off the headphones.

"Hi," the voice said from the doorway.

No reaction seemed too extreme in this place and under these circumstances. Cinnamon shrieked aloud, threw the headphones across the room, punched the communications desk and shrank back in her chair with a bump. Then she burst out laughing, her face going red with embarrassment.

This new figure was a small woman dressed in utilitarian clothes, with a round face, her hair tied back severely. "Are you okay?" she asked, raising her eyebrows – her accent quietly American with a certain touch of the northwest about it. She didn't look particularly disturbed or surprised.

"I thought I was alone," Cinnamon managed after a moment. "Sorry … I …"

She dug her nails into her face, struggling to make the necessary mental adjustments. This person's somewhat scruffy clothes told her that she definitely wasn't hotel staff.

"Almost," the figure said. "I don't think there is anyone else left now. Just you and me. I was thinking I should come and introduce myself. And I need to fix the electrics so …"

"But, but, but … okay … where the fuck were you? I thought the staff had all buggered off without me."

"The science crew left immediately," she said with a touch of crispness in her voice. "Mandated procedure. In the event of a total communications shut-down, you put the labs to sleep and evacuate. The chef guy went too – maybe a bit premature but it was all very confused. As for the rest of the staff … I'm it."

She hesitated. "You are … it?"

"Yes – I am the keeper of eyes," she said with a thin smile.

"Wha?"

"The one who keeps an eye on things. Fixes stuff. Sorts out anything that only a human can sort out … but you seemed to be doing just fine." There was a glimmer of amusement in her face at that. "Everything around here is so automated that I am all they need to run this fun palace most of the time." She patted the laptop bag hanging round her shoulder. "My name is Ola by the way."

"Aha. Well … hi."

"I should know your name, but I've forgotten."

"I'm Cinnamon."

"Um … Cin…?"

"Yeah, yeah, as in the spice. Exactly as in the spice. Don't ask."

Cinnamon thought back, trying to remember who she had seen since coming up here. Ola's face seemed entirely unfamiliar, however. All she could call to mind was the young man who had met her on arrival. The 'chef' Ola had mentioned? Hovering in the background of her life, bringing food when food was ordered or occasionally performing a few small acts of stewardship. She'd tried to keep him at a distance, embarrassed at the attention and politeness, but when he vanished, it was as though a vast door had slammed shut.

"Why didn't someone come and find me?" she asked, her voice dull. "You're telling me he just ran off and left me to it in low earth orbit? With no fucking communications?"

Her voice was rising a little – partly, she knew, fuelled by relief. She could feel a tremble taking root throughout her body – a threat of tears that she fought down hard.

"They left me too," Ola said. "They never cared about the lowly technician either. All a bit confused. To lose communications to that extent is entirely unprecedented."

"We – have an escape pod though … right?"

"We do. One. Which is just a little bit lacking in redundancy for my taste, but what can you do?"

"Fuck," Cinnamon muttered under her breath. "Ok, so what about you? Where have you been? I've been going half out of my mind trying to work out what the fuck's going on, trying and trying to get through to someone … anyone."

Ola just stared at her, an oddly cool expression on her face.

"I mean … you knew I was here, right?" Cinnamon demanded after a moment.

"I did. Your visit was scheduled, of course. And there are enough cameras on this thing."

"Oh," she mumbled. "You were watching me?"

"It's kind of my job."

"Yeah but …"

Memories of a bit of naked swimming and wilder stuff was in her mind. Cinnamon fought with her rage for a few more moments and forced it down again. There were more important things to worry about. Far more important.

"Ok. Ok. Never mind. But … do you know what happened?"

Ola drew a long long slow breath. “No. Not in any detail.”

“Fuck detail – was it nukes? Did they really …?”

“I would guess so, yes. There were certain signatures detected. The gamma ray detector experienced substantial interference.”

“Gamma ray detector?”

“It’s looking for gamma ray bursts in space and it went wild. You know, the blasts produced as gigantic stars collapse into black holes.”

“Oh …”

“Or maybe as neutron stars collide. We’re still not quite sure.”

“Oh.”

“Ironically, they were first detected by satellites monitoring for covert nuclear tests on earth – and now it was our space detector that provided some spectacular data on a nuclear war. Though there are also some things I don’t understand about it …”

Cinnamon put her hands to her eyes for a moment. “Yeah … nukes. That’s what I … I … also … thought, when everything went silent. And the scars you can see. So they actually went ahead and … they really were that stupid?”

Ola nodded, while Cinnamon stared bleakly at the wall for a long moment. “Kind of hard to know what to say to that,” she muttered at last.

Ola nodded again.

“I guess we … what can we do? Stay put?”

“For now … yes. I think so.” Ola drew a deep breath.

“You think there are still people down there?”

“I find it hard to imagine otherwise,” Ola said, again with that crisp town of voice. “One way or another. But what state they are in … that’s another question.”

“How long can we stay here? How long will … will the supplies last?”

"Maybe two years," she said. "With just the two of us."

Cinnamon felt a hint of relieved surprise. That was much longer that she had expected. A lot could happen in that time.

"It's all nicely self-contained. Lots of water – especially if I shut down the pool. Lots of food. Though some things will go off sooner," she added. "You might have to lower your standard of living a bit over time."

"Huh?" There was a tiny hint of a sneer in Ola's voice, which she registered instantly.

"Well – there's enough food for a while, but you may have to forget some of the wine, champagne and three-course dinners."

Cinnamon stared at her, feeling a wary tension rising within her. "I sense a crack of some kind," she said, "but I am not sure why? You think I care about fucking champagne?"

"No?"

"Where I came from, a salt beef butty or a kebab was a treat," she said sourly.

"Oh? Where do you come from?"

"East London," she said. "Deepest, darkest Tower Hamlets. Heard of it?"

"No …"

"You don't remember any lovely politicians banging on about 'no-go areas' in London?"

Ola frowned. "… maybe."

"That's Tower Hamlets. Where the fuck-nuts fear to tread because there are too many poor people or something. Otherwise known as 'where I stroll down the road of an evening for a takeaway'. It was a good place, by and large – and funnily enough …" She spread her arms with a wry grin.

"Ah," Ola murmured. "Then I apologise. I had you down as another of the rich brats who come up and stare down their noses, even as they are puking their guts out."

"Not me, Guv," Cinnamon said, dialling up her accent slightly. "Barely 'ad two pennies to rub together, did I. Come on, you must know how I got here?"

"I know that you won it in a promotion, but …"

"Well, not quite. Didn't they tell you anything? I guess they weren't getting as many visitors as they wanted so they decided to raffle a few holidays to interesting and photogenic creative types …"

She tossed her hair with another mocking grin.

"… so we could do their advertising for them. And I guess I was just famous enough. Cinnamon Thorns ring any bells?"

"No," Ola said with a hint of embarrassment that Cinnamon hadn't seen on her face before.

"No surprise. Experimental Post-Post … Post-Punk … Whatever singer. But yeah – I was supposed to upload a bunch of photos and keep a vlog and blog for the duration. There was going to be a camera team joining us. A documentary, documercial of some kind. I guess all that's scuppered now."

"I see," Ola said. "Cinnamon … Thorns?"

"Yeah. Cinnamon's my real name. Thorns isn't."

"Interesting. And rather – ironic. After all the nonsense, after all that this place represented, it's us two who end up on the ark."

Cinnamon glanced at her, feeling a momentary crawling of the skin at the word. Ark? Crazy visions were buzzing in her mind of two humans stranded in the sky having to repopulate the species like a Garden of Eden scenario. Not that Ola and herself were going to be any use for that. But surely even a nuclear war couldn't empty the world of human life to that extent?

Could it?

She shut her eyes for a moment and swallowed hard, forcing down a blast of emotion. "I just had a jolt of how surreal this is. Us – sitting here – in space – in one of the most expensive objects ever created – talking like this."

Ola smiled again – and now her face looked warmer and more welcoming.

"Is that why you left me alone here?" Cinnamon continued. "Couldn't face namby-pambying some brat of a guest on top of everything else?"

"I'm sorry," Ola said, her smile broadening into something more mischievous. "Maybe. I had … more important things to worry about for a few days. Like going completely mad in the communications room and chewing on the carpet because every single relay station on the planet seemed to have gone offline simultaneously. I'm surprised you didn't hear me swearing."

"Ok – I sympathise. I think."

"Thank you," she said. "But to be honest, I dislike most people. All races, classes, creeds and genders equally. I don't generally like our esteemed guests much … but you might call them first among equals in terms of irritation."

"Oh yeah. How are you with bad-tempered artists?"

"Hate 'em," she said, grinning even broader.

Cinnamon laughed. "Oh we're going to get along just fine." She nodded in silence. Then: "communications room?"

"Oh yes – the main communications centre of the station."

"It's also … down?"

For a moment, Ola's face changed – just a flash of very deep emotion. "Yes. Ground control, the InterSpace headquarters, the relay stations, the reserve control centre, all seem to be … either offline or – or shut down."

"Ok …"

"Yes," Ola said, her face grim. "It was a powerful system, multiple layers of redundancy in case we lost any equipment up here or if anything went wrong on the route to Earth. But we never imagined that we could lose Ground Control. The entire Ground Control in multiple locations around the world."

"There must be something though? We can't be completely cut off, surely?"

"We have radio systems," Ola said slowly.

"And?" Cinnamon cried.

"And … complete silence," Ola said, her voice shaking for a moment. "I have sent many messages to various possible destinations on many, many frequencies. But as yet no meaningful contact. No contact at all in fact. I find it hard to imagine what is going on. You can't just wipe out all the technology on a planet. You can't wipe out all the people either. And yet – silence."

"What the fuck has happened down there?" Cinnamon said in a low voice.

"I must admit," Ola said, "I am mystified. That's why I am still here. Aside from needing to look after you and this fun palace. I didn't want to go back down until I had some idea what I would be going down to. I think the others were a little bit – precipitous. Sometimes you have to throw out the procedures."

There was a silence.

"You know," Cinnamon said eventually, "you may be right."

"About what?"

"I might miss that champagne when it's gone. I need it – I really fucking need it."

Ola snapped into laughter – a fuller laugh than anything she'd produced yet, albeit with a very dark undertone. "Oh, me too," she cried, shaking her head.

More silence, while Cinnamon stared vaguely at the computer screen, then clicked to shut it down. There seemed little point to this machine now.

"You know," she said softly, "it's weird but … I don't really feel sorry right now. I feel … weird. Kind of beyond any of that."

"Yes," Ola muttered. "I think I know what you mean." She bent and picked up the headphones and returned them to their charging station. "Anyway – I came out here to check the electrics. I've been getting error alerts."

"Oh yeah. The pool. Wave machine. Heater." Cinnamon shrugged. "I … really don't care about …"

"Nor do I. But any error could prove a problem under circumstances like this. It's probably an electrical failure but the last thing we need is any kind of domino effect. A short circuit or fire in space is … really, really not good."

"Oh – yeah." Cinnamon frowned, feeling stupid. "I suppose."

"So if you're ok, I will leave you to it and have a look."

"Of course. But now you've found me … don't be a stranger, ok?"

Ola nodded with a tight-lipped smile. "I'll be back, yes. I ... I'm quite glad not to be alone." Her eyebrows flickered again, almost embarrassed. "And if you want to come and help me in the communications room, that would be … good."

"Sure."

"I have been trying to get messages out hour after hour …" Ola shut her eyes for a moment, her entire body clenching.

"Of course. Where is it?"

"Level three, it's signed on the door." She turned away, tiredness radiating. "Maybe we can one day find someone to talk to," she said.

Blog 3 - Politics

Day 19

What happened down there? I mean – it hardly seems surprising. For decades now, we've been feeling the end of the world – by which of course we mean the end of our own particular civilization. The end of our world since other worlds have been ending forever. We've always felt its fragility. And yet, though it lingers in the back of the mind, that feeling of your future evaporating under the influence of forces completely beyond your control and as uncaring as the stars, maybe you can barely process the concept. You intellectually analyse it. You consider that hmm, the chance of things going tits-up within your lifetime is actually a thing. Maybe. The likelihood of you dying of old age or normal sickness is actually going down. Maybe. Whether you lived under the shadow of the Cold War with its absurd forces that could snuff you out of existence without an atom of caring – or under the spectre of climate change and its impending slow destruction – or under the era of rot and madness spear-headed by Trump and others a while back when the always rather fluid concept of truth and reality became completely meaningless – or under the breakups and deteriorations and total insanity of more recent times – either way, you still somehow delude yourself that it's going to be fine. That there's no problem at heart. Intellectually, you know something's coming one way or another. Maybe. Everyone warns you. From the protest movements, to the doomsday clock at the witching hour, to watching the scientists desperately buying land in Greenland, while people fight to the fucking death against any and every effort to fix things.

And yet still you go on living, almost blind, almost on instinct like an amoeba just doing its thing until the droplet of water it lives in evaporates.

And truly, what else can you do? You can yell and scream and fight and protest – and I suppose you should – yet even then can you ever grasp the reality of your own death? Even the fighting is an act of privilege, if I may use that word. It's always too late when you realise the almost brain-melting futility of thousands of years of history. Even this floating fun-palace and all it represents doesn't change that.

I am feeling barely coherent now.

Fuck you, planet Earth. And fuck you, each and every one of you, personally.

STARS

The next day, she found Ola in the main communications room – a small space, cluttered with equipment, with a couple of portholes looking down on the planet below. She was working on something – on all fours with her upper body deep in amongst the wires and technology.

Cinnamon remained there for a moment, watching her, eyeing her arse appreciatively. Her scruffy, stained and torn overalls were sexy, at least right now, but they also came with a touch of fellow feeling. These seemed to be the clothes of a pragmatic person – a fixer and tinkerer. And even though she was an artist, she felt closer to that than to the more cerebral or philosophical headspaces. She also liked to get her hands dirty and she could respect this skilful technician for that, every bit as much as any of the great scientists that had haunted this place, or any number of more abstract creatives and thinkers that had surrounded her back home.

Whatever had become of them now …

Then Ola came reversing out of the narrow space and scrambled up, several wires clenched in her teeth.

"Hey," Cinnamon said with a smile.

"Mmmm …" She spat them out. "Just need to replace an air compressor. The absolute last thing we need is for this lot to get messed up." She waved at the clutter around her.

"No … messages or anything?"

"No. None at all. I still don't understand it. There's no way – no fucking way every radio system on the planet can have been knocked out. And I don't think there is anything wrong up here …"

"Very strange."

"Hang on," Ola said. "Almost done."

She grabbed a device of some kind – presumably the air compressor – and crawled back into the hole. Cinnamon watched her with a smile, then eased herself carefully into a chair, holding onto the arm-rests. The artificial gravity was considerably weaker here and, though there was no danger of floating, there was always this strange feeling as though both she and the room around her were changing shape – drifting gently in a roller-coaster path through dreamland.

"You enjoy this kind of work?" she asked.

"Yeah – always did."

"You certainly look at home there."

"Do I? Like a little rat making her nest out of wires?"

"Maybe."

Or … like a human being, doing what human beings do …

Ola soon came scrambling out again and stood up, shoving a last few cables into her bag. Then she flicked a few switches and watched with a frown as several lights came on – a small cooling fan started up somewhere. She nodded with satisfaction.

"It's safe to say I don't understand one knob of this stuff," Cinnamon said. "Hey – I built my own computers back on earth; I practically lived in recording studios. Just so you don't think I am a complete idiot, but this …"

"This takes years of training. I wouldn't expect you or anyone to. And anyway – much of it seems to be useless now. But, essentially, this is the radio transmitter." She pointed out one rack of equipment above a small desk. "This is what we can use to talk directly to Earth without any faff with satellites."

"Directly with … earth-based radio operators?"

"Yes. Ironic, really – so much technology and all we have now is one of the oldest methods of all. It's a bit hard to use because we are moving so fast. It's hard or impossible to have conversations lasting longer than about ten minutes."

"And … I presume … it's definitely working?"

"Yes."

"And yet … silence?"

"Yes.

"Ok. Well – I can maybe come in here and … broadcast. But you'll have to show me how it works."

"Yes, sure. I'll show you the basics."

"Thanks." Cinnamon took a notebook from her bag.

"This thing can act as a basic two-way radio with some filtering so you can kind of talk over each other – but it's not that great to be honest. Or it can work with both uplink and downlink frequencies. But that's not much use for randomly finding signals. You can set the frequency or the two frequencies here – and here. This one first. Then you make sure that switch there is on. And use this to adjust the volume …"

Cinnamon was writing down the instructions as best she could. This equipment looked terrifying, but hopefully with a set of explicit directions, she could find her way through it all. It couldn't be crazier than a professional mixing desk, surely?

"To broadcast, you set this knob to M for microphone. The microphone switches on here. Adjust the level with this if needed. And you're good to go."

"Ok – so it's live now?"

"Yes. You just broadcast that."

Cinnamon smiled.

"And this frequency is what?"

"A standard international distress frequency. That seemed as good a one to try as any. But of course – try anything you like."

"I have no idea what frequency does which of course …"

Ola pointed to a computer screen and opened a file. "Here's a basic directory." Cinnamon stared at it, feeling her mind slowly starting to spin. Global Maritime Distress Safety System. International Air Distress frequency. Aeronautical Auxiliary Frequency. U.S. Navy emergency sonobuoy communications. Emergency Centre of Activity frequencies. Space facilities. Ground stations. Emergency Channel 9. As well as a whole listing of specific facilities and centres, airports, ports, science stations, military installations, hospitals, taxi companies, police, railway … it just went on and on. Hundreds. Thousands.

"It's worth trying random ones as well – just skimming around and listening. You never know."

"I am starting to feel very dumb," Cinnamon said with a sigh.

"Just stick to some of these and you'll be fine."

"Ok then. I'll … try."

"I've been broadcasting for the past three hours," Ola said. "I always feel as though something in my brain is going to snap at about this point. So please … take over."

"I will."

"Oh, and by the way …" Ola stepped across the room and leaned into a box. "I've got something for you." She held up a pair of binoculars. They looked sophisticated – powerful – and Cinnamon fixed on them in surprise.

"Found them in a stock room," Ola continued. "A stash of them. I've been using them. Maybe we can see better what's going on down there."

"Oh," she said, taking the device and turning it over in her hands – then she put them to her eyes, leaning over to the porthole and peering out at the blue sea. "These are great."

"Maybe useful."

"You're telling me that we are on a – a thing worth more than a small country, orbiting at seventeen thousand miles an hour …" Cinnamon shook her head with a bemused smile. "… and the only way we have of getting a close look at Earth is this thing?"

Ola looked uncomfortable. "Well, there are some sophisticated cameras in the science hub. Can get good resolution imagery of the ground. Could get infrared and other wavelengths as well."

"Why haven't we used them? Maybe we could see how all this happened."

"I've tried several times," Ola said. "But … I don't know how to operate the things."

"Oh …"

"Hey – I was the technician. I fixed things, repaired things … nobody ever showed me how to use that room-sized camera. I sat down several times to try and work something out, but couldn't even see how to begin."

"Fair enough," Cinnamon said with a smile.

"And there's no GRID High-Res Imaging Device for Dummies anywhere on board either," Ola said, a little defensively. "Or a Unity Telescope Quick Start Guide for that matter."

"You never know – we might figure something out. Not as if we're short of time up here."

"I'll keep trying," Ola said, still looking embarrassed.

"And I will lie on the beach with these and watch the world. Thank you. Think I can see people from up here?"

"I doubt it. You can see individual fields clearly, larger buildings, roads, railways … just more details."

Cinnamon nodded.

"I've been using them to watch the stars," Ola said, her voice going dreamy. "Just … losing myself in them. It's very calming."

"I know what you mean. Here?"

"No. They spin like wheels and it's just exhausting. There's …" She hesitated, as though about to reveal a deep secret. "There's one place in the Unity Space Telescope where I sometimes go – a viewing point, really out of the way and strangely comfortable. I'd probably be fired if I'd gone in there without authorisation when everything was normal – but it hardly matters now."

"Oh wow – can I see?"

"Well sure. You mean now?"

"If you like. If you're done working."

"I'm done. Alright, let's go and relax there for a bit." Ola stood up and stretched – reaching for the ceiling, then bending over and grasping her ankles.

"You don't get dizzy?" Cinnamon asked. That manoeuvre would have had her holding her head when she first arrived, and feeling pretty vile even now.

"Sometimes. But I've been on and off this damn wheel of joy for a long time. I suppose I am used to it. Come on, I'll show you the way."

Cinnamon followed her out into the gently curving corridor and along it for a few minutes. Then Ola opened the hatch to one of the main shafts. These were cylindrical tubes equipped with ladders that led what felt like up – towards the centre of the complex. Other corridors would branch off them, letting into the science areas, the crew quarters etc. Cinnamon had been part of the way up here but never climbed all the way to the centre. There was no profound reason for this – it was simply that she had been working her way further and further, but always with the definite goal of finding things or scavenging.

"Up here," Ola said. "After you."

Cinnamon began to climb, hand over hand, foot over foot. It was a long climb, but her weight was continually getting less. Soon it felt as though she was swimming, using the ladder to gently tug herself along. She was starting to feel sick again, but forced that down. Throwing up in low gravity seemed even worse than it was normally. A fall would still not be a good thing either. No doubt she would drift gently outwards – and if she couldn't grab hold again, she would just fall faster and faster until she smacked into the ground with all the force of a fall from the top of a building on earth. At least, she presumed so. The intricacies of the artificial gravity had always been a mystery to her. Either way, she was very careful not to let go of the rungs, no matter how light she felt.

Eventually they reached the top – a small cramped space with several hatches opening off. She scrambled into it and ended up clinging on to one of the railings with a white-knuckle grip, for now she felt truly weightless – the totally unreal dreamlike feeling of zero-G. She'd felt it before on her way up here as the shuttle docked, and she wasn't sure she could ever get used to it.

Ola came drifting up beside her, casually and easily clambering around. She swung herself across to one of the doors and opened it – a complex, heavy opening that suggested an air-tight seal, though there was no hiss or change of pressure. No doubt this was a form of protection in case what lay beyond ever malfunctioned – for the room beyond was slowly rotating. This was presumably the stationary area around which the whole complex spun. It was a strange sight, and moving at a speed that, while it would translate to a hefty spin out at the rim, was here little more than a slow creep. It ought to have ground and groaned like a pestle in a mortar but instead there was nothing more than a faint hum and swishing sound. With no external reference and no down, it seemed pretty much up to her which room was still and which was moving. She could switch them in her mind with relative ease – though as she passed through the transition, as the switch reversed in her perception, it only added an extra layer of confusion.

"Through here," Ola said, opening another hatch, which looked as airtight as the previous. "Not far now." She swung herself into this new corridor and went sailing down it, a casual kick-off sending her floating free in exactly the right direction. Cinnamon followed, though much less smoothly. Her attempt to push herself off sent her banging into the wall, then bouncing in the other direction. She flailed in empty air, turning head over heels for a while until she crashed a second time, then finally managed to haul herself in the right direction, bouncing down the corridor while Ola watched, a faint smile on her face.

"Yeah, yeah," she said, momentarily surprised to hear her voice carrying pretty much as usual. "A fine ballet this …" She grabbed hold of a rail, swung herself in vaguely the right direction and scrambled breathlessly to her side.

"Never gets old," Ola said.

"I bet. Well, always happy to provide the entertainment around here."

Ola gave a brief but wide grin. "I don't care how big and tough you think you are …"

"Well, I ain't either …"

"Not talking about you. I don't care how rich and cocksure you are, you get into zero-G for the first time, you are floundering around like a confused kitten, just like the rest of us. I always kind of liked watching that."

"You mean … you hoard enough wealth to fix the problems of several small countries, yet Ola still has to grab you and turn you the right way up while you flail at nothing?"

Ola chuckled. "Yeah – maybe something like that." She dragged open yet another hatch, beyond which was yet another short corridor. They scrambled through this and then into a room with some of the most complex equipment Cinnamon had seen yet. Rank after rank of hardware, and more screens and keyboards than she had ever seen in one place. It would have felt like a classic control room, familiar from numerous films, except that there was no down here. The seats that people had once used faced every which way – up, down, sideways. Floor, walls and ceiling, like something out of an Escher drawing. Ola flew across the room to the far side, and Cinnamon followed, trying very hard not to crash into or kick any of the equipment. Ola had opened yet another hatch, this one barely large enough to squeeze through – and Cinnamon watched her legs disappear into the darkness.

"Hang on," Ola called back. There was a fumbling, then a gleam of light. A small, portable looking gleam – a lantern.

"Bloody hell," Cinnamon said, squeezing through. Her hips barely fitted – the metal scraping her on all four sides. "Not many fat scientists, I take it?"

"They like small people in this business," Ola said. "We're priced per kilogram after all. But anyway – welcome to the Unity telescope. Please try not to bang into anything.

Just in case anyone ever takes any more snaps with this thing."

"Oh gawd …"

The place was indeed just one giant machine, she realised. Huge equipment all round her, wires everywhere – and ahead what looked like the outside of a vast cylinder. It did cause a throb of awe.

"Anyway – the viewing room is this way."

Ola continued into the bowels of the telescope. Now, being weightless was helping, because Cinnamon could see no easy way to get up here by normal scrambling. They climbed through a narrow square duct, then round a few corners – then one last hatch, and they emerged into a small round room. And there, at last, were the stars.

"Oh, wow," Cinnamon murmured.

"They built this so we can visually check the telescope without doing a spacewalk. It's not the most comfortable area but … it's basically the only stationary viewpoint in this direction. And I love it."

The room was polyhedral and set like a small blister in the exterior of the structure – the half on the outside consisting of what looked like tough glass, the inner half metal. There was some padding, but most of it was hard, and there were a few items of equipment as well – a screen, a keyboard and a few other controls. There was just room for the two of them.

"There you have it," Ola said, switching off the small lantern and plunging the room into deep darkness. "The best view of the stars we have here. Give your eyes a little time to adjust."

Cinnamon drifted up to the glass, if glass it was, and stared out, feeling at a loss for words. The night sky was not entirely alien to her, even given the light pollution down on earth, but this was unlike anything she had ever seen. The sheer depth of it. An endless infinity of shining dust motes against a blackness that seemed able to consume all things.

"It is rather good to look at this after all that has happened," Ola said. "Everything back there seems so small …"

"I don't think I have even begun to process it. And you know … I'm not really sure what will be waiting for me when I do."

"I think I know what you mean," Ola said with some hesitation. "Maybe I am still wrestling with the feeling of it. Especially … us. Here."

"You called it an ark yesterday," Cinnamon said.

"I did, didn't I."

"Is that what this place is?" she asked with a laugh. "A combination of Eden and ark? And us two … what? There must have been some slight miscalculation by fate though. Or whoever is telling this story. Not quite in a position to fuck like rabbits and repopulate the world, are we?"

Ola drew a short breath in the darkness. "I suppose not."

"Well, fuck that. I never wanted kids – even less now."

Ola was silent. Cinnamon could see nothing of her, not even a shadow, but she could still detect a faint hint of tension.

"You?" she asked at last.

"Well," Ola murmured, "I suppose I always assumed that time and commitments would prove an impediment to such things."

"That's one way of putting it. Though – I suppose the fucking like rabbits bit could be arranged, if needed."

The response to that was a nervous laugh. "I would suggest that there are more important things to worry about for the moment."

"Oh you," Cinnamon teased. "Does everyone who comes into space have to be a stuffy arse? Part of the training?"

She was grinning with a hint of challenge, pointless though that was in the dark. It was a faint relief, however, when she heard Ola's laugh in return.

"Well, there are reasons," she said. "You want 'chemistry' running wild in a tin box with nothing but a million fiddly buttons and routines between you and the unforgiving vacuum of space?"

"I take your point. Still – one should be able to relax, right?"

"Well, I can categorically state," Ola said, "that our guests managed it quite well. They were definitely not stuffy arses. More the zero-G orgy and drunken bellowing type as often as not."

"I'm kind of with them on the first," she said, pulling a comically intrigued expression that she knew Ola couldn't see. "You ever tried it?"

"Um …" Ola sounded embarrassed, shifting and moving her limbs. "No. I mean … not many opportunities for that up here. Most of the time, I was the only staff, remember?"

"Ah yes. Various opportunities for a zero-G jerk-off though, surely? I always meant to test that one out."

Ola gave a nervous giggle.

"Ok," Cinnamon said, taking pity on her. "Tell me more about these legendary guests. What wonderful shenanigans did they get up to?"

"Not so wonderful, Ola said. "Some were very nice, don't get me wrong. You'd meet some giant of the computing world or the CEO of some vast company making, I dunno, fuses or car tires … something or other. And they'd treat you like a human being and with impeccable politeness. But then again, some were … well, there was something creepy about them. As though something was missing. Completely excised from their soul."

“Interesting,” Cinnamon said. “I can’t say I’ve met many, even in my business.”

“I have no idea what they wanted from life.”

“Save that they hadn’t found it?”

“Yeah, maybe. It had all dwindled into a ritual. And so utterly isolated that it was surreal. So isolated that they hardly knew they were isolated. Coming up here with their plastic wives or high-end prostitutes … or who the fuck knows what they were? You got the feeling they were on a quest for something they didn’t know how to find – and had been questing for so long that they had forgotten quests should even have ends.”

“Woah …”

“And … they’d bring people with them. Friends that felt like them – or their tools. Sometimes … stranger things. Young boys whose purpose I could never quite work out. Or … objects. One came up here with a car once. Would you believe it? He had a shiny sports car of some kind. He couldn’t drive it – he couldn’t even switch it on – or even bring petrol, oil, battery in it. But he insisted on having it there. Must have cost him millions. We had a pet cheetah up here as well once, that was fun.”

“Holy fuck. It’s bad enough getting used to this place when you know what’s going on.”

“Yeah.”

“They let him?”

“Her. And yeah, they let her. Money talks.”

Cinnamon sighed bitterly. “And the sex workers?”

“You know … I got on ok with them. Some of them, anyway. We’d have a drink in the private areas sometimes, and talk. And when they’d get drunk enough, they’d open up a bit. And yeah – they were also searching for something. Though definitely not the same thing as their clients.”

“I can imagine.”

"They'd talk about college degrees that led to nothing – or, I dunno, some kind of communities or scenes that they'd left behind."

"I can imagine it," Cinnamon repeated. "They progressed from the alternate communities to higher-paying things? And then realised what it cost them?"

Ola hesitated again. "Maybe," she said almost reluctantly. "It certainly seemed a cold life."

"I live with a few sex workers back in London," Cinnamon said. "Um … lived with, anyway." She swallowed a brief cold feeling. "Most of them knew what they were doing perfectly well, but of course, in those communities, that's maybe a bit easier."

There was a silence, Ola sitting quietly with no detectable reaction.

"I even knew a surrogate therapist once," Cinnamon continued, "who sometimes provided services for the disabled. One of the warmest souls I ever met. But what you describe doesn't sound so … healthy, not to put too fine a point on it."

"It wasn't. A fat savings account, and that means a lot in this world, but …"

"But up there the air is so thin you can hardly breathe."

Ola sighed. "Yeah – we'd talk a lot. I preferred them to their clients, I'll say that. Then it was back to being a piece of meat for a few hours. Pretty horrible really."

"I think we're all pieces of meat, one way or another. It's a question of what's going on in here. And yes, I'm tapping my head."

Ola gave a nervous laugh.

"I think many, many people suffer from diseases they never know they have," Cinnamon said. "Diseases that would leave their flesh dripping and oozing off their bones – if they weren't diseases of the mind."

"I can tell you are an artist," Ola said, a smile in her voice.

"Hey – I worked hard for it. And sitting here, looking up, those diseases suddenly seem … just so clear. Did none of them sit here? Look at the stars? And ask what the heck was going on?"

"No," Ola said simply. "This place didn't change a single one of them. As far as I know."

Cinnamon sighed again. "You know what?"

"Hm?"

"When I hear stuff like that, I'm really so tempted to jump into the escape capsule and go that way instead," she said, pointing up at the stars.

BROADCAST

The air in the communications room felt stuffy. Maybe she would have to find another fan, but for the moment she just shrugged off her robe, folded it and used it to make a cushion in the chair, then sat down. Why not? With Ola asleep, doubly why not? It was good to let the body function as it should for once – process the warmth naturally.

She stared at the equipment, trying not to feel overawed. She'd followed the sequence of instructions, hoping that it was all working as it should, but now she was saying nothing. She could imagine Ola sitting here, firing off crisp messages with that vaguely military lingo that always seemed to orbit around radio systems, and she sighed. It was a sad image. The symbolic death of the really quite wondrous interconnectedness of people expressed in one terrified woman spouting formulaic utterances into the void. The power of communication always seemed to offer hope for the future and an escape from the dark side of existence – but now silenced.

No doubt, Ola would know precisely what to say, and precisely the best way to broadcast it. She didn't – but that had never stopped her in the past. In the end, she drew a deep breath.

"Good evening ladies and gentlemen, is anybody listening? No? Nothing? Well, welcome to your late-night opera from the skies above. I guess whatever people do, a watcher must remain and I guess that's me. Even though I can't fucking see anything."

She glanced round the room. The light never really changed here, the dancing sun and moon not having much connection to day and night as she thought of them. But still, by some internal or external clock, this was late. Very late. The silent station only seeming eerier, by some mechanism that she didn't really understand. Could you have witching hour when the sun rose and set a dozen times in a twenty-four hour cycle?

"It's remarkably restful being the only person around," she said. "Is that what it's like on Earth now? Have you made a hell down there? Or have you made an Eden by ceasing to exist? Is that what utopia always was? Somehow rooted in complete destruction? There were a lot of contradictions surrounding that word – as a concept it always seemed to come back to some kind of authoritarianism. This, the utopian would say, is how the world must be. This is how it would be perfect. But you can bet utopia breaks down pretty quickly if what you are lies outside that perfection. The moment you define utopia, you kill it. And yet … what have people been dreaming of all these centuries?"

She paused. Talking felt good – though as the words came, she almost hoped nobody was listening. This felt more like a stream of consciousness rather than anything she could argue with another.

"Maybe it always was simply about minimising evil rather than pushing for good. I know it always felt as though we had to settle for that – but maybe that was the most profound thing of all."

She sighed, taking a drink from her bottle of water.

"Anyway – never mind. There have been enough words in the world. I can't do words anymore. So … hmm. Would you like me to sing for you?" A thin smile. "Well tough, cos I'm going to. The acoustics here stink – and I've no idea if this equipment can do any processing. So you're going to have to put up with my voice as raw and real as it comes."

She hesitated, staring at the microphone – then out of the window. Below, she could see land, though she had no idea where. Again, was anyone listening? Was anyone picking up the passage of her meandering mind as it passed high overhead?

Maybe that uncertainty helped – there was indeed something almost relaxing about the void.

And Cinnamon Thorns sang. What came out of her mouth was strange. It started off as a melange of existing songs – old folk songs, revolutionary ballads, songs of solidarity and love and freedom, Punk melodies – but it soon tangled its way into something completely improvised. Words of her own, sometimes bitter and aggressive, sometimes filled with a desperate warmth. Words that pined for a world of beauty and life. All set to strange winding almost random melodies.

As she was winding down, she was aware of a figure entering the room quietly. Ola – looking at her in astonishment. Cinnamon glanced round, her voice wavering for a moment, then she mentally shrugged, turned back to the microphone and allowed the last few phrases to drift to a halt.

"Goodnight to the lovely people down there," she said, her voice slinky and sweet. "It's always the lovely who get broken first – so yes, goodnight. Sleep tight. Don't let the politicians bite …"

She switched off the microphone and leaned back with a sigh.

"What are you doing?" Ola demanded, a flicker of amusement on her face.

"I'm not doing anything, I'm sitting here."

"Yes but, why are you naked in my chair?"

"Can you honestly give me any reason why I shouldn't be? Anyway – I thought you were in bed."

Ola was silent, her active eyebrows rising even higher.

"Hey, you were spying on me for days anyway – so I ain't disposed to fuss about it much."

Ola went crimson. "Yes, well, it wasn't really like that …"

"Like hell it wasn't," Cinnamon said with a huge grin, plucking the robe out from under her and putting it on.

"Anyway," Ola said, dragging the subject back to somewhere she could control it, "what was that singing about? I thought we were trying to communicate?"

"I just wanted to give anyone who was listening something to, well, listen to. This might be my last song to the world. My opera, broadcast to whoever happens to still have an ear."

"It was … rather beautiful," Ola said, almost reluctantly. "You are a pro singer?"

"In my own sweet way. I was … kind of famous among those who cared about such things. Started off in Alt-Punk, then started exploring more personal stuff. Lots of a capella and experimental electronic music." She gave a brief wistful look at nothing, remembering working in the studios far into the night, not as some wild angry rebel but as an almost owlishly serious craft-master, feeling increasingly frustrated with the people around her – wanting to stretch them open and have them follow her into worlds of intricate wonder that were increasingly hard to classify – only to be left more and more alone.

And now, of course, was a world in which all genres had died.

At least, so she assumed.

"But I guess enough people were still interested in me for InterSpace to take me on," she finished. "I suppose they wanted someone edgy but not too uncooperative. Boy did they read me wrong."

"I must say, I never ever expected to have someone like you up here. Ever."

"And yet, here I am. Funny how these things work out."

Ola shook her head with a grin. "No communications picked up, I suppose?"

"Nope. Silence. Nothing heard, nothing coming in. Maybe I am just singing to an empty room."

Blog 4 – Kemories and Scars

Day… I have no idea right now.

I can see the scars. Just.

It's weird – massive space station, billion quid's worth of technology, yet I am staring down at Earth using a pair of binoculars. Not very powerful – but yes, I can see the scars. I can see them in much more detail now. And … it's hard.

It's the one in London that gets me most, of course. I know that city. I used to explore it a lot – I'd walk or cycle for miles, poking around new neighbourhoods or cruising long-distance from east to west, south to north. And now, I can see the damage cutting my routes in half, but I can't make out anything really useful. I can't see whether there is anybody alive down there. The actual scar is hard to describe from up here. As though someone took a photo of the city, then let the paper get wet, so that the ink smudged, the details blurred and went flat. It's not even overt. The pattern of the roads are still mostly there, just overlaid by a decay. A dissolution. A rot that makes my head swim and sends my imagination into overdrive. Also, it seems safe to assume that, if those scars mean what I think they mean, the actual damage stretches much further than anything visible.

I presume my home no longer exists.

The East End was my world – an entire universe. I don't mean I never travelled outside it, but somehow the east end was all I ever wanted or needed. From the glitzy money-stinking Thames to the subtle decay of Bow to the wonderful alt artscape of the Wick to the marshes of Walthamstow. Life was hard in many ways – expensive vampire-London did its best to suck us dry, but somehow the East End was. In spite of all, it was.

And I have faces in my mind – friends, the scene, watching eyes, thronging crowds. And a strange numbness. The processes of the world were always too big to grasp – billions of people, far too many to ever hold in your head – and now their end, in whatever way, is only more so.

Fuck fuck

fuck fuck fuck fuck fuck fuck fuck fuck fuck fuck fuck fuck fuck fuck fuck fuck fuck fuck fuck fuck fuck fuck fuck fuck fuck fuck fuck fuck fuck fuck fuck fuck fuck fuck fuck fuck fuck

POD

Below – beside – beyond … outside, down on the surface of the Earth, there was nothing but an endless carpet of green. Some forest or other, she was not entirely sure where. She stared at it feeling a blast of yearning, some of the strongest she had felt since coming here. She wanted to be in those trees. She wanted to run through them, the dappled sunlight strobing in her eyes, the sound of birdsong, the feel of the wind on her skin, the sound of droning insects and the occasional glimpse of some scurrying creature. And the smell – the smell of earth and life …

She splashed out of the curved pool and up the beach to where the jungle was green and lush, maintained and watered by the automated systems.

"There's nothing here," she wailed aloud. She was scrabbling around in the soil, her hands deep in it, dragging leaf-litter aside, digging through the compost. And yes – there was nothing here. None of these plants were edible, as far as she knew. They were all ornamentals, none with a useful purpose, as far as she knew. Plants yes, but they all somehow screamed at her as alien – artificial. Unreal. Also, nothing crawled through the undergrowth or buzzed through the air. Everything here looked fundamentally wrong – as though just a little bit out of place, just a little bit off. Whatever verdant feel it was trying to create was clearly on an artificial foundation.

It was maddening.

After a few minutes, however, she gave a yell of triumph. She had found a snail. A rather unusual snail, very long and thin, in a tight spiral like a unicorn horn. About two centimetres. It looked alive, though retreated inside its shell. No doubt it was a stowaway – a greenhouse alien. A while later, a couple of beetles scurried away from her invasion – and what looked like a centipede. There were a few spiders as well. And the odd smaller thing that she couldn't identify scurrying or jumping away. They were a relief, a comfort, and she watched them with haunted eyes.

"What are you doing?"

She glanced round. Ola had appeared behind her, quiet enough to avoid detection.

"I just needed something alive."

Ola shook her head with a smile. "I thought they were nuts building this greenhouse thing when I first came up here. Half the plants died and some of them cost as much as a small house to get up here. Now I'm rather glad though."

"So am I," Cinnamon said, scrambling to her feet.

"Let me show you something," Ola said, waving her to follow. "At least – if I can find it."

Ola led her to the very edge of the jungle area, to where the walls rose up. Here, the plants had grown densely against the panels, and when Ola tugged at them they pulled away in a solid flat mass of pale stems. She tried a few times in various places, then gave an exclamation.

There was a small brown worm-like thing and Ola picked it up gently.

"What is that?" Cinnamon asked. Thinking earthworm.

"Look closer," Ola said. Cinnamon took her hand and did so – and realised that the creature had eyes – tiny black dots.

"What is it?" she repeated in surprise.

And then the creature yawned – opening a tiny mouth.

"It's a thread snake," Ola said. "It must have come up here with the plants and now there are quite a lot of them. That means plenty of small things for them to eat as well."

Cinnamon stared in wonder. She had never heard of snakes this small. And leaning in close, it looked beautiful. A tiny life that had somehow fit into this place, probably far better than she had. It twined around Ola's fingers, puzzled at this strange new world of warm skin, but not seeming particularly disturbed. And eventually, Ola released it back into the stems.

"I feel better for that," Cinnamon said with a laugh. She glanced up at the windows again, but the vast forest had long-since faded behind them, and now there was nothing but blue ocean. She smiled faintly, glancing at the water a few metres away. There was little point hoping for any kind of watery balm as well. The pool was definitely sterile.

"What have you been doing," she asked, as much to chase away that thought as anything.

"Oh, just my usual checks. There's a lot to check in this place."

Cinnamon nodded with a small surge of grimness.

"At some point, I will even need to make an orbital correction," Ola said. "I'm dreading that – but will cross that bridge when we come to it."

"Orbital correction?"

"Yeah. Nobody ever trained me to do that." She sighed. "But … we'll be fine."

"What is it?"

"You know, we're not actually out of the atmosphere here?"

"We're not?"

"The atmosphere stretches out a long way from the Earth. It's just very, very thin. And this attenuated gas outside exerts drag on the station, which means we steadily descend. So every so often, we have to fire some of the thrusters to boost the station back to a higher orbit. Otherwise … well, we'd eventually burn up in the heavier air below."

"Oh, fucking great," Cinnamon muttered. "I never even realised. We can do that?"

For a moment, Ola's face went blank. "I … think I know how. I'm less sure about when. Week or so. Month maybe. The atmosphere out there is changing constantly and we have to ride it. But I'm monitoring the altitude, atmospheric density, solar cycle, solar weather etcetera."

"Bloody hell. I thought that you just … put the thing here and it orbited."

Ola gave a wan smile. "Noooo. Put a craft in one of the Lagrange points way, way off and it will be very stable – but in low earth orbit, it's not far off a piloted vehicle. Highly automated but I still have to keep a careful eye on things. I guess I'm driving this thing now. How exciting."

"Thank goodness you're here," Cinnamon muttered. "Why is everything so fucking complicated?"

"The mechanics are just insane. So many variables to take into account. There's the presence and varying strength of earth's gravity as well. The earth's geoid. That slowly degrades our orbit in subtle but cumulative ways."

Cinnamon's brain felt as though it was starting to spin, ice crystals forming behind her eyes. Ola watched her with a hint of mischief in her face now.

"All it really means," she said, "is that if we drift too low, we need to go higher again. But that's for the future. For the moment, I'm just making sure all the systems are still working, that nothing has broken down. Just got the escape pod left to do. I check that every day – really really don't want anything happening to that."

"Bloody right," Cinnamon said. "Come with you?"

"Sure."

"I should probably see the thing since those fuckers went and left me here."

Ola smiled faintly. "Won't take long. It's up in the hub."

They walked out of the hotel area to where the ladder led to the centre. And the now-familiar climb, her weight decreasing by the minute. Then through the airlock into the central hub where, on the opposite side to the Unity Telescope, the last remaining escape craft waited with a patience that was comfortably inhuman. Their only hope of ever seeing the surface of the Earth again.

She placed herself in one of the seats, strapping herself in to prevent herself drifting away. It was built to restrain its occupant and keep them safe during who knows what wild journey downwards, yet it was still comfortable. Silky and cushioned – no doubt suitable for the arses of the swankiest of guests. The carpets and panelling were also luxuriously padded and soft, and a couple of small portholes gave her a view of the stark metal wall of the chamber in which it was held.

Ola propelled herself across the room and unlocked an almost hidden hatch in the wall. A click as the laptop was plugged in – and then left floating in space. The screen flashed up a window. Click. Click. Process started – a long list of technical-sounding components and a status bar. Presumably it was performing some kind of diagnostic, for every few seconds or so, another item on the list would display a green tick. It all seemed remarkably mundane for what was not only a spacecraft worth more money than she could easily conceive of in her mind but also their only means of ever returning home. At one point, one of the diagnostics threw up a yellow indicator instead of green and Cinnamon felt a momentary unease – but Ola barely glanced at it.

On the wall at one end were a large red lever and an equally large red button – the one a little bit like an emergency leaver on a train, the other a metal mushroom that could presumably be pushed. It was almost cartoon-like –

and somehow all that was needed? And now she sat there staring at it, trying to understand how she felt. Would she ever press that button? Should she? Should she press it right now?

It seemed to her that staying forever in this hotel fulfilled a primal need that she had always felt. The need to rise above the insanity of the world and find a safe plane of existence. Now, of course, that need was simple and clear – a refuge. But it was more than that – and older than that. Far far more and far, far older. Maybe even eternal. It was the yearning for a safe distance while life muddled onwards, politics chewing up people's lives like a great beast, while people bickered and argued, while a grey corruption spread through all corners of life that she could never balm for herself by imagining past glories or future enlightenment. And now, if she could forget the basic facts of her isolation and precarious future, being up here felt peaceful. Even if this hotel proved to be an orbiting coffin, it still had that same sense of peace.

And yet … how could you process that feeling? What did it mean? She had never been suicidal in her life, yet something about the fact that of all the human beings on the planet, great and petty, wise and insane, she had been the one to end up here – a place and time unique in human history – had totally floored her. And the thought of staying here in space witnessing the end of all things came with an almost mythological touch to it that left death barely even significant. Pressing that red button almost felt like something forbidden.

"Whose cack-handed idea was it to build this thing anyway?" she asked at last, a grumbling tone to her voice.

"Hmm?"

"This hotel? It's just … surreal. A place that maybe fifty people on earth could afford to visit? And most of them were more concerned with building bunkers or fortifying islands. They were trying to … do something, weren't they?"

"Something?"

"Yes. They wanted to somehow … elevate a sinking civilization in the only way they knew how. That's what I think. Trying to make something bigger as our horizons were shrinking smaller and smaller?"

"Interesting," Ola said. "It is possible."

"Everything on Earth was so bad that they wanted to open up something off it. But by that time it was too late and even this just feels sick. So they drag me out here instead, in the hope that I would be some kind of ambassador – show the world all about it. Oh boy could I do that … if anybody was listening. You want to argue my contract now, InterSpace Corporation? Seriously … fuck them."

"You may still get the chance," Ola said with a smile.

"Yeah, maybe. I can tell them all how insane things were … before."

"And … how wonderful. Let's not forget just how wonderful."

"This place?" Cinnamon asked with a frown.

"Among others."

"How, for fuck's sake? When has there ever been anything wonderful about all this elitist crap?"

Ola glared at her, eyebrows knitted for once. "You see the hotel," she snapped, "I see the Unity Telescope, the labs, the microwave detector, the supercomputer, the gravity wave research project, the gamma ray detector, the blazar project, the dark energy project … To me, the hotel was almost an add-on."

"I suppose," Cinnamon said, nodding reluctantly.

"The simple act of learning – of discovering. Understanding. That's more important than pretty much anything. More important than any of the politics."

Cinnamon sighed. No doubt that was true. The hotel had dominated the news– and much of the time not in a good way. Debates, arguments, blather. The costs of spaceflight had been coming down significantly, but even so, launch after expensive launch devoted to carrying luxury equipment and fittings had raised plenty of eyebrows. Scientists had been angry at the crowding out of scientific missions. The public had been angry at the incredible cost, regardless of who was actually footing it. But yes, there seemed little reason to trust the perspective of the media over the scientifically literate Ola.

"To me the place always stank of death," she said. "But … I suppose I know what you mean."

"Death? How?"

Cinnamon hesitated, unsure how to express what she was feeling. "I think I was talking about money," she said. "Money always smelt of death."

Again, Ola shrugged. "A few expensive tickets from the super-rich to help cover the costs of this fun palace never did any harm."

"Maybe," she said – and mentally shrugged. How many people in history had swum in a pool that curved? And the pool was not even Earth water, she remembered that much. The hotel had been expensive enough without ferrying an entire swimming pool into orbit. It was asteroid water, a by-product of one of the first asteroid mining operations. A small space pebble had been towed into a lunar orbit, then slowly dismantled – and as well as all the metals and minerals, there was a good percentage of ice. It had been far less work and expense to ferry a few giant bladders of that over here than to lift it from the surface below, gallon by precious gallon. Maybe that was enough to make one feel dizzy with awe.

There was a polite beep from the laptop and Ola glanced at it.

"All good?" Cinnamon asked.

"All good."

"So how does this thing work? That lever is really all you need?"

"Yup. It's all automated. It's designed to get people back down to Earth so simply that even a rich brat can manage it."

Cinnamon smiled. "Even an arty-farty brat like me?"

"Yeah. Just seal the door, yank that lever to activate and press the button twice when asked – to confirm. Strap in and get ready to write a song about g-forces. Computers will automatically take you down into the Atlantic Ocean just off Key West unless someone like me changes anything." She patted the laptop, sending it drifting away until it reached the end of its cable and halted again.

"We could go anywhere?"

"Probably. Up to a point. You want to land in the estuarine Thames, I could do it, I think. I hope. If I fail, we'll never know. You want to land in the river at the bottom of your garden, probably not. Boy, has spaceflight changed since I first started."

"I believe you."

"A million fiddly little things to do and check, using a million fiddly bits of equipment, in a box you could barely see out of. It was like flying into orbit inside your desktop PC strapped on top of a rather large bomb. Every damn bodily function pawed over by at least twenty scientists down to the smallest detail and with toilets that would make even a budget airline recoil in horror."

Cinnamon chuckled.

"I kind of miss it," Ola finished with a small smile, reeling in the drifting laptop and snapping it shut. "Ah well – this thing's still here if we need it."

"Yeah … maybe. Maybe."

"I'll probably go and lie down now – read a bit."

"Then I will have another swim, then head to the communications room and try a few more things."

"More singing?"

"Maybe. Can you honestly think of anything better?"

"I'd go for something like 'InterSpace Hotel, do you read me?' repeated about five hundred times on various frequencies."

"I bet you would. I'd go for bizarre rants and a bit of opera."

"You know – it's not much like any opera I've heard."

"And just who says what opera is?" Cinnamon demanded with a frown. "I'm telling a kind of story – or some kind of fucking requiem. And I'm singing. I'm not sure what else I could call it."

"Fair enough," Ola said.

ABERYSTWYTH COMPOUND

The voice came crisply: This is Aberystwyth compound …

Ice crystals formed down Cinnamon's back. Muscles clenching. She had been drifting idly around the frequencies, listening to the silence. Until suddenly the silence went away.

"Oh hi," she cried. "I …"

… issuing report dated oh two, oh eight. Reporting successful completion of defensive measures. Friendly casualties eighteen. Territorial security maintained. No prisoners taken.

"What?"

Freedom is maintained.

"Can you hear me?"

No response. The voice just continued, speaking slowly and precisely. With shaking hands, she scrabbled for a piece of paper and wrote down the frequency and the current time. This frosty and rather inhuman broadcast was the first human voice she had heard from Earth.

I repeat, freedom is maintained. Incoming persons are advised to report to the compound perimeter for vetting. This has been a recorded message. Message repeats …

Cinnamon stared blankly at nothing, then scrambled to her feet. She stumbled over a metal support and went flat on her face, though the gravity here was so weak that it barely hurt – then she was running, bounding, flying down the corridor.

*

"Ok," Ola said sharply as they stepped back into the communications room. "So it was just repeating the same message, over and over?"

"Yes – it's stopped now."

"It would have – we're quite a way further round the world." She examined the scribbled note of the frequency and time. "You didn't write down the co-ordinates?"

"No – should I have?"

Ola shrugged and slid into the chair, rapidly fiddling with the equipment. "Aberystwyth," she murmured. "Where the hell is that?"

"Wales. Quite remote."

"That would make sense. Somewhere far away from any effects of whatever attack happened."

"Attack," Cinnamon murmured, her voice trailing away. She could feel a tremble taking root inside her.

"Ok – the time fits. We'd have been approaching roughly that area when it first came through. I guess we can assume that it is located somewhere near the city."

"Town."

"Whatever. And they said …?"

"Oh – some kind of defence. They mentioned friendly casualties. And … no prisoners taken."

"Ok …" She leaned back in the chair looking jittery, her voice sounding a little strange. "So … hum. Well, at least we know there is somebody down there."

"Yes – oh and …"

"Hmm?"

"And freedom is maintained. Those were the words."

"Oh …" Ola glanced at her with a frown. "Those kinds of words always make me nervous. But who knows. Interesting. Nothing we can do now until we are somewhere near Aberystwyth again."

"When?"

"Might pick it up in about an hour, or we might have moved too far on. Most likely sometime tomorrow. I will need to check precisely when."

Cinnamon nodded slowly.

"I will stay here for a while," Ola said. "Just in case. I … don't suppose I'll be sleeping again."

"Then … I'm going to bed," Cinnamon said.

"You ok?"

"Yeah, fine," she muttered as she scrambled into the corridor. "We'll … tomorrow, right?"

"Right."

She stumbled out into the corridor and back into the hotel area.

*

In her room, she switched the fan on full power and let the breeze blast over her, clothes beating her skin like a gentle but enthusiastic sadist. She lay and stared at the ceiling, trying to analyse what she was feeling. She was used to trying to understand rather than just reacting, but this time she was confused. No idea why she was shaking so – why she almost wanted to cry. There was a sense of relief, of doom, a burning exaltation and a feeling so strange, even so treacherous that it made her mind curl up in horror. Disappointment?

That was insane.

There can't have been many people in human history who had wrestled with emotions such as this, she thought. The universal grief of a species – your own species. It was slightly like the feeling that arose when you read that another animal, insect, snail, plant had gone extinct, but amplified a million times, and still applying even though there were apparently still people down there. At least, assuming that hadn't just been some mindless recording repeating over and over surrounded by graves.

"You don't know anything," she told herself aloud. "You don't know what's happened. You still don't know …"

With a twitch, she dragged the bedding over herself, reducing the fan to a blast against her face. Closing her eyes, she undid her trousers and kicked them off, then her fingers were gently caressing herself, rubbing at her labia, slipping around and inside – and she shivered. Within her, something was burning – a storm – and she lay there masturbating, unsure precisely what thoughts were driving it. At the very least it might shut her whirling mind down for a little.

*

Cinnamon studied the display. It still read the same frequency – that of the Aberystwyth compound. She and Ola had both tried several times in the last few days, when the hotel was in roughly the right place, only to receive the same recorded message. The orbit of this thing was complicated – certainly not as simple as passing over Aberystwyth every time it swung round the planet. In a polar orbit over a rotating earth, every passage it moved a little further east, slowly covering the entire surface of the Earth. The result was that it would pass within range of a specific point a few times in quick succession, roughly every 90 minutes, before leaving it behind for a while until the process had circled all the way round and approached again. The details made Cinnamon's head swim, but Ola seemed to know at least a rough timetable and had written down a list of times. And Cinnamon was more than happy to keep listening. As their only contact with the ground, as their only proof that there were even any people still down there, that message sent a shivering thrill across her skin every time she heard it.

This time, however, as the start of the designated time window approached and she tuned in, she was met with nothing but silence. She stared at the equipment, reluctant to start fiddling with it in case she lost them forever somehow. But the silence was intense.

"Um … hello?" she tried at last, feeling weirdly self-conscious.

There was a faint murmur from the speakers – then a male voice. "Aberystwyth compound, go ahead."

"Um …"

Totally frozen, she stared at nothing for a moment, trying to work out what to say.

"Is there anybody there?" the voice said.

"Yes," she said with a gasp. "Who are you?"

"Aberystwyth compound, receiving you weak but readable. State your position and intentions."

"So there are people still alive down there?" she asked, her voice breaking.

"Confirmed. But who are you and where are you located. Identify yourself please."

"Um …"

Flickerings of a deep unease thrilled through her mind – a hint of warning, though she wasn't sure why.

"I am – I am in the InterSpace Hotel," she said at last. "What is happening? Should I come back to Earth?"

There was a brief pause. “Say again …”

“The InterSpace Hotel. High overhead. In low-Earth orbit.”

Another telling pause. At the very least, she had surprised whoever she was talking to.

“Received,” he said at last. “Please stand by.”

“Um … sure.”

It felt weird. What should have been a moment of extraordinary human connection – the first contact with Earth after an apocalypse – was playing out more like a telephone call to the local council. Trying to get through to the right department, waiting on hold – the only thing missing was some bad music playing in the background. She wondered whether she should run and get Ola or try talking again, but she did neither. She just sat there, her heart racing as almost two minutes ticked by.

Then finally the silence broke. “InterSpace Hotel, are you there?”

“Hello,” she cried, the word coming out in a rush. “Yes.”

Was the voice even the same one? She had no idea. Just a generic BBC English accent and with no detectable emotion.

“Please state your intentions,” he said. “We request that all incoming report to the perimeter for full vetting and I must warn you that the vetting is quite strict.”

“Ummmmm,” Cinnamon attempted, feeling sweat starting to oil her skin. “Do you … know what the InterSpace Hotel is?”

“Confirmed.”

“I am … currently in orbit. Around the earth. You are my first contact with the ground. I really have no fucking idea what my intentions are at the moment …”

“I would ask you to mind your language please.”

Cinnamon fell silent, puzzled, then she screwed up her face in a weird blend of intense annoyance and embarrassment. The swearword had come with no conscious intention, but the thought that this was somehow more important than the circumstances made her clench her fist. After a moment, however, she decided to just ignore the remark and press on.

"But … what is happening down there?"

"Happening in what sense?"

"In pretty much every sense. I am trying to decide whether or not to come home."

There was a silence on the radio. Then the voice started again, with a new dose of weariness, as though trying to recite a well-learned spiel but unable to quite hide the exhaustion underneath: "Situation is currently calm. The area of land we control is approximately seventy miles by fifteen miles and encompasses a long stretch of coastline. There has been little unrest recently – most of the more disruptive elements have been neutralised now. We occasionally receive new arrivals and there remains a small capacity before we must close, barring any further expansion. So if you wish to apply for admission, we suggest that you do so quickly. We ask you again, what are your intentions? And if you could give us some idea of what you do and what you believe, that would be helpful."

Cinnamon listened to that, her brow furrowing. She wanted news on a much wider scale than this, but it was enough to chill her. Control, calm, neutralised, close, believe …

"I don't understand. What do you want to know? And why?"

"What can you contribute? And please state your political and other leanings."

"I am trying to find out what happened to the planet," she said carefully. "I … have no idea about joining any organisation."

"Please answer the questions if you can."

Cinnamon frowned, wondering whether something was more seriously wrong here. Was this guy suffering some kind of delusion or mental breakdown? It would make sense given the presumed devastation that had occurred, but a hint of anger and confusion was starting to grow within her, an anger that she carefully squashed. "I'm sitting here – in space, wondering whether I should stay here or go home – why are you asking me what I do?"

"You will understand that we have to vet all incomers."

"But …" She hesitated. Absolutely barking, she thought. "Well, I do a lot of things. Or did. Do you want the list?"

"Please."

She shrugged massively. "Well – I'm an musician, artist, writer, dancer, clothes-maker, potter, gardener, language expert, therapist, street artist …" She wracked her brains. "Woodworker, night-owl, activist, I can handle figures, I did some guerrilla knitting once …"

"Thank you. Some of those are potentially useful, some are neutral."

"I … dare say."

"And some are, shall we say, rather suspect."

"Huh?"

"Please state your political leanings."

"Well, I dunno." She was silent a moment, trying to decide what on Earth – or off it, really – to say. "Nothing specific. I suppose … that everyone should be free to be who they are."

There was a long silence, while Cinnamon rubbed at her face, trying to dispel the feelings of unreality. This was definitely not how she had imagined her first contact with home would go.

"Hello?" she said at last. "Are you there? Look, I'll be out of range soon. I really need to know what happened. It was a nuclear war, right? Or is there something else? Why are things so … quiet? What is left? What is happening?"

"I fear we have no choice but to reject you."

"What?"

"We advise you that you should avoid the Aberystwyth compound," he said, his voice taking on that same weary tone of one repeating something from memory. "We advise you that if you arrive here applying as an incomer, you will be turned away as an undesirable element. We advise you that further contact after that may be seen as an act of aggression, to which we may respond with terminal measures."

Cinnamon just stared at the radio equipment, feeling totally frozen. "Is this some kind of joke?" she managed at last. "I'm trying to ask you what's going on, not …"

"What part of that sounded funny to you?" There was a certain change in tone there, from bureaucratic drear to something more personal.

Cinnamon drew a deep breath. "I would ask," she said, in a harsh imitation of his formal tone, "what the heck you mean by all this?"

"Space is limited, vetting must be strict. We cannot allow degenerate elements and those responsible for recent events to infiltrate."

Definitely, definitely delusional. Is there even a compound or is this guy just sitting there raving?

"What degenerate elements?"

"You fail the vetting on seven counts. Your kind may not be allowed to exert any further influence."

"My kind?" she demanded, her voice going shrill. "And what the fuck do you mean responsible? Are you telling me that pissed off artists nuked the planet? Are you out of your mind?"

"Using such a tone will achieve nothing," the voice said.

Cinnamon shut her eyes. There was something in his voice that was like a pin stuck into her soul and she took a few deep breaths, fighting hard to keep the anger down.

"Alright," she said. "Alright. Let me try this one more time. What happened three weeks ago? Please explain."

"Degenerate global elements forcing confrontation that led to a nuclear exchange, which some of us had been expecting for some time."

Cinnamon swallowed, a deep, deep feeling in her stomach. "Nukes," she muttered. "I suppose I always kind of knew it was that."

"And a few other events as well," he said. "The nature of which remain a mystery. Maybe you would know more about it than I do."

"Would I?"

"I would imagine so, yes."

"And why is that?"

"Merely because you and your kind are more responsible for it than anybody around here."

A deep breath. Cinnamon contemplated the well of anger rising up inside her and shrugged. Let it explode. Why not? Why fight it? It was enraging not because it was wrong, but because it was nonsensically wrong and thus almost impossible to defend against. What defence do you have when someone accuses you of being purple? Or of causing a hurricane? Or of conspiring to move the houses of parliament one yard to the east? Or of replacing every road sign in London with an exact copy of itself? There was a dose of utter farce about it – cartoonish logic that seemed disturbing enough under normal circumstances, now given a hugely amplified harmonic series by the end of the world.

"Oh don't be fucking ridiculous," she yelled, much louder, her entire body tense and shaking. "I don't have a 'kind'. Or if I do then it wanted unity and generally not fucking hurting people so yeah – of course we're responsible for … a world war?"

"There is nothing more to say," he continued. "Your kind will not be tolerated. You have no further place in this world, I am happy to say. One of the few good things to come out of what happened, though I don't expect you to ever understand that."

She stared at the microphone. "Understand?" she muttered, aware on some level that she was losing control dangerously. "Oh no. I understand. I understand fucking perfectly. I know what drives all this. I know the cowardice and lack of emotional intelligence – the need to drag the world down to your level because otherwise you have no meaning or point whatsoever."

"Nonsense," he said. "You sound quite mentally deranged. I would suggest you do not delude yourself any further."

She drew a deep breath. "Why the fuck am I sitting here, in fucking space, arguing about the psychology of selfishness? I have better things to worry about, like whether to come home and fucking die surrounded by morons or stay right here and fucking die alone."

"I suggest you stay where you are."

"Fuck you," she said. "But you may be right there. Though …" She laughed grimly. "I don't expect you to ever understand that. You are too much of a coward."

"Coward?" the voice cried – obviously stung.

"Yeah. Too caught up in your universal all-encompassing pants-wetting fear."

"We're the survivors. We are the ones who will make it through this. We're the ones that will take control and may be given a reason to hope for the future."

At that point the door opened. Cinnamon flinched and glanced round.

"What the hell are you doing?" Ola cried.

She ignored her. "Oh maybe," she snarled into the microphone. "But you know as well as I do that sooner or later that cowardice and fear always bites you on the arse. Now – later – sometime. Whenever people get a good hard look at you. The one thing you can't deal with – anyone looking at you."

"Give me that thing," Ola growled. "Our first contact with Earth and you're having a row?"

There was a brief scuffle and then Ola had the headset out of her hands. Cinnamon found herself barged sideways out of the chair. "Give it back," she cried.

"Shut up. Hello? Hello?"

Cinnamon stared at her, breathing heavily.

"InterSpace Hotel speaking, do you read me? What? Yes, never mind that. Who am I talking to?"

Cinnamon turned away and stormed into the corridor, the full expression of her rage somewhat muted by the reduced gravity. She was shaking all over, feeling a white heat of fury that even embraced Ola at that point. She was feeling worse after that ridiculous exchange than at any time since she'd come here – even during the first creeping realisation of what had happened and what the silence meant. No doubt, there had always been some level of blindness to events that had been numbing her, but here, farcical though the conversation had been, it also contained a harsh trumpet of reality – of what silence meant. It rang and echoed through her mind leaving her feeling dizzy and cut wide open.

PLAY

Drunk enough for the stars to swim, she lay on the beach – flat on her back, staring up at the disk of the earth, tears soaking her face. Empty bottle by her side. She had yanked down her light top a little, exposing one breast, and over her nipple crawled a snail – a larger garden snail that had somehow found its way up here and probably the biggest living thing she had encountered yet. It crawled across her skin with a wet tickle that was not unpleasant. In general, however, snails do not like human touch and react as though it pains them – and this one was rearing up with a hint of reluctance. She watched it with a smile – then plucked it up and moved it down so it would ascend the mountain again.

"You're a long way from home, my friend," she murmured, her voice husky with misery, her eyes wandering upwards. Outside one of the huge windows, endless stars. Outside the other, the familiar blue and brown and green disk spun with its usual disorienting speed. And again she was marvelling just how normal it looked. Humanity and its eternal muddling barely even registering from up here. A species that could live or die with barely a murmur. All its eternal strife and bickering, festering and boiling, pain and harshness as pretty much nothing beyond a few faintly visible scars on the land.

Then there was a scuff in the sand.

"Hey," Ola said softly, barely raising an eyebrow this time at what she was doing. "You ok?"

Cinnamon lazily turned her head, staring at the bare feet that had planted themselves beside her – then picked up the snail one last time and put it back in the nearby undergrowth. "I dunno really. What happened?"

"We talked. I … got a little more info before we were cut off for the last time."

Cinnamon just shrugged – not even sure she wanted to hear. "What a … waste," she muttered.

"Yeah," Ola said. "One stupid minute and …"

"I don't even mean that, though," she said, with a wet sniff. "We – never really found what we were so frightened of losing. We never even seemed to want what we so were frightened of losing. It doesn't make sense."

Ola stared down at her, head on one side, but Cinnamon didn't care if she was coherent or not. "I just don't understand why the decision to live or not live, to hurt or not hurt, has to be so hard," she wailed. "In the space of a few minutes, I went from a member of an amazing species – capable of such wonderful things – to … completely invalidated. There's nothing left now. It was all rendered … it's all gone. I mean – even if most people survived, it's still all gone. It's not even a tragedy, it's just too stupid. It's … a farce, that's what it is. We should be shrieking with laughter at a bunch of entities so blind that they just decided to stop existing for no reason. It's like a whole line of caterpillars walking down a twig into a pond – and just crawling on not even aware that they are drowning …"

She rolled over onto her front, resting her face on one arm.

"I think you were right anyway," Ola said, after an uneasy pause, sitting down beside her and placing one hand on her shoulder. "We should probably stay here for a while."

"What did you find out?"

"Hints. After some rather more diplomatic questions." She smiled wanly. "They didn't know much either, but things sound a little rough down there. At least in Aberystwyth. Not very friendly. Lots of fighting and violence. There seems to be some muddled war going on on various levels … I have no idea why."

"Told you."

"Yeah … I guess you did." She lay down beside her.

"So … we stay here?"

Ola nodded. "For now. I wish the others hadn't just run off home. Maybe things will calm down given time …"

"Good. I never even wanted to go back anyway," Cinnamon said, aware of the childishness of her tone. She gave a drunken giggle. "I was going to say 'I'd rather stay here where I am alone'. But you know … I'm quite glad I am not alone, actually."

She reached out and squeezed Ola's hand.

Ola nodded. "I'm also quite glad. It would be very cold out here if you weren't … here."

"Awww," Cinnamon said. "How sweet – a nice bonding exercise in space. Hug?"

Ola rolled over and grasped her and the two locked together for a while, Cinnamon relishing the feel of Ola's weight on top of her. And when they separated again, they ended up lying in the sand, side by side, staring up at the blue, brown and green disk of earth.

"I sometimes wished I'd read more as I was growing up," Ola said out of nowhere. "For a while, I quite enjoyed science fiction. Then I … moved on. Lost it all in the nitty gritty of science fact. But I suppose that point where science meets the imagination and the human soul is way more important than I sometimes thought."

"I hate sci-fi," Cinnamon said.

Ola gave her a comically pissed off look. "There's no pleasing you, is there," she cried. "I'm trying to wax lyrical about the old arts vs. science thing …"

"Which always was complete bollocks."

"My point exactly."

The two stared at each other for a moment, then both started laughing quietly.

"You know how to reprogram that escape capsule? Make it less idiot-proof?"

"Up to a point. Why?"

"I was just thinking. Maybe we should load it up and go that way instead." She waved at the stars. "I dare say we'd be doomed, but maybe we could see something beforehand. Mars or …"

"Have you any idea how long it would take that thing to get to Mars?"

"Well … no."

"Months and months and months … I'm not sure I can cope with that amount of time stuck in a box with you."

"Oh that's nice, that is. I thought we were bonding."

"Besides, the air wouldn't last more than a few days. These things are only made for short trips."

"Fuck. That's the problem with science. Always something pragmatic has to come along and ruin my dreams."

"That's the problem with you fantasists … always spinning off into cloud cuckoo land and who is it that has to pick up the pieces?" Ola pointed at herself with an emphatic jab.

"Fuck you."

"And fuck you back again."

Cinnamon chucked a handful of sand at her and bounded to her feet – then, while Ola was still spluttering, went belting down the beach towards the water, dragging off her clothes as she went. A quick glance back confirmed that Ola was also on her feet now and pursuing. Exactly what would happen if she was caught she had no idea – how wild was Ola under that crisp clinical surface? But she was going to push the game a bit further before finding out. A running jump at full speed in the direction that dialled down her weight a little and she was hurtling through the air, then cannonballed into the mirror-like water with a massive splash.

On the beach, Ola had come to a halt. She stared after her for a moment, then gave a massive shrug and started stripping as well – readying herself to break the mirror a second time. Cinnamon watched with interest. She'd been running around naked so much that it felt like a small triumph to have Ola follow her.

And besides, Ola's body was definitely worth looking at.

A second dive and she was approaching at high speed, swimming strongly. Cinnamon gave a wild laugh and splashed away up the curved surface of the water. It seemed that Ola was a fast swimmer, however. Capture seemed inevitable, so Cinnamon gave up trying to escape and instead dived under as she approached. In the flurry of bubbles, she caught Ola by the feet and yanked her down below the surface, before striking shoreward. Ola bobbed up with a spluttering shriek and again pursued. And again Cinnamon dodged away. Not too fast though, because maybe she wanted to be caught. Maybe a bit of rough and tumble seemed the most perfect and beautiful thing in the world, right then. Maybe.

It was a delirious swim, as dizzy and dreamlike as any dance on land, but slowed and confused yet further by the curving water. And maybe there was a hysterical touch to their laughter as they swam and played together, the vast form of the earth turning overhead, always a bit faster than it should have been.

What else could you do?

*

And later, the two lay side by side on Cinnamon's bed.

"Whatever," Cinnamon said, still feeling very drunk. "If this is the end of time, then I'll still be singing."

"And think of the scientific observations to be made," Ola said. "Not every day you get to watch a civilization implode. I should be writing all this up."

"Of all the times in history we could have been alive, we managed to be here at the truly defining moment. And of all the places to be, we managed to be up here with the best view in the house."

Ola glanced at her, then smiled – a smile Cinnamon returned before burying her face in Ola's neck and giving her a kiss.

Ola went slightly stiff for a moment – then Cinnamon could almost feel her shrug internally. The technician's arms locked tight for a moment in a comforting squeeze.

EARTH OPERA

"Three more radio broadcasts so far," Cinnamon said. "In English. And a couple more that I can't understand. I think one was in Korean. It's as if … something switched the world off, and now it's coming alive again."

Ola shook her head. "I have no idea. Something very strange happened, I think. Something more than just nukes."

"What would it take to shut down communications technology globally?"

"Electromagnetic pulse would do a lot of damage, but to shut down the entire world, you'd basically have to nuke the entire world. And that would shut it down pretty permanently, I would have thought. And it'd be beyond our capability anyway, I'm sure. Simple answer is, I have no idea."

Cinnamon sighed. "I have just been sitting here, drifting. Twiddling knobs. Mostly on the old emergency frequencies. Every so often some little clip comes through. It's surreal."

Ola reached into her bag and pulled out two silver foil pouches, one of which she tossed to Cinnamon. It had a short stubby straw protruding from it. Obviously fluid. She caught it with a question in her face.

"Drink," Ola explained. "Rather more standard space fare – not quite what you are used to from the bar. Just push the straw in like this to open it."

Cinnamon followed her lead and sucked. It required a little more suction than a normal straw would – no doubt some sophisticated valves to keep the stuff inside until needed – but she easily got a mouthful of sweet fruity liquid. Ola, meanwhile, had settled down on the floor, cross-legged, leaning unconcernedly against a rack of instruments.

"So what have you heard? Did you talk to anyone?"

"No. Of the three I could understand, two seemed pre-recorded and one was out of his mind."

"Huh."

"One said ..." She glanced at a scrap of paper. "One said ... all it said was 30 45 82 18 over and over."

"Coordinates maybe. I'll check them later."

"One was saying – fuck, I wrote it down. Oh yeah – Tallahassee is dry. Move North. Make for Tired Creek Lake."

"And the out of his mind one?"

"Some religious hate-twaddle. I didn't listen for more than a few seconds."

Ola nodded. "People trying to regroup," she murmured. "Maybe."

"Yeah. I wonder what is at Tired Creek Lake?"

"No idea. Never heard of the place. Though I wouldn't mind being somewhere called that when the world goes mega-fucked. Oh well. Let's keep twiddling. Where are we?" She glanced at the instruments, then the window. "Ah – Atlantic ocean. I guess we have a few minutes' break anyway." She took another sip of her drink with a lazy stretch.

Steps must be taken, the voice cried, shrill with fanaticism.

"Or not," Ola murmured.

Steps taken to … to cleanse the skies. That was the great mistake. The great blasphemy. We must take down the satellites, destroy the space stations. We must restore purity through cleansing fire. The fire of rockets …

"Bloody hell," Cinnamon said. "Another one."

"I wouldn't worry," Ola said. "A person like that wouldn't even be able to open the door mechanism, let alone get the systems on and fire any rockets."

"I suppose. Though maybe if he took up with some insane ex-military type …"

"No. Hitting anything in space would be a major undertaking even with a huge team of scientists and engineers. Even some bonkers general …"

"With a hard-on."

"… with a hard-on would have a hell of a time doing it."

"Ok," Cinnamon said with a smile. "He does sound just the kind of swivel-eyed loon who would once have been yelling at Speaker's Corner."

"Must be from somewhere on the East Coast," Ola said, glancing at the instruments. "Northern end. Just reaching us out at sea."

Cinnamon stared dully at the window for a moment as the voice faded out. She was still unsure how to read most of these instruments, though the radio itself was quite familiar now. "How long until the UK?"

"Not long – this thing moves fast. Maybe about quarter of an hour to the edge of the range."

"Yeah – no wonder we can only get brief clips." She stared again at blue below – a blue unbroken by any scraps of land.

"What say we try and pick up your old friends in Aberystwyth?"

Cinnamon growled with a certain sardonic inflexion. "Sure. But you can talk to them this time."

"Shall I take the driving seat? I might as well start messaging."

"By all means." Cinnamon drained the last of her drink and stood up, reeling as she was reminded yet again of her reduced weight. Ola slid in and spent a few minutes adjusting the knobs, running a few checks. Then she picked up the microphone. "InterSpace Hotel, do you read me?" she asked crisply.

Silence. Ola checked the readouts and repeated the greeting into the void. Cinnamon watched as she said it over and over again, her voice barely changing its inflexion, leaving several seconds between each message.

Then the voice came through, crisp and recorded.

… homosexuals, atheists, false thinkers and any other degenerate elements continue and our message to you is that you cannot hide.

"Oh for fuck's sake," Cinnamon said.

We will find you and there is still plenty of room for you all, high on our walls and in our trees of fire. We repeat, you cannot hide. This has been a recorded message. Message repeats. Aberystwyth compound is now closed. I repeat, Aberystwyth compound is now closed. We are at capacity until further notice. Any attempt to make contact may be seen as an act of aggression, to which we may respond with terminal measures. In the area of the compound, freedom is maintained. I repeat, freedom is maintained. Outside, operations against deviants, socialists, homosexuals, atheists, false thinkers and any other degenerate elements continue and our message to you is …

The two just stared at each other.

"That's … a lot of ways they could find to kill me," Cinnamon said with a strange laugh.

"I'd rather like to see a list of what they think is 'deviant' as well."

Cinnamon sighed as the slowly repeating message faded out of range. "It's like some kind of deranged cartoon," she said at last.

"Uhuh."

"I always tried to avoid politics, just to protect my sanity and not … kill myself or whatever." Ola's eyes darted round to look at her for a moment and she gave a bitter laugh. "It never avoided me though. And when you see what you're up against, it's hard to keep out of it. In fact … If anything, keeping quiet hurts more than any stupid pointless row."

"Funny thing is, they probably think much the same thing." Ola waved at the radio.

"Yeah. So? It just boils down to moral decisions, that's all. Not who shouts the best or feels things strongest."

"I guess, but where's morality without reality? Neither side seems particularly good at that," Ola said, wrinkling her nose. "That's what gets me."

"What?"

Ola stared at nothing for a moment. "One really wants to exist in a nice cerebral world focussing on important things. The way things are, the nature of reality, as far as we can find out – and what we don't know, we don't know. We don't make stuff up, is what I am saying. You just want to laugh at the anti-science crap that people blather – blathered … whatever. But … then they end up shaping policy and everything around you. They fill peoples' heads with unreal ideas of what we are, they get things banned or turn public opinion against some of the most important things humanity has ever achieved – against the only chances we have to save ourselves … or … had …" She broke off, blinked a few times and stared with burning intensity at the coordinates displayed on one of the screens. "Fucking hell," she muttered.

"Both sides?" Cinnamon asked, after a moment.

Maybe that wasn't the right thing to say, for Ola's face contracted into a black frown. "You fucking bet," she said. "Have you listened to them in the past few … decades?"

"I … suppose."

"I've just had it with the lot of them and their insane dreamlands, whatever they are. Were. Are. And you know, I don't care if you call me intolerant or not respecting people's fucking beliefs … I don't respect people's fucking beliefs. Just – no fucking patience left."

There was a sound from the speakers and Ola sighed and grabbed her pen.

… from the Camden Town sewing club. We are barricaded in and for the moment, safe, but we estimate supplies will last for a maximum of two weeks without further excursions. We invite all to join us. Sewing skills not required. Please be aware that we will need to meet on neutral ground first. Message repeats …

"I ain't calling you anything, you can believe that," Cinnamon said as Ola noted it down.

"Oh, I know, I know. It's fine – I just really really hate beliefs. Opinions."

Cinnamon watched her uneasily. She had never seen Ola looking quite this dark. The normally unruffled technician seemed filled with a rage that she had never suspected lurked there. Of course, strong emotions were nothing unusual – she had felt enough of them herself. She'd felt something similar while arguing with the Aberystwyth Compound – she'd felt it while staring down at the scarred cities. Seen from without, it came with a weird sense of futility, yet also a massive compulsion. Was the ideal to try and maintain cool crystal logic and not give way to emotions? Or was some expression of rage, even to irrational degrees, an inevitability of life?

Maybe both were true.

But then Ola smiled grimly. "Ok, you've got an opinion," she continued. "I'm happy for you. Now for fucks sake, zip it away and stop waving the thing around."

"We all have them."

"Yeah. But I don't need to see them, do I?" Ola shrugged. "Especially the stupid ones. Ok, ok – if I say too much, I'll start sounding like those morons in Aberystwyth … I'm just pissed off, like you. I just wish people would fucking reality-check what they fucking believe just occasionally." She grinned a crooked grin, which Cinnamon returned with some relief.

"It's almost refreshing to see you rant."

"Oh yeah, I can do it. Occasionally. When the mask slips. The world is complicated – and just because something makes you feel good, doesn't mean it's true."

"… yeah …"

Then, out of nowhere, music. A violin. Just that. A single line of eerie, slow, classical melody. It cut through the fizzing atmosphere and Ola sat up, blinking several times and looking more startled than one might expect.

"It's … what is that? It sounds quite atonal." Cinnamon wrinkled her nose in surprise. The high violin sounded faintly familiar and came with an odd poignancy – a sound that shut down the conversation and fit well with the cold black vastness of space.

Judging by the playing, which was good but not without the occasional hitch or hesitation, it could have been live.

"Violin … solo …" Ola said, patiently writing it down, along with the time and coordinates. Cinnamon glanced at the window and the revolving Earth beneath. It was hard to tell where they were from the land below, but they must be well away from the UK now.

There was one more message, a few minutes later – a brief clip of a language that she couldn't recognise – all sharp edges and uneasy frightened inflections. It came crackling through the speaker for a few seconds and the only word she could pick out in any detail was the word zapaljen repeated several times.

"'Zapaljen?'" Ola murmured. "That's something about fire, right? On fire?"

"No idea. I don't even know what language that is."

"The only second language I am any good at is Arabic," Ola said. "But that sounds Croatian. Or something." Again Ola wrote it down, then rose to her feet. "Another drink?"

"Thank you. Though after all that, I am tempted to have something stronger than squash. Maybe you could use it too."

Ola smiled and produced a bottle of wine from a bag – an actual bottle rather than a plastic pouch. "Shouldn't booze too much up here. Can't be drunk in charge of a space station. That would be bad."

"Oh, I can," Cinnamon said with a laugh, sitting down on the floor and leaning companionably against the chair at Ola's side. "I'd love to be drunk in charge of a space station."

"I bet." Ola poured wine into two plastic cups and handed one over. They sipped in silence for a few minutes. It was hard to relax though – a storm of tension remained. But at least the atmosphere between them was clearing, even before the wine started to cloud her mind.

"I don't really hate everyone," Ola said at last, with a small smile. "I just succumb to frustration sometimes."

"Oh, I know. We all do it." Cinnamon rubbed the back of her head against the chair and stared up at her. Maybe ranting was no bad thing, she thought – but likewise you had to have an exit strategy. A path to a place where you could leave it behind for the quiet plateau of rationality. Otherwise the mind would barely function.

But Ola would be well aware of that.

Then Ola turned to the window. "Talking of Arabic – here it comes."

The two leaned against the glass, staring out. Below them, the land was slowly losing most of its green and transforming into a strange but beautiful scarred warm brown. Desert. They were orbiting too low to make out much of the familiar shape of the Arabian Peninsula but the desert passed beneath them, filled with complex textures. Scattered dark blotches – strangely regular dots of green that a close look revealed to be perfectly round irrigated fields … unlike many places, these dots of green and the occasional hint of town or city were the only signs of people living their lives that were visible. The scars of roads and railways were not standing out very well against the overwhelming scar of the desert itself – nothing more than a beautiful tracery of dry valleys and sand dunes.

"Is that … home?" Cinnamon asked softly.

"No. My home is Oregon. Portland."

"Ah …"

"But I do have some connections with Kuwait. I have only been there a few times but … I suppose I do have a certain bond with the area."

And at one point, another message came through. Cinnamon had even less chance of understanding anything from this one, but she noted a tiny frown settle on Ola's face.

"What is it?"

"Nothing important."

Cinnamon watched her curiously for a moment, but shrugged it off. And then there was nothing but sea.

"We're off," Ola said, putting down her notebook. "If the orbit crosses the UK, you also get about as long an ocean journey as is possible on Earth – across the Indian, the Southern and then right over the Pacific.

"So much water," Cinnamon murmured.

"Yes. Might conceivably get some broadcast drifting over from Australia if we're close enough, but not sure I can be bothered." She stretched. "The Pacific is pretty stunning. Not so much an ocean as a water hemisphere. You know what an antipode is?"

"Ummm …"

"The point directly on the other side of the planet from where you are standing. If you tunnelled right through the centre and out the other side."

"Ah yes – they used to talk about the Antipodes."

"Everywhere has an antipode somewhere – oddly, the vast majority of land at this point in history has its antipode in water. But the Pacific is so vast that it contains its own antipodes in a few places. You dive down into the Pacific ocean, tunnel right through the earth and out the other side – and you are still in the Pacific."

Cinnamon stared out of the window again at the endless blue, feeling a distinct thrill. That did indeed bring home the scale of it rather. "And of course," she murmured, "at heart it's all one vast ocean …"

"Yes."

Cinnamon blinked, shivered. Like the stars, the sense of insignificance and vastness felt good, but it was still only lying on top of her roiling mind like a layer of oil.

"Maybe enough for today?" Ola said at last. "It's getting late and I need sleep. We can ride the carousel again tomorrow."

"Yeah," Cinnamon said. "Though I might stay here for a bit and just watch … see if I can find any islands passing."

*

Except that there were none – at least, not that she could see. She leaned against the window, staring out and down at the expanse of blue and the occasional cloud. It was a quiet, meditative sight but now she was alone, she could feel the tension returning. A nasty knot inside her. Her mind felt restless and eventually she withdrew to the corridor, climbed downwards/outwards a level and entered the kitchen.

Part of the art of this place had clearly been creating meals for the rich, pampered pallets of the guests using ingredients that wouldn't fill up an entire cargo capsule. A lot of the food in storage here was preserved in various ways – dried and packeted, rehydrated with asteroid water as needed. Or was it recycled urine? The asteroid water sounded more romantic, but in reality it would all be mixed together now in one watery soup of pragmatic realism.

However, there was also a freezer filled with meat and fish that she was eating her way through without restraint. Even frozen, it would not last forever and she hated the thought of it going to waste. One did not waste food. Especially meat. Not in East London. Not in low Earth orbit. No doubt, over time, she would be reduced to eating the preserved food more and more, which was a gloomy thought, but she'd deal with that when the time came. For now, she just gathered some ingredients and began chopping them, then slung them in a pan and cooked. Simple food, but deliberately rich in the hope that it would calm her storming thoughts a bit.

Memories were in her mind now of doing this before, though. Cooking late night meals for herself or her friends. Her London apartment had been … ok. She had been luckier than many, even though Cinnamon Thorns had never earned her anything even close to a living wage. The result had been a tangle of odd scraps of income – gig economy, freelancing at any of half a dozen different jobs, while exhaustion gnawed and her music got angrier and angrier. Now though, there was a huge wash of homesickness. In spite of everything, she had loved London. The city had been a strange almost-living entity, sick in some ways, vibrant in others. The people likewise. And in her circle, they had been fantastic – as wild and energetic and varied and original a crowd as you could ever hope to find.

And where were they now?

She had moved a fairly comfortable chair in here – one from the main hotel area – and it sat looking rather surreal against the gleaming aluminium surfaces and the utilitarian pots and pans of the kitchen. She sat and ate quietly – not the most inspired food she had ever cooked, but she was too lost in memories now to cook high art. Memories of life in London. The bustle, the activity – markets, events, art, uprising. She remembered the shouting and ferocity in London as people took to the streets, protesting against creeping fascism, against the housing situation, against environmental carelessness, against a thousand other things. It had been only a few blocks from her home that Oswald Mosely and his Blackshirts had been run out of the East End way back in the 1936 Battle of Cable Street. Now, a gigantic mural to the event adorned the side of a house there. And the same spirit still burned in the East. She remembered watching flares and smoke bombs colouring the air – the carnival atmosphere of the marches. People taking the opportunity for street performances – capering around in ludicrous costumes. Slogans everywhere. Tories Out. Smash the Fasch. And she'd loved it. She'd loved it from a distance though, it was true, caught up in her own little world of music. But yes, there was something miraculous about human beings. In spite of everything.

Scrappy, messy, chaotic, beautiful, beautiful East End.

And where was it now?

She dumped the bowl in the huge washbasin and tramped grimly to her room. It all seemed so far away now, in every possible sense. In time. In distance. In thought. In style. In life.

Occasionally, as she walked down the street, people would yell Cinnamon Thorns and wave – and there was no denying it felt good. It felt good to be known. She remembered working the venues around the East End – smaller places with an industrial vibe or dark back rooms in the London pubs. Excited crowds with herself at the focal point. The exhilaration of performing, of standing like a sorcerer over a thundering mass of human bodies, energy flowing from her to them. And back again.

And where were they now?

Preparing for bed, she still felt tight and anxious, as though something vast was building within. As though there was some vitally important task that she had to do, but she was prevented because she was stuck waiting on others. Only the others in this case were the whole human race. Or maybe it was a task that, through her own carelessness and theirs, was now too late.

But what could you do with thoughts such as those?

In bed, the shutters closed to provide some semblance of night in this world of strobing sun and stars, she could only toss and turn. She tried telling herself simple stories to relax herself, but they just went dark. She tried masturbating, imagining everything from old memories of erotic euphoria to Ola naked – but gave up. There were too many ghosts – and it was hard to imagine sex with an invalidated species.

Faces of old friends came and went. She could have no way of knowing whether they were alive now. Maybe they were. Maybe the East End still burned with the same fire, in spite of the apocalypse.

She felt naked in her head – the massive thing growing larger by the second and manifesting not in grief but in stark terror now. It seemed as though they had been flatly murdered, as directly and personally as by a knife. Murdered by everyone on the planet – an entire species that piloted itself straight into oblivion. She felt a deadly guilt that she herself had not been more politically active. Why had she not fought more? Millions had – by no measure were people blind, and yet the rails the vast homogenous mass of humanity ran on had proved impossible to either cope with or sway.

As she lay there, she imagined the UK politicians stripped naked and marched through London before being tarred and feathered and chucked in the Thames. She imagined the Russian elite bound and handed over to the rage of the artists and activists they had persecuted for so long, who stood waiting grimly, spray-paint and razors in hand. She imagined the Communist Party of China each plugged into a million wires and cables, their blood draining across the internet as they screamed their lives out. She imagined the Japanese Jimintō all bent over and fucked up the arse by the raging J-underground. She imagined stripping the president of the USA naked while TV cameras rolled, tying him down and reaching for a long leather whip …

She curled over in bed feeling sick. It was a mad storm of thoughts, driven as much by guilt as anything – by her own inability to ever expiate the toxins of the world. But most of all, there was a massive sense of futility. It seemed utterly insane to imagine that the species as a whole was in any way in charge of its destiny when you realised how helpless it was against its own forces, how fragile society was in the face of shocks and disruption. It had been feeling like a snowflake or a soap bubble, even before she had left the planet – years before, and that had been a hard thing to cope with. People came, people went – that never changed. The flux and background chaos of individual people and individual interactions was familiar enough. But she had grown up with the notion that society itself was something stable and permanent. That was the delusion – and the pain of watching that crumble had been unique. Homo sapiens may be a survivor species – a spectacular opportunist that could function in a wide range of environments and conditions – but that meant little on individual, personal terms when disaster struck. That never assuaged tragedy. The grief on a societal level, however, was entirely new and burning – a very strange shape to fit into the hole that was her head.

She deliberately tried to imagine more amiable faces. Her last boyfriend and what it had felt like early on as he stared into her eyes as he fucked her. The first time she had eaten pussy and felt a woman orgasm. Hugging crying friends with desperation as they tried to find a way out of their lives. Popping MDMA and feeling an ocean of love flowing through her, hugging everyone in the room over and over again, tears in her eyes at the magic of what they were, then waking up sick and dry-mouthed.

… those dark days watching as her gentle and extremely intelligent musician friend with the sandy hair slowly gave up any interest in existence – drifting like a feather on a fat, oily river – options, hope and resilience dwindling. And then that far darker day when she'd suddenly gone quiet – until the news of her suicide had finally trickled through …

"Fuck," she yelled, shockingly loud, and sat up.

In the end, she just opened the shutters and watched the spinning stars, trying to recapture the sense of insignificance that they could provide. This time, however, even that seemed to be failing her. People were insignificant enough, no doubt … the argument could be made. But to her, from where she was standing, as one of them, the significance was inevitable and vast.

SPACE OPERA

"Ok," Cinnamon said rather shortly as she joined Ola in the communications room as they did most days now. "Let's see. Maybe this is where we hear something positive for once."

"I'm not sure about that," Ola said. "Aberystwyth Compound is still ranting away. They do love the sound of their own fucking voice."

"Huh."

"And … they seem to really dislike artists. I mean yeah, they hate all the usual targets – gays, people who threaten their rickety belief systems … but artists?"

Cinnamon just stared at her for a moment, something black surging up inside her. Then she turned to the window, watching the world below.

And the speakers crackled into life. Ola grabbed her notebook.

… And you shall eat salt, for it feels no pain. And you shall eat fruit, for it is freely given. And you shall eat wingless flies because they have no soul. And you shall eat horse leeches for they likewise. And you shall eat the harvested roots of plants, but not more than sixty percent. And you shall eat zebra mussels for they have no eyes. You shall eat purified clay, for it feels no pain. You shall eat mushrooms harvested with a knife, for they are freely given. You shall eat charcoal made from deadfall. You shall eat the excrement of vultures because they consume carrion …

The pen had come to a halt over the paper – and in the end, Ola wrote nothing. Shut the notebook with a snap. Placed it on the desk beside her. Sat staring into space.

A full minute passed.

"You sure you don't agree with those fuckers on some level?" Cinnamon asked.

"Who?"

"Aberystwyth. I'm … was … just some pretentious waif wasting my time trying to express things? Living in cloud cuckoo land?"

Ola stared in surprise. "No, actually," she said, her body language radiating wariness. "I think most people can't express much at all, so it makes a change to at least try."

"And I've fucking succeeded too – better than them. Better than you. You may know a lot of stuff, and it's great, but what use is any of it on its own?"

"I ain't arguing," Ola said with a smile. "Though I'm sure that goes both ways."

"Oh, sure. But as for those fuckers …" She waved at the radio. "Aberystwyth and others. They not only don't try, they glory in not trying. They've turned cowardice into an ideal."

"… maybe," Ola said, still looking uneasy.

… 68 23 88 56 37 22 84, the radio announced. I repeat, all marked with the following numbers must report to Stony Creek Road: 05 06 18 68 23 …

"At least they survived," Ola murmured, as the numbers kept counting.

"What point is there in surviving like that? Knowing what we could have been – no, what we fucking are, yet shrugging off everything?"

More silence. Cinnamon didn't know what part of the earth was passing below the small window, but the last two accents had been American.

"You know what?" she said at last, and Ola looked round. "I don't want to go back down there at all. I just want to stay here until we can't stay any longer, then open an airlock or something."

"Don't say that …"

"What the fuck is the point of anything else?"

Ola was silent. "We don't know," she said at last. "We don't know what's going on down there. Or what will be."

"If all we heard wasn't enough, we've had thousands of years showing us exactly what's going on down there."

"At some point," Ola whispered, "I want to go home. I am not giving up. And when I do … please don't make me leave you behind. I … don't think I could do that."

Cinnamon made a dark sound, but said nothing.

Ola stepped up behind her and slid her arms round, squeezing hard. "I don't think I could do that," she repeated.

"If I tell you to bloody leave me behind, you can bloody leave me behind," she growled.

"No."

"Why?" Cinnamon yelled.

"Because … I don't want to," Ola whispered, hugging her tighter.

Cinnamon shivered, stared at nothing for a moment – then there was an abrupt crack. A sob. There are few pains like one who is contemplating oblivion being told that they are needed. Nothing rips you wider open. And in just a few seconds, Cinnamon collapsed. She was not weeping, she was bawling – almost screaming as she sagged out of Ola's arms and into a hunched and shivering ball on the floor among the trailing wires. Ola stared down, then, looking almost weary, knelt down behind her, continuing the hug. Stroking her gently.

For several minutes, Cinnamon lay there, hunched and shaking, given over to an outburst of grief, then she slowly quieted. "Gawd sake," she muttered at last.

"You feel better for that?" Ola whispered, stroking her hair.

Cinnamon gave a tiny nod. "Thank you," she murmured. "I think I … that's been … for a while."

"Let it out. It's always good to let it out. I can tell you, I've had few a good cries the last week or so. I just hid away in a corner."

Cinnamon glanced at her with a faint smile, then sat up. A shaky sigh. "What are we doing here?" she asked.

"Hm?"

"Some utterly random … fucking ridiculous fluke put … me here. Us. In this place. Role. I suppose I shouldn't just sit around weeping and wailing." She waved at the audio equipment. "You can record stuff with this lot? And broadcast a repeating loop of it like those fuckers in Aberystwyth?"

"Yes, sure."

"Multiple frequencies?"

"Yes. Some."

"Audio editing software?"

"Ummm … yes."

"Good – set it up please."

"What are you going to say?"

"Set one of the frequencies to that fucking Aberystwyth compound."

"But …"

"Just do it."

Ola shrugged a small shrug, slid into the seat and spent a few minutes starting up the equipment and software. "Ok," she said at last. "This is ready to record. It won't be live."

"Good, thank you. You can show me how to do all this, to edit it sometime, but for now, just record."

Ola handed her the microphone, pressed a button, then sat back rather diffidently in the chair, legs crossed. But Cinnamon stood there, still soaked with tears, still shaking, and stared at the ice-cream-shaped mystery in her hand. "I don't know," she murmured at last. "I don't know what to say and I'll have to edit this later, but fucking hell. What does everybody think humanity is? You lot. All of you. I never knew – except … this. This," she cried, her voice rising for a moment. "One big fucking wound that you pick at and beat and rip so it never ever heals. It bleeds and oozes pus constantly and every day we chew at it a little bit more." She fell silent for a long minute, aware of Ola watching her with piercing eyes. "I don't know what to say," she managed at last. "I should find words – some kind of magic, beautiful words that could bring all of us together. And yet … I have no idea. What can I ever say that is more … more … affecting than what happened? I mean … what do you want, people?" she asked at last. "Now? Is history enough for you? Is this enough for you?"

She paused again, gathering her tangled thoughts. "Do you know who I am?" she asked at last. "You don't need to – of course you fucking don't. All you need to know is that I am overhead. I am crying with inexpressible grief, but I still have a promise for you. Every day, I'll be here. For everyone who needs to remember what we are, what we were … and what we can be. On the frequency … what the fuck is the frequency, Ola?"

"Which?" Ola mouthed.

"Fuck." She closed her eyes for a moment, then waved at Ola to stop the recording, which she did in silence. "I'll … sort that out. Find some better words." She closed her eyes for a moment, then opened them again, her face grim. "Now

– one more please," she said, aware that she was slipping into her professional studio persona from the days of Cinnamon Thorns. But Ola seemed happy enough to be ordered about. The button was pressed, a new audio file opened on the screen, and she signed her to go ahead.

And Cinnamon sang.

She had performed many kinds of music in her time. Classical training had given her a lot of skill, supplemented by various musical scenes, her alt-punk style, and further into much more experimental music. Singing unaccompanied was not so alien either – she had done a capella songs in her various albums and rather liked the freedom and nakedness of it. In this cold and rather flat-sounding communications room, she was only sounding more naked, but even that could be embraced. The utter humanity of the sounds she was producing – far removed from anything electronically processed, accompanied or even massaged by acoustics. It almost seemed primeval – a delicate wandering melody with few modern inflections – a melody that might have drifted through the rocky hills accompanying the dawn of human life. And she let the melody flow – no particular sense of a beginning or an end – a melody that sounded as though it could go on forever, and what you heard was nothing more than a small window into something that had always existed.

Ola just stared in silence, her face somehow more intense than Cinnamon could ever remember. And when she stumbled to an end, she ended up blinking for a moment, numbed.

"Cut," she said at last, and Ola switched off.

"That was … beautiful."

"I'll make more," she whispered. "I feel I can produce that stuff forever. Who needs fucking bands or backing tracks?"

Ola nodded and the silence again stretched out.

"I'll … edit that soon if you can show me how. Ummm – ok, just one more please."

"Sure …"

One last time, the button was pressed, a new file opened. Cinnamon gave a faint smile this time, feeling the exhaustion of artistic creation draining away her devastated mood. After a moment, she spoke.

"This has been your brief opera from the skies above … passing at seventeen thousand miles per hour. So please listen in when you can. I shall be here – and I will sing for you. I shall sing for everyone who needs to remember what we are, was and can be. For everyone who needs a human voice. And I'll be here until the end of time if necessary. I'll be here … until I am no longer needed." She broke off and glanced uneasily at Ola – but she was just sitting there, her face frozen, maybe even spellbound.

She drew a deep breath. "This is Cinnamon Thorns wishing you all a good night. Sleep tight. And try not to let the monsters bite …"

THE OLD NEIGHBOURHOODS ON MARS

J. J. Steinfeld

Mars-Monitoring Station on Earth, August 21, 2120

"Life imitating art…life imitating art…life imitating art…"

"What in the universe is the commander talking about?" one of the Mars monitors, listening to the latest transmission from the Bradbury III expedition, asked his supervisor.

"Your guess is as good as mine," the supervisor said, both head-shaking bafflement and deep concern in his comment.

"I stopped counting at fifty times. He just keeps saying those confusing words, over and over…"

The surface of Mars, August 21, 2120

While the first two human missions to Mars—the Bradbury expedition in late 2115 and then the Bradbury II expedition in early 2118—had landed successfully on that planet, communications from both expeditions were lost within a week and never restored, the fate of both crews remaining a mystery. But success or failure, communication or non-communication, was of secondary concern, the desire to colonize Mars taking precedence over any exploratory impediments or unforeseen setbacks.

The Bradbury III, the most advanced spacecraft ever built on Earth, with its forty-person, international crew, landed on the surface of Mars on the last day of July, 2120, and the population of Earth, numbering fewer than a billion for the first time since early in the nineteenth century, celebrated for the third time in less than five years as a world holiday was declared even though the projections for population decline and environment degradation were growing bleaker by the day, had been since well before that momentous first human Mars mission. Most scientific projections were that by the middle of the twenty-second century the population of Earth would be fewer than a quarter-billion, and that was without factoring in even more deleterious conventional or nuclear warfare which only the most optimistic believed would cease. Population decline, drastic average life-expectancy reduction, and adverse human-habitat conditions on Earth had been deteriorating steadily since the end of the twenty-first century. The previous two Bradbury spacecraft, certainly full of hope and enveloped with the marvels of technology, left too many questions about Mars colonization unanswered and unrealized. The third Mars mission, two-and-a-half years after the second, whether it was prayerful luck or miraculous science, at least as far as communications were concerned, which had gone on almost uninterrupted since landing, confirmed the viable prospects of colonization. The plans for more spacecraft and the colonization of Mars accelerated with the successful landing and preliminary favourable reports back to Earth, optimism fuelled with each Mars-inspired descriptive word and mind-stimulating transmitted picture.

Unfortunately, there was no trace of the first two spacecraft or their crews, not a single trace, even after three weeks of exploration using the most advanced technology and exploratory equipment. The biggest advance over the previous two Mars missions was in the portable breathing systems, now lighter and longer lasting, as were the space suits and fully-computerized helmets. A recent transmission from Earth indicated that the next Mars mission could be ready in a matter of weeks, with a crew of one hundred.

As celebrations on Earth continued and a new era of global cooperation seemed to have begun, wild speculation getting wilder on how many humans Mars could eventually accommodate and how many spaceships could be constructed within the next crucial decade, estimates ranging from 500 to 1000 passengers each, the crew of the third Mars expedition carried on their exploratory work, each day venturing farther from base, which had been named Green Town, in reference to the fictitious town in the novel

Dandelion Wine, based on Ray Bradbury's hometown of Waukegan and the Bradbury III, like the first two Mars-destined spacecraft, named in honour of the venerated and prophetic author. Even though books were no longer printed on Earth, no books were more valuable or coveted than the old print editions of Bradbury books, especially *The Martian Chronicles*, *Dandelion Wine*, and *Fahrenheit 451*, regarded by many as literary bibles from a distant and strangely idealized time.

It was on the twenty-first day of exploration, when a fully-equipped seventeen-person group lead by the expedition's commander sighted the first built structures, something no one had anticipated, science fiction stories and speculative Mars films notwithstanding. Nothing in the initial reports from the first two Mars expeditions had indicated any form of life or construction other than Earth-originating rockets and equipment from earlier robotic or human Mars missions.

"We have all read *The Martian Chronicles*," the commander said, immediately thinking of the sixth story in that collection, *The Third Expedition*, then ordering no one to go near any structure, which were organized in clusters he thought of as strange neighbourhoods. How many times had he read or heard read that magnificent story, and felt he knew the characters Captain John Black, David Lustig the navigator, and Samuel Hinkston the archaeologist as friends. His parents, both agronomists who dedicated their lives in attempting to protect the Earth's food supply from atmospheric contamination, had introduced him as a precocious child to Bradbury's work, often using the great writer's stories as bedtime reading. The last thing he remembered his father talking to him about before he died in a horrible house fire was *The Martian Chronicles*.

"Exactly like the house I grew up in," youngest crew member said, and the other crew members voiced similar observations, but pointed at different houses. The common thread of their comments was references to Ray Bradbury's book *The Martian Chronicles*, which all the crew members had read at one point of their lives and often enjoyed discussing at various times, having heard read on audio-systems or watched on video during their lengthy and intensive training for the Mars mission and during their long flight. In fact, the crew had brought along an old first edition of *The Martian Chronicles* in a capsule and had buried it not far from where the Bradbury III landed. It had been one of their first acts after disembarking, full of solemnity and reverence, as if placing any offering to the deities of interplanetary travel. All of the crew members had spent time during the voyage reading and rereading on their electronic screens all of Bradbury's work, in different languages depending on the crew members language of choice, as if Bradbury's stories and word-pictures were necessary to making this Mars mission a success. Each crew member had her or his favourite story from *The Martian Chronicles*, and even during the most recent exploration the names and plots of stories were mentioned as spirit-warming or psyche-stimulating. The story titles *Rocket Summer...Ylla...The Summer Night...The Tax Payer...The Earth Men...The Third Expedition...And the Moon Be Still Bright...The Settlers...The Green Morning...* sounding like fragments of a potent mantra. Until this sighting, despite a few minor problems with malfunctioning ground equipment, the mission and its initial over fifty tasks and scientific experiments were going smoothly, too smoothly the crew physician said with a punctuating laugh. "I have a hell of a lot more problems on Earth," she joked.

The chief technical officer, seeing his childhood home where as a boy of twelve declared to his parents that he was going to be an astronaut and visit Mars, pointed out that tomorrow, August 22, 2120, was the two-hundredth anniversary of Ray Bradbury's birth, yet others disputed his claim, offering different dates. This turned into a contest as to who knew the most about Bradbury's life and work, the commander acting as the quizmaster, ever attentive to the psychological states and needs of his crew members, repeatedly cautioning his crew members not to go any closer to the structures regardless of what they thought they represented.

"We don't want life imitating art," he said, pausing at the sound of the odd old-fashioned expression. attempting to sound calm and even jovial, knowing all too well the tragic outcome of that story. The second in command, whose twin brother had been on the first Mars expedition and he desperately hoped to find, pointed out that he was married on the hundredth anniversary of Bradbury's death, on June 5, 2112. His wife, also an astronaut, was back on the spacecraft, monitoring atmospheric and weather conditions on the planet. Another astronaut was born in Illinois, not far from Bradbury's Waukegan birthplace, and another in California, close to where Bradbury is buried, noting that the author's gravestone had the words "AUTHOR OF FAHRENHEIT 451" on it in capital letters. A Swedish crew member was pleased to make a connection to Bradbury's mother, who had come from Sweden to the United States. A Russian astronaut claimed that an ancestor of his in what used to be known as the USSR had worked on film adaptations of several Bradbury short stories for television. The communications officer from the United Kingdom, the oldest crew member at forty, went on about a cousin who had not only a successful line of clothing based on characters from Bradbury stories, but also a popular drinking-and-eating establishment called The Dandelion Wine Pub. One of the five crew members from an African country was especially proud that his great-grandmother had written and illustrated a black graphic-novel version of *Dandelion Wine*, transforming 1928 small-town America into a 1998 African village. Not to be outdone, a Canadian astronaut boasted that his great-grandfather had translated into French both *The Martian Chronicles* and *Dandelion Wine*, winning literary prizes for the translations. The connections to Bradbury's life and work and death went on full throttle, even as all the crew members slowly moved toward the structures.

The commander repeated his "we don't want life imitating art" warning several more times, each time more ominous and serious. Despite their commander ordering them back to the Green Town base, each crew member recklessly removed space suits and life-sustaining helmets, calling out that the air was like Earth's, or at least how they remembered the Earth's air and atmosphere from their childhoods, and entered a structure. The commander thought he saw the house where his father had died in a fire but his mother and he as a teenager had somehow escaped, a house he hated. He heard his parents reading to him, from *The Martian Chronicles*, but he fought getting any closer to any of the built structures, his childhood house or any of the others.

Then the commander saw three men standing on the porch of a house, thinking they might be crew members from the Bradbury or the Bradbury II expeditions, but as he stepped closer, he heard them talking to each other, the names Black, Hinkston, and Lustig occurring prominently in the conversation. These men seemed as real as any of his crew members and he yelled at them that they were characters in a story, creations of Ray Bradbury's astonishing imagination in *The Third Expedition*.

A few hours later, still unable to locate the missing crew members, or offer a rational explanation for their disappearance—going over and over the theories and possible explanations in *The Third Expedition*, the commander remained baffled as to what had occurred—he confined the rest of the crew to the spacecraft. The commander filed a report that sixteen crew members had disappeared, and emphasizing the need for replacements from Earth as soon as the Bradbury IV was completed, neglecting to mention that the loss of his crew was the same number as had perished in *The Third Expedition*, his favourite *The Martian Chronicles'* story.

In the midst of making his latest report, the commander suddenly remembered that *The Third Expedition* was originally published in 1948, with the title *Mars is Heaven!* His mother had told him that, or was it his father, he wasn't certain, but it felt important to pursue accuracy. He knew that if he returned to the site of the built structures he could find out the answer. He instructed the crew to monitor activity, especially at the coordinates of the built structures, and left the spacecraft alone, wanting to talk to his parents one last time, continuing to transmit to the Mars-monitoring station on Earth as he walked toward the site of the built structures, his voice increasing in desperation and urgency with each word-accompanying step on the Martian ground: "Life imitating art…life imitating art…life imitating art…"

THE GRIEF ENGINE

Terry Grimwood

ONE

Mummy? Are you there?

The ship hung above the gleaming, blue-white expanse of earth. It was gossamer, womb-like, translucent. It was both utterly beautiful and grotesque. It was butterfly and chrysalis, both and neither. Its umbilical, trunk, tentacle, whatever it was it, ended in a claw-like appendage, splayed and sealed over one of Star Lab III's airlocks.

Laura had been warned that the ship would disturb her, even more so than its pilot. She had been sceptical about that, as much as she could find the mental energy to be sceptical about anything. Grief drained you of resources, of thought and feeling for all but the object of your hurt.

"Why should it disturb me?" she had answered. "It's a space ship, for God's sake. A machine, an inanimate object."

She had been wrong.

The ship, viewed through the side port of the shuttle, disturbed her a great deal. It was hard to define why. The semi-organic feel of the thing, the shape, the way it clung, leech-like, to the Lab? Everything about it was wrong, non-human.

Perhaps that was the crux of this.

Non-human meant someone else. And she knew who that someone else was.

The shuttle's steering thrusters erupted into a brief, dull roar. The ship slid from view. Earth was replaced by the white and grey chaos of the Lab. The Lab had no shape or form. It was utility over aesthetics, a joining of a thousand disparate parts, representing, both metaphorically and literally, the fragile union of human nations.

Docking gate. Contact. Laura felt a gentle, distant bump and shudder. Then silence, but for the radio chatter up at the shuttle's control station.

A second shudder, a dull thud. Airlocks open. On the other side, the Lab's interior would be clinical white.

*

Like the Cytherea mission prep room.

Where some of the ten-person crew had already been struggling into their suits, while others, like Laura, made their last, brief calls.

A few moments to say farewell (not goodbye, never goodbye) to loved ones.

"Good luck," Leo answered her. "And I love you too, darling."

Corny, but it worked. Laura felt a little better. "Can you put Marcus on the line?"

"He's feeling a bit rough. Hang on, I'll take the phone over to him. He's lying on the sofa." Leo's words became muffled, indistinct as he spoke to their eight year-old son. Then Marcus's child-voice burst out of the earpiece. "Love you Mummy." He sounded groggy. Not right.

"I love you too sweetheart."

"Mummy, where are you?"

"I…I'm about to climb into a giant rocket, like the one I showed you on the iScreen. I'm going to another planet, remember? I'm going to Venus."

No answer. Leo returned.

"Is he okay?" Laura tried to sound casual.

"Yeah, of course he is. Just a little under the weather, that's all. You know what kids are like."

Yes, she knew what kids were like. One moment feverish and out-for-the-count, the next, up and tearing around. So, why did it unsettle her like this? Oh come on, of course it rattled her. She was taut, frightened and exhilarated. The voyage, trained for, yearned for, lived for, was two hours from its beginning. Anything was going to knock her back. Marcus was under the weather. That. Was. All.

She could back-out. There was a chance. Her last chance in fact. Every crew member had an understudy, waiting in the adjacent prep area, fully trained and mission-ready. All she had to do was tell the Crewmaster, who was God in this room, and it would be over. It had been drilled into them from the start; any problem, any hint of illness, any reason for not going, other than natural raw terror at what they were about to undertake, and you had to step down. There would be a next time.

But no more first time.

"Okay," she said "I have to go. I love you. Tell Marky I love him." She was not sure if she managed to keep the tremor out of her voice. She glanced nervously towards the Crewmaster, who was talking to Schneider. They laughed, briefly, at some shared joke.

"Look at the sky tonight. I'll blow you and Marky a kiss."

Connection cut.

The Crewmaster turned her attention to Laura. She nodded. "I'm ready. Suit me up."

Line crossed. No turning back from this moment on.

*

Star Lab III was all smooth walls and clean lines. The pipes and cables that formed its venous and nervous systems were neatly hidden. It was also busy. Weightless human traffic torpedoed along its corridors, fast, nimble, and intimidating for Laura as she attempted to follow her meeter-and-greeter, a lanky, pale-skinned technician named Johansson, without collision. Weightlessness disorientated her. It had been a long time. She bumped into walls, tumbled and groped for the handholds. There had been no-training for this mission. After Cytherea, she had tried to hide in a small Australian town on the edge of the Outback. It was a quiet, discreet but friendly community. Laura made a living teaching science in a high school. She thought she was safe from the past, until the arrival of two men in suits and an order, thinly veiled as an offer. Five days later she was driven, bag's packed, to the nearest shuttle launch site.

Now she was back in space.

And it was a terrible thing.

Johansson showed her to her cabin. There was a bunk, complete with restraining straps to prevent her floating away in her sleep. A porthole, through which she could see the vast blue-white sweep of Earth. And little else.

"Briefing's in three hours, get some rest." Johansson said, and left.

Laura allowed herself to float in the centre of the tiny space and her body curled slowly into a tumbling comma. She closed her eyes and saw cracks in the wall of red darkness that enclosed the inner sanctum of her mind. Beyond the wall, lay a seething chaos of unreason and guilt.

And grief.

So much unutterable and debilitating grief.

It couldn't be allowed to seep out, not up here, in this lethal, frozen nothingness.

*

Venus was hell.

Venus was a toxic, deafening, scorching wasteland. The temperature could boil blood, its dust storms flay a human body to the bone within seconds. Yet here, viewed from inside the visor of her suit, there was brutal beauty about the place. The red-orange flare of distant volcanoes, the racing, lightning-veined canopy of cloud, the torn, rocky landscape, all were redolent with primal grandeur. And, impossibly, Laura was the first to ever walk its surface. In sight of the landing pod, of course, and linked to it by lanyard. Her huge suit was more vehicle than garment. Its limbs and appendages operated by internal touch pads and servos, rather than by human muscle.

Laura heard the dust rattle against the suit and once again tried to comprehend the reality of this moment. She was on Venus.

"You need to come in Gold, over."

"I've still got twenty minutes -"

"In. Now. Do you read me? Over."

It was an order.

Laura made to swing the suit round and head back.

And saw a figure.

Human, or, at least, humanoid. Dear God, out here? No suit that she could see, indistinct, possibly even a rock formation…No, a figure someone, naked, on the Medieval Hell surface of Venus. Someone watching her. Then gone.

"Gold, do you read me? Over."

"Read you. Coming in."

For a moment, Laura's mind was clear of foreboding. The figure, had been real. Solid, three-dimensional. Male, female, she had not been able to tell. The sighting terrified and exhilarated her. She would not, of course, be believed. But that didn't matter, not at this moment, because at this moment -

The sizzling mix of euphoria and fear dissolved. She had been called in. Something was wrong. She knew what was wrong. Dear Jesus, she knew exactly what was wrong.

"They've launched a supply ship. It has a passenger pod fitted, to take you home." Schneider told her after she had listened to the voice-comm from Earth. From Leo. The mission commander's voice was husky, dry and awkward. "I'm sorry Gold."

"What's the point of me going home?" Laura answered, her own voice dead. Every word was a supreme effort to form, a collection of sounds and syllables to be forced out of her mouth. "It's too late. Marky's -"

"To put it bluntly, you're a liability now."

"No -"

"For Christ's sake, Laura, you're son's dead -"

Meningitis, it was fucking meningitis.

The living unit went silent.

"I'm sorry," Schneider said.

Laura shook her head. "…right." She had not been able to form the first words of the sentence. Guilt had arrived, suddenly, shockingly, and speech was no longer possible. It brought with it, the realisation that she should have followed her instinct back on Earth, in the prep room when Leo had told her that Marky was ill.

Venus hurled dust against the thin-but-strong walls of the living unit. Lightning flashed. Laura understood, somewhere deep beneath the smothering burial mound of grief and self-hate, that the figure was back, close by, watching. Waiting.

Then the awareness was gone. Everything was gone and she broke down and it would be a long time before any of the pieces could be put back together.

Mummy? Where are you?

TWO

Johansson stopped at the door to Star Lab's conference pod.

"There's something you need to know, before you go in."

"Yes?"

"You saw the ship, you were warned about it."

She nodded. "Of course I was."

"And that its pilot is here, on the station."

"Yes." She had thought very little about that fact. "I'd assumed he, or she -" or it " -would be."

"The alien…the pilot is in the conference room, with the others."

"And?"

"I thought I should warn you, that's all."

"Thanks, now, can we get this over with?"

Johansson twisted back round to the door and keyed in its code.

There were three humans buckled into the room's chairs. The Lab's careworn commander, Colonel (US Air Force) Alex Conran. A slender woman with red hair and movie star looks who introduced herself as a Cortez, a psychologist. And a square-jawed, too perfect male who announced that he was;

"VanGuest. UN Representative for Scientific Advancement." A politician then. No jacket and tie though, just the same anonymous jump suit worn by everyone up here in the Lab.

Then she saw the alien.

She had known, of course, from the brusque mention of First Contact made during the sparse preparation she had received on Earth. She had known that the alien was the same entity that had watched her as she struggled across the surface of Venus, seven years ago. She was certain of it.

The pilot, as Johansson had called it, was almost human. Same height as Conran, human features, two eyes, arms and legs. It was hairless and its skin, (*it*, because it was impossible to give the being a sex) was porcelain white, and webbed with a mesh of fine blue and red vessels. Other differences were harder to define, the barest angle, the slightest movement of its eyes or head. The pilot was naked, but as sexless, on the outside at least, as a manikin or a doll.

"Laura," it said, in faultless Earth Standard, better, in fact, that most humans over the age of thirty could manage. Earth Standard was new enough to be spoken fluently only by the younger generations, who were born to it. The pilot's tone was friendly, polite. It smiled slightly as it spoke.

As she strapped herself into the remaining seat, Laura nodded. "Hello…"

"Thomas," said the pilot. "Call me Thomas. It will have more meaning to you than our own way of identifying ourselves."

"Thomas," Laura said.

"We have already met, Laura."

"Yes, yes we have." Laura glanced at Conran, expecting surprise or scepticism.

Instead he said; "I'm aware of your first encounter, on Venus." He shook his head. "On Venus. Christ Thomas, I still don't understand how you could survive down there."

"We have a lot of attributes you don't possess," Thomas said "And you have a lot of attributes we don't possess."

"Which is why you're here, Laura," Cortez said.

"Any attributes of use to you people, have been gone a long time," Laura answered. "I'm strictly a Surface Crawler these days."

"It isn't your considerable spacefaring skills we need," VanGuest said. Laura disliked him on sight, and sensed that the feeling was reciprocated.

"Whatever it is, you can't have it. I want to go home. You have no right to keep me here, or force me to go into space, or whatever it is you want me to do."

"You're right," Conran growled. He seemed increasingly uncomfortable. An ally perhaps? "Although we're hoping that you'll, at least, hear us out."

Laura sighed and sat back. "Okay. I'm listening."

"I am the one who chose you," Thomas said. "You are the inspiration for this endeavour."

"I'm the inspiration? I'm a wreck, Thomas. I'm damaged goods."

"No, you are hurt. But you are not broken."

"How dare you judge me."

"Laura," VanGuest snapped. "Thomas is our guest -"

"I don't care what he is. I want to go home."

"You can," Thomas said, gently. "But it won't change anything for you, or your people, or my people."

"Why should I give a fuck about your people?"

"Listen to him, please," Conran said. "Laura, just hear him out."

"Okay, okay. I'm sorry. All right? I'm listening."

Thomas waited a moment before speaking. "Like all my people, I was mass-birthed. My concept of parent, of a bond between mother and child, is from observation only. I was assigned to a ship the moment I was weaned, my lot, to be a traveller. I have wandered the galaxy for thousands of years, my body, maintained by the ship. My mission, is to make contact with others, to gather and share knowledge. But if I find one significant fragment of knowledge, one event or technology, that will change everything for my race, then I can return home. I think I've have found it. You, Laura, you represent something unique. Something I have not yet encountered anywhere else on my journey. I read it in you even before it was fully formed." Thomas paused. Its smile faded to the merest hint. "Grief."

Laura felt anger burn inside her. "What the hell is -"

"I feel no grief. Our race is a hive mind, we have a hive loyalty, but no idea that loss can cause pain. Death to us, is inevitable and simply creates material to be recycled and reused. But you, you feel."

"I envy you," Laura said.

"Perhaps you should. But your grief, this emotion and all that it entails, is the key to your reaching the stars."

If she was expected to comment, then Thomas would have a long wait. This sounded like mystical claptrap to her.

Thomas resumed his speech. "The need you have to see your lost ones is an overpowering one. I've made it my mission while here, in your solar system, to create an interstellar drive. I believe that, if harnessed correctly, grief can provide the energy -"

"No, no this is sick," Laura couldn't stay silent any longer. "I don't know what the hell you're talking about, but bringing me here, using…using what happened to my son…I want to go. Now."

"You can see him again," VanGuest said.

"What? What did you say, you callous bastard?"

"I said, you can see your son again."

Laura sat back. She shook her head. "This is…" She struggled for a word, for some way of expressing her outrage.

And hope.

Dear God, there was hope mixed up in her anger. Was she really that weak, that gullible?

"I'll be straight with you," Conran said. "We call it the Grief Engine. Thomas claims it will enable his ship to cover interstellar space in a matter of minutes, hours at the most. It's powered by…" He glanced at the others, and it was if he had to force his next words past a barrier of raw scepticism. "It's powered by the need of its pilot to get to their lost loved one."

Laura laughed a cynical laugh. "You really believe that need can power a spaceship across billions of miles of space? Christ, this is, I don't know what it is, insanity is too mild a word for it."

"I know," Conran answered, with obvious feeling. "But we have reason to believe it will work. Thomas has already given us several technologies based on scientific principles that are more like magic than physics."

"Okay, okay, let's pretend this is real. You say that it's driven by the need to see a loved one. Well, Marky…my son, is dead. Gone. Annihilated. He isn't anywhere."

Cortez spoke this time. She leaned forward, held Laura's gaze. "But, he is somewhere, Laura."

"Oh come on, don't give me that 'he's in your heart' shite. He's gone." Laura was beginning to cry; rage, renewed grief. The cruelty of this madness.

"We've found the dead Laura."

"All the dead," Thomas said. "Not just yours."

VanGuest took his turn now. Interjecting quickly, before Laura was able to answer. "You've heard of the Sir Patrick Moore?"

Of course she had. The Moore was a largest radio telescope ever built, set into solar orbit just beyond the moon.

"A year ago, just before Thomas came to us, the Moore picked up some astonishing signals from..." He waved ceilingwards. "Out there. It took a while to untangle it all, but when we did so, we discovered that the signals consist of...of voices."

"Someone trying to make contact?"

"Not someone as in an alien race, no, but human voices. Recognisable individuals."

"Oh, for God's sake, can this get any worse?"

VanGuest reached for the audio player that sat at the centre of the table. "We've managed to distil this one from the general chatter."

A moment, then a voice issued out of its microspeaker.

"Mummy, where are you?"

"Christ," Laura sobbed. "You fucking bastards. You fucking, fucking bastards..."

THREE

She entered the alien vessel through the umbilical cord. There was breathable atmosphere in the tube and, so she had been told, the ship itself. No need for a suit. Laura pushed herself towards the ship's entrance hatch. The gristly structures of the cord flashed past and she was glad not to get too close a look at their fleshiness. The hatch itself was more wound than doorway; a tear in the mummified material of its hull. Laura baulked at the prospect of passing through into, what suddenly seemed like, the belly of a whale.

They had given her no choice. They had torn cooperation out of her with emotional blackmail so brutal, she could not help but give in.

Because she might see him again. She might feel him and tell him how sorry she was.

There was gravity inside the ship. Of sorts. It was not full gravity, not the solid pull and weight that held you to the surface of a planet. This was more like the buoyancy of water. She fell gently to the floor of the craft, which yielded and was warm and thrummed with some energy that soothed her and made her want to curl and sleep.

The ship's interior was vast and cavernous. Its integrity maintained by a rib-like framework that heightened the illusion of being marooned in the belly of Pinocchio's cartoon whale. There was warmth and light, but where it came from she couldn't tell. There was no seat, no bunk, no control panel.

Up onto her hands and knees, Laura saw the supplies promised to her by Conran. A neatly stacked set of gleaming aluminium containers filled with food, water and a full suit, for emergencies.

Beyond the supplies was what she supposed was the ship's nose, or prow. It was transparent and gave a view to the outside. As she walked towards it, she was unnerved by its clarity. It was as if the ship was open to space itself. Ridiculous, she knew, because there was atmosphere in here, and warmth.

She stopped a few metres short of the vast window. Glass? A force field of some sort? Transparent flesh, like the surface of a gigantic eye? Whatever it was, the vista was stunning, even to a hardened astronaut like herself. Spread out below was the blue and white glory of Earth. Protruding in from the top right hand corner was part of the Star Lab's superstructure. And all painted against a backdrop of perfect, unending black.

Her comms earpiece crackled. Conran. "Casting-off in twenty seconds. Stand by." The umbilical was about to be detached. At that moment she would be alone.

"Standing by." Her voice sounded shaky, even to her own ears. "Conran…What do I do?"

"You'll know," he answered. "Thomas said that you'll know."

There was a dull thud, a slithering sound, faint, muffled by the ship's hull. Then nothing. Silence.

He's waiting for you, Laura. Go to him. Go…

She waited for the gut punch of acceleration, the roar of engines, the sickening unrealities of some hyperspacial jump.

Nothing.

A tremor. A moment. A ripple passed through the ship.

Mummy? Where are you?

"I'm coming, darling, I'm coming -"

FOUR

She drove too fast. The night was rain-lashed and, somehow, darker than it should be, treacherous. Her need to get to her son was too great for care. Instinct and reaction, carved into her by her training, kept her alive.

The road wound through wild country. The sky was cloud-dense and starless. The trees were black claws, thrust from the earth on either side of the road, bent at their wrists by the gale. Branches, torn free, tumbled across her path. She swerved, straightened, swerved again. The landscape, glimpsed as lightning flickered, and reduced to yellow-white snapshots by the headlamps, was alien. Wrong.

There were mountains, brutal jagged peaks. Some glowed, like dying coals on a fire.

Rain slashed at the windscreen. The rain rattled and the glass cracked. Not rain, dust, a dust storm, so savage, it would tear her flesh from her bones if the glass broke open.

She wrenched the car to the left and there was the hospital. St Martin's, somehow transported from its city centre location to this place. It stood, alone, at the end of the road, a brutalist concrete block, its night-dark façade, broken only by scattered pinpricks of ward light. Those odd mountains were frozen waves that bore down on either side of it like the cupped fingers of a giant hand.

The hospital car park was deserted. Laura skidded to a halt, as close to its entrance as she could get. A moment, an indrawn breath, then she was out and swearing with pain as she was pummelled by the storm. Her coat tore, her sweater, her blouse, her flesh. Inside. She stumbled into the reception area and the storm's howl was silenced. A woman sat at the desk. She wore the uniform of a security guard, dark blue vee-neck jumper, clip-on tie. Laura ignored her, made for the lift.

"Excuse me, hey, excuse me…"

Laura spun round to see the guard hurrying towards her.

"Baker Ward," Laura said. "I need to get to Baker Ward." That's where he was, and the clock was ticking. She tried to keep the frustration and panic out of her voice.

"It's three in the morning -"

"My child." Laura turned her back on the guard and slammed her fist against the lift button. "I have to see my child."

"I'm sorry, you can't go up there."

Laura felt the guard's approach. She felt her aggression. Heard her breath, an animal pant, a low growl.

Come on, come one…

"Step away from the door, please -" No politeness in that last word. No concern or kindness. The voice was cold, inhuman.

Hold your nerve…

Ding! The doors opened. Laura jumped inside and punched the door-close button. She glimpsed the guard. Glimpsed…then fell back against the back of the lift and covered her face with her hands. She almost broke. No, not yet, not here.

Up.

The lift was slow. Too bloody slow. It bumped and shuddered. Laura paced, clenched by her frustration and by the pain from a dozen dust-storm wounds tattooed on her arm and across her back. The lift's trembling and rattling grew louder and more violent.

It stopped, with a jolt that almost knocked Laura off her feet. She fell forwards, her palms splayed against the smooth, cold wall.

Stopped…

The fucking lift had stopped.

Laura pushed herself away and stabbed at the door open button. Nothing. Doors jammed. Lift jammed. Oh Christ. Oh Jesus.

She pummelled her fists against the door.

"Help! Help me! Please, someone, help me. Help me!"

Nothing but the closed-in deadness of her own voice. Exhausted, she stumbled back. It was three in the morning. No one was going to help her. The corridors would be empty. The staff were in their wards, huddled in their little pools of light at their desks, focussed on their sleeping patients.

Laura stood, arms tight about herself. She was going to cry. She must not cry. She bit down on her grief and closed her eyes. Think. She had to get to Marcus. There was a way. There had to be a way. She opened her eyes and looked up; trapdoor, in the lift car ceiling. Out of reach.

Not out of reach, not if she stretched upwards, if she willed it not to be.

She shook her head, puzzled by the thought. Of course it was out of reach. No amount of willpower in the world would change that.

Would it?

Mummy, hurry up. Where are you…

She raised her arms and stretched until her joints hurt. She filled her head with the need, the will, the want. She cried out his name and it was the cry of a wounded animal and she felt herself distort and felt herself rise.

From the floor.

Startled, she dropped back. Her legs gave way and dropped her to her knees. She panted, her heart beat wildly. Her head felt light, she was dizzy.

Again; blood roared through her skull, the edges of the world bled. She cried his name again. The word a single elongated howl of agony. She rose once more. She shook from the effort and it felt as if every part of her was about to shatter like glass.

She felt the smooth surface of the hatch under her finger tips. The contact broke, she fell, a few inches, strength failing.

Marcus. Marcus...

The name pushed her back up to the hatch. Fingertips on metal. The hatch gave, lifted. She screamed his name and thrust upwards and the hatch fell away with a clatter. Her fingers curled about the edge of the gap. She clung on. Her feet dangled above the floor. Escape was a million lightyears away.

Lightyears. Yes…

She waited, gathered her strength. She was mission-trained, strong and fit. She. Could. Pull. Herself. Up. By. Her. Fingers. The pain was immense. Her arms trembled. It felt as though her tendons would snap, her joints unhinge. This was not possible - No, any doubt, any wavering from her purpose would end this.

Up. A final hissed exhalation of effort, a final agony of strained muscle, ligament and tendon and her shoulders passed through the gap and she was able to slip her hands outwards to grab at brackets and hooks and at the grease-wet lift cables. No rest. More effort, until she doubled forward at the waist and dragged herself out on the roof of the lift car.

The cables smeared grease onto her storm-ripped coat, but it didn't matter. Panting with effort, on her hands and knees, she waited for her heart to slow, then looked up to see the tight-shut doors of the next floor. They were just above her head, cut into the sheer concrete of the lift shaft wall and illuminated by dull, industrial-looking bulkhead lights. The lights offered a stark, uneven glare that was broken by deep, black shadow.

There were rends in the wall, their grey, dusty edges frayed like cloth, that exposed the pulsing white inner surface of the shaft. The oddly organic wounds were familiar to her. They stirred memories she couldn't comprehend.

Laura grabbed at the nearest cable. It was slick with grease that squeezed coldly through her clenched fingers. She used it as a support as she clambered up onto the lift car's pulley mechanism. From here she could reach the narrow inner ledge of the lift shaft doorway, which was now at shoulder height.

She clawed at the join between the doors.

Solid, immovable.

Mummy? Where are you?

Mummy?

Mummy, please…

She screwed up her face in effort, gritted her teeth and pushed her fingers into the join. Impossible. But there it was, her fingertips, vanished into the thin dark line. Then it hurt, suddenly and she yelped and made to snatch them back. The pain was the pain of a hand trapped in a slammed door. The pressure bore down on her nails and was enough to make her weep. It was a relentless, throbbing hammer blow.

It was the only way.

She pushed her hand further into the join. And saw the flesh peeled from the bone as she rammed it home. The agony was exquisite. Somehow perfect, a clear, crystal thing that erupted through her in an immeasurable firestorm and tore a shriek of raw, primal shock and terror from her throat.

Her flesh. That bloody, white rag crumpled about her wrist was her flesh.

But she could bear this. Because every beat of that white, shimmering pain, brought her child to her. Marcus; youthful face, round, already handsome, smooth-skinned, wide-eyed and guileless, his smell, a soft milky smell, underlain with the tang of sweat, his voice, his breath, the feel of him. And the greater the pain, the more vivid his presence.

Pressure. Translated into hot, scalding light by her maddened nerves. A light sliced through with dazzling yellow-white. Pressure. A tug to her right. Something gave. The doors, it was the doors! Another effort, another tsunami of unutterable agony that brought her child's lips to her ear.

Mummy, hurry, please…

The doors slid aside and she collapsed, head bowed, arms supported by the ledge and the cold, smooth vinyl floor beyond. Her heartbeat was a pummelling vibration that echoed through her and forced blood, all her blood, to the source of her agony.

Hurry…

Laura groaned as she pulled herself up over the ledge. There were no handholds, but she didn't need those did she? She had her will and the pain and her son's urgent, pleas.

She lay, belly-down, face down. The pain was everything. She daren't look at the remains of her hand. She was exhausted. She couldn't go on.

She felt the hard corridor floor grow soft.

No.

She forced herself up onto her hands and knees. Around her, the bare, pale green corridor walls had cracked to expose more of the white fleshy surface below. She surged to her feet and, clutching her wounded arm to herself, broke into a shambolic run.

A figure blocked her way. Dark indistinct, a blurred silhouette against the light.

"Laura, no," her ex-husband said. "It's too late. Let him go, let him die in peace. It's not worth it."

Leo was right. She was tired, hurt, possibly bleeding to death. She wanted to fall into his arms, let him protect and care for her, let him soothe the pain.

Leo? Was it really Leo? She was unsure. The figure was too indistinct, it shifted and flickered. She saw darkness rather than clothes and flesh. Stars, scattered like dust against the black.

She broke into a sprint and slammed into him and for a moment the two were locked together in a struggle, then she was past.

Another door.

A window. She fell against it and peered through and there was nothing on the other side, but a bed, a small bundle motionless beneath a sheet, and all bathed in bright light. An island in the utter, impenetrable darkness that surrounded it.

She lifted her arms and splayed her palms against the door and saw the butchered wreckage of her right hand, and hissed against the pain as she pressed it to the door's surface and pushed.

She stumbled through and threw herself onto the bed and gathered the tiny bundle into her arms and sobbed and bled.

Mummy -

FIVE

- you're here.

She jumped back from the soft tissue of the ship's transparent prow. She staggered, reached out to the ship's walls for support and stared at what lay beyond. Space, yes. And a planet, its surface lit by a faraway blue sun. Laura could see whirls of cloud, patches of yellow brown and deep green. Its poles were ice white. Seas glittered.

It was not Earth.

She had travelled to the stars.

The grief engine…

Laura moved slowly back to the prow and reached out for the transparency, carefully this time. She noticed the scarring on her right hand; a network of freshly healed wounds, as if the skin had been torn then carefully repaired.

But even this was not the focus of her full attention.

It was what filled the space beyond the planet's atmosphere that transfixed her and was the engine of her tears; a nebula, lightyears vast and lit by myriad points of clear, yellow-white light.

Mummy, you're here…

Yes, yes I'm here Marky darling. I'm here.

It was him, Marcus, and a million, million others. Out there, souls, the dead. Souls that whispered and sang.

They say we're the stuff of stars…

Where was he? Laura pressed her fingertips against the prow and felt the ship move. The planet slid by then was gone. The nebula enfolded itself about her, hot and titanic. Laura spoke her child's name, over and over again. Not grinding it into herself this time, but, rather, tasting its sweetness.

Infant suns blazed with urgent, impatient energies on either side of the ship, their lights diffused by the drifting cobweb trails of gaseous matter. There were smaller globes, strung out in the spaces between them, shrouded in swirls of multi-coloured gas. Some were gathered together, slowly fusing, coalescing into larger, foetal suns.

The ship stopped.

Mummy, you're here…

Laura spun round, ran to the stacked stores and dragged out her suit. She fumbled at catches and struggled with the thing's weight and cumbersome geometries. Everything took too long to pull on, to clamp shut and to check. She bit down on her impatience. Her life depended on thoroughness, on check-and-re-check. Air filled the helmet. She breathed in. Cool and sweet. No dizziness or nausea. She looked down at the life-support status panel on the suit's left arm. All green. All go.

Outside, the nebula was a terrifying, infinite cathedral. Its roof was a vast arch of gas and matter, it walls, multi-coloured columns, and star-spotted washes of blue and red and green. Tiny globes of light swirled about her like snow.

They whispered.

Laura pushed herself away from the ship and experienced that familiar sense of disorientation, of falling, of crossing an unimaginable chasm that had opened out below her.

Infinity. A fall that would never end.

A lanyard snaked out behind her; salvation, lifeline.

She fired the suit's miniature steering rockets, adjusted her course and slid across the cold nothing and through the swirl of whispering globes. She knew which one she needed. Instinct. Telepathy. She didn't care.

It was this one.

The sphere glowed red and tumbled, with a thousand others, towards a distant clot of proto-suns. A gleaming, sparkling rain of souls. She caught it easily and it fitted into her palm. She held it tight.

Mummy, you're here…

There was no heat, only light. Laura trembled within the suit and cried openly now. She felt static crackle over her skin. The globe's surface boiled, arcs reached out like glowing tentacles. And there was his voice. And his little boy smell of soap and sweat. And the feel of his soft hair and skin and him. She felt him. Inside the suit. She wept and held him tight to herself.

I'm sorry…I'm sorry…I'm sorry…

She murmured his name over and over again until it was her breath and the beat of her heart. She felt herself tumble through the giant archways and corridors of the nebula. She folded herself about the globe, and about his presence. She reached for her belt and the lanyard's clasp.

Mummy…

Her gloved fingers closed about the hook. She applied pressure and felt the locking clasp give.

No mummy…

Open now, she began to slide the hook from the eye on her utility belt. A few centimetres and she would be with him forever.

I love you…I'm sorry…I love you…

No mummy, not yet…

The tip of the hook slid over the metal of the eye, two more millimetres, one -

No mummy. NOT YET…

She jerked her hand back and felt the lanyard slip free. It floated up, past her visor. She watched it, transfixed, puzzled. Then afraid. It was still within reach, if she let go of the globe. Of Marky. Now -

She couldn't, not again.

Mummy, please…

She fell. The lanyard hook bounced against the top of her helmet.

She fell.

The lanyard was gone. Christ, she was lost. Fear turned to panic. She was going to fall forever and suffocate and die. Not yet. It wasn't her time. Not yet…

I love you Marky.

She released the globe and reached up. The hook glinted in the maddened light. She reached up and touched it and it snaked away from her. She cried out and snatched again.

And caught it.

She clung on and panted from exertion and sobbed with grief.

And joy.

I'll come back…

As she hauled herself along the lanyard, towards the ship, she looked down. The globe was lost now in the glare of the embryonic stars into which it was falling. Marky wasn't lost though. He was here. He would be here forever. They were all here. Waiting.

BASTARD SPACE

Ray Daley

Man had always looked upwards to the heavens at night, eyes raised to the vast expanse of stars ehich stretched off far above him. Even in his earliest days, *homo sapiens* had wondered what was up there.

Until about ten years ago.

We sent the first ship through the rift entirely automated. Sensors of every possible type and description. If we had an instrument for detecting it, one of them went aboard the *Serpent*. Obviously, we could have risked sending people on that first ship, but why would you? Why risk human lives unnecessarily? We were sending a ship through a region of space we had only previously theorised actually existing. It was impossible to know how people would react in such a place.

We placed cameras everywhere, both inside and outside the ship, as well as the most sophisticated A.I's we'd ever created to crew her. All but one of our eggs into that particular basket. *People*.

We made our predictions, ran billions of probability studies, numerous scenarios. A journey through normal space would have taken eleven million years at our current level of engine technology. The average of all our estimates said it would take around seven days to pass through the fabric of space, and appear safely on the other side. Light years travelled, in a week.

*

We named it J space, the area where interstellar jumping was about to become possible.

Of course, we had previously sent a large number of sensors and probes to map and record the interior of the rift. At least we called it a rift. Our data told us it was more like a subway to the stars, not just between planetary systems, but between galaxies and universes too. We would be capable of travelling to places our scientists hadn't even given names to yet. Any number of exits and entry points existed, all of which appeared stable. So we chose to try the closest, cosmically speaking.

Once the *Serpent* had entered the rift, it immediately fell into a communications black spot. As far as we could tell from our records, the rift contained wildly fluctuating EM fields, prone to disrupting all transmissions. When we initially sent out those sensors and probes, we assumed we had lost them all. Until they came out the other side. So we could send data through the rift from an exit point, but not whilst inside the rift itself.

That week was one of the longest mankind had ever lived through. *Up to that point.*

As each station in Mission Control suddenly died as a single entity, we held our collective breaths. Until...

A single male voice spoke across the seemingly immutable silence, almost unsure of his own words. "Flight, I think I'm getting telemetry over here?"

Then mere seconds later, another voice spoke out, equally as hesitant as the first had been. "Same here, Flight. Local star map currently being received."

Then suddenly a hundred more voices in rapid succession, each was just as excited about the information they were now receiving from the *Serpent*.

It fell to one lone female voice at the Logistics desk, to ask the question everyone else had been wondering about, but dared not voice. "Flight, about that data? Has anyone checked the send time?"

It turned out there was a delay of seven hours, from transmission to receipt back on Earth. One thing the experts agreed upon, if men were going to be sent out there, they'd have to try to do something to massively bring that delay down to something far more acceptable. Every possible expert alive spent the next year scrutinising every iota of data. What were the radiation levels like? Had the cameras recorded anything likely to upset the human psyche? All these questions and many more were asked until the experts were as satisfied as they could be that the journey through the rift was safe.

For a given value of the word safe.

*

Mankind spent the next six months creating the definitive crew list.

The *Serpent* was duly returned through the rift, arriving back in our solar system after another blackout of seven more days. She was inspected in minute detail, before finally being refitted to carry human passengers. Don't let yourself think *Serpent* went through a massive reconstruction at any stage. Far from it. A few monitoring stations were removed, to accommodate crew positions.

Eventually, a minimal crew of fourteen was agreed upon. And just before her relaunch, the ship was optimistically renamed *Eden*.

Eden took three days to reach the rift, during which the fourteen-person crew gave her the best shake-down trip they could manage, given the minimal staffing level. Until she reached the blackout point.

"This is *Eden*. About to cross the terminus. We'll speak to you in seven days. Wish us luck, don't hold your breath. *Eden*, out."

*

The first the crew knew of any problem was shortly past one P.M. ship time (synced to Greenwich). As he had done every other day up to then, Captain Willis called to each section for an afternoon update. As they had before, the first ten reports came through as normal. Nothing new to report, no changes had occurred, the ship was still operating according to known parameters. Then came the next call, to the engine room.

"Bridge to engine room, your report please?"

It was normal procedure to wait for anything up to a few minutes to allow each section to answer. That had been agreed upon during the shake-down cruise to the terminus. Everyone had pointed out that several areas were manned by only one crew member, and that there was no possible way for them to be at their station all the time. People needed breaks, time to use the toilet at least twice each day, and be allowed to eat or sleep too. The crew had worked out that they could automate most stations for at least seven hours, to allow themselves an uninterrupted sleep period.

They had also agreed that if they thought they might be stepping out for longer than a few minutes, they'd tell that to whoever was manning the bridge. No such report had been received from engineering.

As protocol dictated, they allowed the three minute grace period to elapse, before calling again.

Captain Willis kept his voice calm, knowing engineering would answer him eventually. "Bridge to engine room. Could you send us your report please?"

Still nothing.

Willis walked over to the security console. "Show me the camera in the engine room, please? Put it up on the main viewer."

The screen showed the large engine room to be completely empty.

Willis was concerned, but not worried. "Give me ship-wide comms, please?"

Taylor at comms gave him a thumbs up.

"This is the Captain, to all stations. Please stand by unless directly ordered otherwise. Engineer Reed, could you please report in? It doesn't matter where you are, even if you're in the bathroom. Just acknowledge this hail."

Another three minutes passed. *Still nothing.*

Willis took a short breath in. "Bridge to Sickbay. You've got a person spare, and you're the closest section. Send someone to go check on Reed, please?"

"Captain, this is Nurse Hill. I'll go and find him. Hold for five."

Willis nodded to himself. She was asking for the maximum amount of time to check the entire engineering section, the mess hall, and his quarters. All of which were within a five-minute walk."

After thirty seconds, the first call came back. "Hill to bridge. He's not in his quarters, sir. I've placed a medical lockout on the door, he won't be able to enter again without calling either myself or the Doctor for access."

A minute passed. "He's not in the mess hall either or rec room either, sir. I've applied the same lockout to both areas until he's located. Apologies to the rest of the crew."

And another. "Not in the corridor bathroom. Checking the engine room now sir."

As Hill entered the engine room, they could see her on the main viewer, looking behind consoles, around bulkheads. She looked up to the camera. "Not in here sir, I'll check the engine bay itself. perhaps he's doing system checks, and couldn't hear you over the engine noise?"

She pulled on a pair of ear defenders that were hanging outside the engine bay. *The only pair there*.

"Sir. Before I go in, I need to report for the record. The only ear defenders in here are still hanging up outside the engine bay. I'm going in now."

Another minute passed slowly by.

When Hill came out, she was shaking her head. "No-one in sight. I checked everywhere, all the crawl spaces. The fuel lines are open, the engines are at max q, he can't be in either of those. Unless he went outside the ship, Reed appears to have vanished into thin air, sir. I'm going to seal the main door after I leave, security and senior crew only. Can someone come down and set this place to automatic?"

*

When he saw it, Captain Willis couldn't believe what he'd just seen. "Run that back again."

Security Officer James reset the loop. Once again, his monitor showed the impossible. Thirty-eight seconds of engineer Reed standing quietly by his station, then suddenly blinking out of existence. No pool of blood, no residue of any kind. There one second, gone the next.

"Bridge, this is Sickbay. Nurse Hill here, sir. Did anyone send the Doc off on a call while I was away? Only he's not here, and the section was left wide open. We normally seal the door if no-one is present."

Captain Willis replied straight away. "No reports that we received up here, Hill. How long did it take you to get back from engineering?"

"About thirty seconds, sir. I ran, on account of the fact I needed to rehydrate."

"Do you want to hold fast there, Hill? I just need to check something."

Willis looked over to James. "Show me the last five minutes and thirty seconds of Sickbay."

They spotted it within ten seconds. Almost as soon as the doors had closed behind Nurse Hill, Doc Jones had also vanished. Just like Reed.

*

Seven long silent days of anguish. Man had thrown himself out into the bosom of the stars. With no contact. Until...

"Flight, I'm getting telemetry here?"

"...come in, Earth! I say again, this is Navigation Officer Docker. Come in, Earth? Do you read?"

"*Eden*, is that you?"

"There's a message delay of two minutes, Flight. It looks

like the amplification beacons we deployed along the rim of the rift worked to some degree. Listen. I don't know what happened, but I'm the only one left. The rest of the crew vanished, while we were travelling through the rift. Somehow I was the only one not affected? I'm going to spend the next day automating the rest of the ship's systems if I can. I'll report back this time tomorrow. There's no point in me staying out here on my own, so I'm preparing the ship to come back. Hopefully whatever kept me safe the first time will work again. I'll speak to you in twenty-four hours. Docker, out."

*

Docker made it back safely to Earth. He'd had little in the way of sleep, even after almost fully automating the rest of the ship's systems. We gave him two days to recover before we started with the first of the several million questions we had for him. The most important of which was, "What the hell happened out there?"

"Reed went first, then the Doc. James went to check on Hill, but she'd gone by the time he got there. I excused myself to use the bathroom. You've only got logs of what happened after that. Because everyone else was gone by the time I came back to the bridge."

We questioned Docker in every possible way, hypnosis, regression, pentathol even. His answers never changed. What he had told us was all he had seen and all he knew. He wasn't trying to hide anything from us. So we turned to the ship's systems next. We stripped *Eden* down until there was nothing left of her. Checking every deck plate, every wall panel, nothing of that ship didn't get scrutinised five ways from Sunday. And then some.

Right down to the atomic level, and below. All logs and digital records were analysed, both by humans and machines, back at mission HQ.

*

Chief Of Flight Operations, Dylan Green looked around the room at his team. "So what are your conclusions, ladies and gentlemen?"

Bill Miles, head of the technical department consulted his report. "Thirteen members of the *Eden* crew were removed during the passage of J space, by forces or means as yet still unknown. We checked Docker's medical records and cross-referenced them with the others, to see what made him so special. Turns out it was nothing, sir. He had the same blood type as two of his crew, so it wasn't that. He had no fillings in his teeth, neither did four of the others. He'd had chicken pox and the German measles jab, likewise half the crew. We even went deep diving, he's gay, so were three others. And it wasn't religious either before you ask. He regularly attended church, as did two of his exact faith. Docker wasn't married either, but neither were Hill or Reed."

Green shook his head. "So what you're telling me is, if there was something special about Docker, you don't know what it was?"

Miles nodded. "Exactly that, sir. And having asked the man himself, neither does he."

Arguments and counter-arguments flew across that briefing table for the next three hours. The only solid decisions made were as following, another ship would be built to the exact same design and automated just like *Serpent* had been. This time all souls manning the ship would be dead bodies.

In hindsight, it didn't turn out to be all that helpful a decision. *Serpent II* was duly dispatched, as soon as we finished building her.

As she went, *Serpent II* was pre-programmed to drop more amplification beacons, bringing the total time delay down the rift to a mere thirty seconds.

We made sure the bodies were all on camera, being recorded twenty-four seven. According to the digital logs, the first three ceased to exist on day three, two minutes after noon. All bar one, placed in the mess hall, flashed out of existence across the next three minutes. So it wasn't down to any known medical condition. Whatever it was, it took the living and dead alike.

We brought her back, with the sole traveller making the return trip as safely as it had gone out.

Chief Green gathered his staff together once again. "Okay, we've got to send living people again. We can't just waste this shortcut through space. Who knows how long it'll take us to develop thrust technology that'll get us so far that quickly in the future?"

Amy Lane, head of personnel stated the obvious. "So where do we look next? We can't afford to waste precious scientific brains again?"

Where indeed? Where could they look, to find people qualified to operate under such high-pressure conditions, to military standards, who weren't going to be missed if they suddenly vanished?

*

Chief Green couldn't believe it when they told him. "Leavenworth? The military prison?"

Lane shook her head. "Not that one, sir. The other one."

They took twenty of us, all told. Sixteen men, and four women who were being held at Miramar. We were given access to all the records of the previous travellers if we wanted them. Of course, I took the opportunity to read everything, former Lieutenant Mike James. If I hadn't, I might never have happily placed my life on the line.

All because of a simple insult. "You know something, Looey, you're always here with your damn files, taking up all the space. You should let someone else get a chance to sit down! You know what, Looey? You're a bastard!"

I looked up at the guy who'd insulted me, former Sergeant Taylor. "I'd have to check with my parents, Taylor. But I've been called worse, and I was here first. If you want a chair, get here earlier. Asshole."

That honest exchange set me to thinking. It couldn't possibly be something *that* simple, could it? Still, it warranted further investigation on my part before we left Earth. It wasn't the type of phone call you wanted to be making from anywhere, let alone a military prison.

Especially not to men and women in their fifties or older. I still made the call in the end, knowing how many lives depended on the certainty of that knowledge. "Yes, the military prison. I think it's quite an important call. It might save lives. It's about your daughter, the nurse? Were you married when she was born? Yeah, I know, sir. It's not a big deal these days, it might matter quite a lot though!"

I made everyone else check thoroughly with their parents before they volunteered. "Badger them until they 'fess up, embarrass them if you have to. Just make sure they were already married *before* you were born. Otherwise, you won't be coming back."

*

"Flight, I'm getting telemetry here?"

And the next voice they heard was mine, sounding extremely glad to be alive. "James here. That's now a delay of three seconds, Flight, and before you ask, twenty out of twenty-one are still alive. Just as I suspected, you'll have to rename it B Space. We still don't even know vaguely how it works, what possible force is able to detect that, but somehow it seems to know which of us is a bastard. The classic definition, born out of wedlock. You'll have to send your apologies to Private Morrin's family. I know he was already on death row, sir. Turns out his father wasn't just a liar. We'll commence scans of the local system shortly. Ending transmission for now, Flight. *Pathfinder* out."

DAY BREAKS ON THE SCHOOL OF NIGHT

Tim Nickels

Never with love…

Alison works slowly with the bone folder, mindful that Milly may break inside her coffin.

The bones must fold gently in, as softly as their colour. Grey soft; the softness of that non-colour grey. Alison's colour. Her favourite. No snap or sharpness here in the little corridor beyond the carers' common room: that place of uplifting brightness; of evangelical memos and Andrea Bocelli. Peace travels behind the hand and wrist that holds the bone folder: not a vacuum but a tiny place of glowing.

Alison pauses to relieve the eczema itch inside her elbow, the bone folder glow roseating her forearm enough to render it almost transparent. Alison has many rough edges: her scalp, her right side beneath the breast, both hands. Chaffed and drying away, the nerve cells running riot through her overgrowing body. Her head feels dizzy beneath its cornflower-coloured scarf.

"Alison?" It's Oskar, the boy. The youngest of them. He leans against the doorway, his skid lid and gloves atop the nursing journals on the coffee table behind him. "About done, old girl?" This Oskar's okay, re-built his own Lambretta; on some government scheme, wants to be somewhere else, seems to make the best of things.

Good at faking it like all the Oskars.

"About done, Oskar." She lays the bone folder on its little green baize pad. "Quite an easy one." She hesitates, plunges in: "I didn't know her very well..."

But helpful Oskar is ready with the clipboard. "Romilly Pennington. Unmarried." He pauses as his finger slips down the sheet. "No. I didn't know her at all. Used to be on the Up, of course. Maybe you've forgotten... Hang on -"

Alison has reached for the crutches too quickly, off-balances herself, slams against the wall a little too hard.

The crack makes Oskar wince.

"It'll heal, boy. More than this bloody itching." A tiny trickle of blood, no thicker than a trail of antique ballpoint, begins the long commute from shoulder to wrist. She tests the broken bone. "A day. Two at most. Come on, I'm missing my daytime."

Oskar helps her through the common room and out into the television lounge. Searches for the remote. Alison bends double as she goes, the top of the door frame a splintered witness to previous passings.

She does not glance back at Milly's coffin; just whispers their lullaby as she limps away into the brightness.

*

Alison now watches Oskar scooter off down the drive at 8.00 pm: the long shadows of September bloom below the hydrangeas and re-cycling bins. She thinks about her husband David - though always a Dave. In truth, a Liam Dave; but even the assumption of a second name as first failed to save Dave from heart failure eighty-three years previously. Alison's thoughts are tearless: her memory of an iceman over-enamoured by the electro-glistering darkness of the age. She glances at his smartphone inside its protective little bodybag by the bed. Smart. Phone. Alison can't be certain the oxymoronic term went unobserved. She half-expects the bloody thing to scream out some forgotten anthem from Ibiza; Dave crowing from yet another Vodka & Bull-fuelled deal closure in the Docklands. A further Tweet of triumph. #gotcha. She smiles and decides to stop thinking. Serenades herself instead with her rasping lullaby; looks in the mirror. Her ears seem bigger today, the lobes plump and pale as they drag on her shoulders.

*

The nine-legged spider quivers on its web over the dressing table.

It reminds her of the ship.

It would be incorrect to say that Alison has woken. She has long ago left sleep behind. Her consciousness obliges by unfocusing occasionally - trips on the train, visits by her younger relations - but true sleep remains a lost de-colonised land.

Blue light from an outside security lamp renders the spider as a child would paint an icicle. The spider smiles with the crescent of its eyes and arcs down onto Dave's PlayStation, boxed now and used as an occasional table. A tiny yellow tea set sits in the very centre on a doily decorated with polar bear cubs. Her relations prefer coffee from the machine in the television lounge these days. No biggie. A classic Daveism.

The shoulder that she shattered that morning has mended now. Quicker than she thought. She reaches up and touches the ceiling. The forearm between wrist and elbow buckles ever so slightly, the skin scrapings hanging in the air like an ivory miasma.

She's heard about the bones on the beach.

*

"Hello, great grand-gran! Gosh, you do look well. Doesn't she look well, dear? I think you've lost a little weight. What do the doctors say? But what do they know anyway? Still got that funny tea set then. My goodness. Do you remember, dear? Do you?"

Her great granddaughter Lisa didn't talk until she was five. Alison makes a golden rule of avoiding little nostalgic moments - but in Lisa's case she is happy to make an exception. There is baby Lisa in her mind's eye, cross-legged and sweetly aghast watching great grand-grannie's fragmenting tapes of Friends. There she is tipping over cups on to the doily and stealing midget jam sandwiches from other infant relations. But here is grown-up Lisa, a melanoma as big as a plum on her cheek, Lisa's own daughter (Alison can never quite remember the name) hovering behind the grips of the wheelchair, clutching extravagant quantities of Kleenex.

A silence. The Oskars tweak the telly in a far corner.

"Oh," opines Alison hopefully. "I think they're going to show Friends again."

There's a pause.

A long one.

"Well, is that the time..?" Lisa hasn't quite rescued her watch from the arms of her teal jumper before the words are out.

"Mmm," Alison murmurs. "Expect it is. Thanks, Oskar."

Oskar has appeared with a tea trolley and Lincoln biscuits.

Lisa's face upturns to the mystery daughter with the tissues. "Such a shame that we can't stay, dear. Mind you, I suppose those Lincolns are full of gluten. Another one of my little no-nos. But then..."

A ghost hangs suddenly in the air between them and the ghost is called You Probably Know That. The conversation of surprise is a pale creature indeed.

"Yes. Yes. Such a shame we can't stay, um, dear." Lisa ceases to wheedle and barks up at the tissue woman: "And such a pity Stella's worried about her precious car after dark."

Alison winces, her skull skin tightens. Lisa's daughter. Her name, of course, is Stella.

Alison speaks: "You still have the car then, Stella?"

Stella is taken aback. Her supernumerary status is never challenged. Alison is speaking to her. She must answer.

"Yes, great, great..." concentration ripples the forehead "...great grandmother Ali."

"They call me Alison now. It's like I'm a child again."

"We keep it for the visits," continues Stella. "The car. The lights are a bit dodgy but we can wait a bit. We got a special form from Swansea." She wonders whether to say more. "It's grey."

"Those forms used to be pink and green."

"The car is grey, Alison."

"My favourite colour."

*

Stella watches Alison as she reclines on the deckchair, her massive dry calves stretched out towards the sea.

Alison's done too much unfocussing; has awoken from sham-sleep to discover too much loss. And now the deckchair's yellow pyjama stripes leap out from the grey pebbles and make Alison's head buzz.

Sunset's some hours away and the headlights won't be needed. Someone's found a day-bed back at the Home so Lisa can have her little lie-down.

Fossils drift in the mudstone cliffs above them. Massive white bones have been revealed by the latest land-slips. The geological layers have been rendered vertical by seismic activity: it's possible to walk through a hundred million years of the planet's pre-history in the space of a brief conversation.

Not that their conversation has been brief.

As Stella carries the deckchair down the path of shattered pink shells, Alison has told her about past lives.

And in turn, her three greats grandmother is pleased that Stella has been named Stella. Without pomp or embarrassment, Alison announces that somewhere out there lies a small galaxy named after herself, one of the new Messier series. Ali Galactica. NM44001. Several thousand star systems, their light curving into a triangular beam of singularities. As many stars as these massive cliffs hold ammonites.

"I love the fossils." Stella stands very close to the cliff face. She is amazed how her thumbnail can indent the soft rock. How it can make a difference.

Alison lets her gaze sweep across the big bay to the very tip of the Up facility; the very end of the faraway Island.

"Take me out again, Stella." Alison picks dry skin from her fingernails. "Drive me out and I'll show you fossils that move. That live in the now."

Stella scans the beach, wonders at the great bones. Notices the scooter parked at the top of the cliff for the first time. "Tell me about the ship. Tell me everything. Tell me about the Oskars."

Alison's eyes close and she can see it all.

*

They were finally sleeping after their busy day in the nursery; bouncing around like gurgling spewing blue and pink asteroids. Ali had chuted the soiled babygros, arranged the soft toys into their accustomed places. She had experimented with one-fifth gravity today. It hadn't been pretty and Ali was grateful that solid food still lay six weeks in the future.

She watched the five small bodies, velcroed to bulkheads and random recesses. Any nook that could give up its micro-space for the babies. They slept peacefully now, even the twins; mouths soft triangles, portly frames barely twitching to the rhythm that pulsated down the fine copper spray into their skulls. Ali smiled and made coffee. Read, ate. Dimmed the light and lay on her bunk. Thought of Milly on the other side of the ship, looking out of her own tiny jam jar-bottom life port into the black and the stars.

Ali awoke to find Oskar had died in the night.

*

Stella and Lisa have departed with the twilight and Alison lies on another bed tens of years later trying to unfocus; following every leg shake of her blue-painted spider.

The door rattles. She realises someone's knocking. It takes Alison ten minutes to cross the floor without overturning the tea set; to avoid tripping on Dave's mess of charger cables.

Milly is standing - no, that would be stupid - leaning there, her great shaven bumpy head grazing the wall over the door frame.

"Romilly!" Alison's cry is a hiss, the sharp passage of air instantly bringing her oesophagus out in a bloody rash. Milly moans like a calf, staggers inside, ribs cracking, makes it to the window sill and looks out on the blue lantern and the night.

"It wasn't time, Ali. I'm sorry. I really thought it was. I really did. I had the rattle. I hadn't pissed for a fortnight. When I closed my eyes all I could see was Oskar. That final film night. The black and -"

Alison gazes into nowhere. "The black and the stars."

Milly has made it to the bed, sits heavily. Her ears lobes catch in her armpits like long empty breasts.

"Do you really want to go?" Alison is trying to pace the room, one hand splayed like a starfish on the ceiling for stability.

"Course I want to bloody go, Ali. We all want to bloody go."

"I don't."

Silence.

Milly whispers: "God, I think I might have snapped two ribs. Bastard body."

"I had a chat with my granddaughter today. Great great great grandwhatever. She's called Stella."

In spite of herself, Milly grimaces a smile.

Alison smiles too. "She's coming back to see me. Says she'll take me out. Got a car. Might drive along the coast. Take in the Up." Alison fixes her friend with a dim yellow eye, slips out the wickedest grin in the world:

"Might go further."

*

Oskar sat in his dish of jelly.

Ali couldn't see him, of course. A silvery barcode announced that she'd selected the correct container from the archive. She must not think of him as Oskar II; must not consider him a replacement for his failed predecessor. He must be nothing beyond ordinary. In fact, the very opposite. The other children will have a head start on him.

He will be frozen by the starlight, thought Ali. He'll be like a root vegetable in winter, growing in the dark, unable to help himself, pushing, thrusting to keep up. He'll be stronger than his five brothers and sisters who came to life within the warm radius of the Sun.

She must study him carefully.

Nothing beyond ordinary.

*

Folded wheezing grasshoppers, Alison and Romilly sit in the back of Stella's Kia compact and stare out of the side windows.

The relic keeps up a steady 40 kph along the curving coast road past windblown-over-backwards husks of trees. Alison murmurs something as Stella glides the car to a halt in a lay-by facing the sea. Pulls on the thing called a handbrake. A sign announces they have reached a viewpoint advantageous to photography. A shuttered ice-cream van peddles the ghost of Mr Whippy.

They are inside the Up zone.

The road these unexpected tourists will soon rejoin descends a steep hill where low gears are advised and continues across salt marsh until it reaches the Isle of Portland. In the midst of this flatness a hill rises, topped by an ancient chapel. The chapel walls ripple in the deep September heat exhaled by sub-tropical gardens that clog the lower slopes.

A spaceship of stone wondering whether it will ever be elsewhere.

*

Baby Oskar giggled as he prepared to latch onto Isobel's arse with his mixture of gums and teeth. Isobel was intent on her spellings, her stubby finger stroking words into life on the steamy glass sides of her bunkette:

IsObALIsObULIsO

The baby's sharp bite took her by surprise: Isobel whirled in zero g, slapping Oskar into a spin that ended hard and nastily on the other side of the nursery.

*

They're on the flat, the chapel passing by.

Alison wheezes: "Can you imagine all of time happening in one place in a single moment? The stillness. The utter sense of rightness?"

Stella stares through the windscreen, knows it's silly. "Can you see your galaxy from here?"

"Too far away. It's around a bend in the sky."

Romilly emerges from her deepness. Smirks. "Bend in the sky? She always speaks like a Ray Bradbury novel. Or some other writer in the school library."

"We never went to school, Milly." Alison glances up through her own smeary window at the invisible stars. "Well, perhaps the School of Night."

*

Two cycles later, Ali found Isobel squidged into the corner of a broken refrigerator, her lifeless nostrils stuffed with damp spinach.

Oskar needed watching.

But Ali would rather watch the stars.

*

They have reached the shattered island.

It has been shattered since the Great Fire took old London and Portland stone built a new one. For seven hundred years it has been a mass of quarries; more un-island than island as the dynamiting threatened to open more voids than the rock could bear.

The history of the Up could be easily traced through sedimentary layers of ancient rocketry. An industrial cliff face. A-frame gantries rise proud of the musty blast trenches: an inner space of mutant knotweed. Untethered umbilicals. Rainbow stains. Elevators stilled midway between pad and escape platform. Shuttle runways to service the orbital constructors now littered with spoil from the quarries to deter joyriders.

Joy. Rider. Smart. Phone. #justsaying.

Stella steers the Kia carefully over the mosaicked blacktop to the souvenir shop and visitors' centre. The Up was always more dirtily alive than the orbital stations. No rust in earthlight. Now brambles curl like questing squid. Stella has never seen such bramble-tangles as those that choke the jetways of the Up facility. It is quiet here. The plexi-glassed cowlings of the guard booths are yellowed and seem to soak in sound; the moist gutterings a haven for barely-murmuring toads.

*

Ali followed the progress of the nine-legged spider across the porthole. In less than fifty generations, the species had adapted to zero gravity - the ninth leg furze-hooked and able to adhere to its web as inevitably as a struggling fly. Those webs were a constant gossamer wonder in the corridors; fine rippling auroras, tripped fantastic by leaf-weight, hand-sized spiders. The twins were fascinated and certainly appeared more fearless than the others. Tunde especially would hold up his hand and flick his fingers into the web.

In the dour middle of her white/grey/white living space, Ali took a rare wet shower: looked at herself; pondered this fatless, sexless thing with the hysterectomy scar. She thought of her eggs sleeping in the bunkers below Salt Lake City and showered without singing, her tongue catching the fine testosterone spray.

Forty-seven years from earth and she could no longer picture Dave.

#whatevs.

Ali grabbed a towel and stared back at Oskar as he studied her through the plastic screen.

*

The Race still surges around the still-intact lighthouse at Portland Bill. Currents clash. The sea kale rises like yellow plumes of smoke. Strange daytime moths. Pink, violet, green. Semi-dismantled dry stone walls whisper their way to the sea. Pre-Up. Ancient.

"This is the place where the fossils suffer their most intense life. There is a glow in the earth and if you know where to look you can see them." Alison leans back against the great lighthouse and pulls back the washed-up kale. Beneath it something wriggles like an embryonic dogfish. Movement is abrupt, arrhythmic as the timeline interrupts itself. And as the twilight deepens, light shafts the colour of bone throw themselves up to the low clouds from the land all around her.

Milly speaks: "Up has bent time and continues to do so. Given time's nature how could it be otherwise? This is the place where forever happens always."

Stella lies back and experiences the fossil-vibration through the wall of her skull. She opens her eyes and stares. And stares again.

*

Oskar never stopped talking. “Is it true Romilly’s got children just like us?”

“You’re not meant to know that. She has children, yes -”

“Just like us? Living on the other side of the ship? With our names, with our looks, with our thoughts? Are you comparing notes? Are you?” Oskar punctuated each declamation with a great gulp of juice. “Like a mirror then. No, that’s not quite right -”

He’s so clever, thought Ali, even as she recoiled. She’d have to give him a proper job on film night. She stared down into his grey eyes, the left iris drizzled with saffron, the right with a colour harder to define.

“No, it’s not quite like a mirror, is it?” Oskar burped triumphantly. “Because we’re all the same.”

*

“You thought of them as cyphers, didn’t you. Isobel, Karl and the others you were telling me about. Not real people. There was no love.” Stella tries to keep her tone measured. They are back in the car watching the turbulence far out in the Channel. The fossils have shut down for the night.

Alison replies immediately. “For decades they were my only companions. I knew every hair on their forearms, the way each one of them breathed. And then they died - just as every pre-ordained molecule of their being screamed out that they should die. At a certain time and - who knows - at a certain place and by a certain hand. Their life was unnatural so why should their death be any different? In the Darwinian world model there are no victims, only survivors. Or rather survivor.” A single blink. “Romilly’s Oskar was destroyed and vivisected.”

Through the heavy air, Alison speaks again quietly. "But love? No. Never love."

Stella rests her head on the wheel and suddenly feels the weight of her lifeless uterus as if it were made of cold, cold lead. So heavy, it feels as if it should drop out of her body to swarm with the billions of other dead uteri all across the planet.

*

Romilly lay in her bunk and thought of Ali.

Ali's love of tones - grey, white, off-white - so different to Milly's own Tangerine Dreamed life bubble. Eno's Music for Airports on continuous loop. Her Oskar would revolve in the egg chair reading Sontag or Ballard and often opined that if Citroën had designed a moonbase in 1972 he was sat in a chair spinning inside it.

Romilly hadn't seen the other children lately but Oskar assured her they'd be fine. He knew she was jumpy after what had happened to Isobel. He'd make her some tea. She could do with a sleep.

He wondered how Alison's Oskar was doing.

Not a mirror. We're all the same.

*

Victims. Survivors. Survivor. Life and death considered in shades of grey.

Stella sleeps on the train two weeks later. The window is frosted with condensation, the sea fog blending and unblending with the glass five centimetres from her nose. The fitfully visible horizon is choked with the spinning farms.

Oskar has messaged her from the care home, his quiet urgent words floating in on a wave of light classical music. Alison has lain herself out in a coffin in the quiet room, waiting to be folded. Stella studies Oskar's accompanying pictures: not quite in a fugue state, Alison is kneading her own chest; massaging it as if the heart beneath can be made to go faster, can increase its stationary rate of once every two and a half minutes. Death in life. Never quite death itself.

Stella blurs her glittering eyes into the outside. Although she is constantly travelling, Stella wonders whether - like the chapel in the sunshine - she will ever be elsewhere.

*

Alison has made it out of the coffin and past the hydrangeas. Has crawled down the path of pink broken shells to the beach and has burrowed her way into the cliff, face in and askew. One arm juts uncomfortably out behind her. She has succeeded in breaking the other and it folds itself in front of her forehead. The Oskars who shadow her can hear the rasp of Alison's slow breath as it echoes around its small recess in the mudstone. Whistling dust. This part of the cliff collapsed a month ago and the Coastguard has been trying to deter fossil hunters - but somehow Alison has made her way up the slide into this shelf, this half-place between earth and air. Death in life. Seagulls bounce around the beach on the look-out for displaced nematodes but are silent and don't fight amongst themselves. The big bones are good for perching.

Alison whispers a lullaby. The one she used to sing to Karl.

*

Karl looked a bit like Garfield.

For years, Alison had retained a photograph featuring her granny as a girl looking out of the back of a purple car. Attached to the rear windshield by suckers was Garfield the cat.

Garfield didn't look very happy in the photo - in contrast to Karl who couldn't help but smile as he peered into the main porthole from spaceside, his grin fixed and frosty. The capillaries in the toddler's hands had burst and frozen simultaneously, causing his fingertips to adhere to the glass with black/pink glue. His eyes were brighter than they had ever been in life: they glittered like the deep smile eyes of a spider.

Alison wondered if she should signal through the life port to Romilly in her Seventies party room on the other end of the ship.

On her next round, Alison noticed a single EVA suit was missing.

*

Alison dreams at midday in her nook in the cliffs. It's that final film night on the ship. The last hours before she knew. She decides to not-dream in her non-sleep; imagines her own film inside her eyelids. The lids are thinner than the wing of the tiniest day-moth, the veins running wilder than the brambles on the Island of Portland. She hears the concerned voices of the Oskars down below on the beach.

Her dream crashes in against her wishes. Milly and she are children running through thickly luscious gardens. A vivarium and forced pineapple sheds. They are racing up a slope now and pass through white gates. Lambs scatter as the girls reach the open meadow and sprint for the chapel on the hill.

Even before they reach the ancient oak door, Alison knows it will be locked.

*

Oskar floated alone in the dim canteen, forcing his overpressed knees and elbows to move and trying not to cry. Was biting hard on a crinkled tube of krill paste. On their two sides of the ship, Ali and Milly permit themselves a thin smile.

The two suits were back in their respective cabinets. The Oskars hadn't quite got the nitrogen mix right.

*

The Oskars are shifting the great bones about the beach. They work in teams with grapples. The bones have come from the cliffs. Or could it be the sea? They are not whale bones or the beaks of giant squid. They belong to human beings. Perhaps they come from an ancient epoch of giants. Or from those recently died who have lived too long. The Oskars stand by with their bone folders. Someone's brought a recording of Andrea Bocelli. Family members huddle in the shadow of the cliff chatting about nothing.

Alison has now descended shakily and sits on the beach atop a massive section of spine. She nurses Romilly. Ali's broken arm is midway through self-repair. She wonders if her own back will ever grow to the size of these vertebrae. And if these great bones might roll off the continental shelf - the drop is dramatic here, just a few metres from shore - to be forgotten and rendered invisible by the depths. How many experiments have there been? How many Alis and Millys? How many lives given?

Why have the bones returned?

*

The four of them assembled for film night. The weekly ritual.

Ali had set the twins to making ice-cream and marshmallows, Oskar to popping the corn. He settled over the gas burner, barking with delight when a smidgen of hot butter whipped Esther in the eye. He made quite a show of trying to help her with a handful of wet wipes; lingered longer than needed. Ali looked up from her notes, worried that Oskar might become more boisterous. That Tunde would disappear even further into himself, his earlier fearlessness a mere memory. Tunde had already settled into a chair in front of the white screen and was furiously thumbing through the battered Halliwell's Film Guide.

"You choose the film, Tunde." Oskar was licking his buttery fingers, his interest in Esther gone, hers in him lingering as she weighed out the marshmallows. "Something funny."

*

The salt-spume hangs in suspension like a web in weightlessness. The wave action super-oxygenates the air. The Oskars have nearly finished; the bones are coming together to form a bleached simulacra of the twin vanes of the great starship. The bones have created resonance points of dream antennae and sensors. Coloured seaweeds adorn Milly's section; on the further wing - Ali's wing - slates of varying grey hues. Those non-colours of Ali's comfort zone. Razor shells are artfully scattered to resemble nine-legged spiders.

*

Ali awoke. The film was nearing its end. She was alone in the hall, her tongue thick with marshmallow. Ali hadn't expected to be alone. She scanned the monitors but the three youngsters had obviously sought out one of the ship's numerous blind spots that had been deliberately created as part of the experiment. But Ali was attuned to them - every forearm hair, every breath - and understood that some epic screenplay had been played out long before the film had begun.

The velcroed utility cover was a smidgen awry. She unrasped it and gingerly slid out into the zero gravity of the ship's service regions. It was musty down here, possessing the multi-generational Xeroxed quality of over-recycling. She paused at the life port and glanced keenly across the vacuum and solar vanes of the ship's exterior to the farther section - but Milly's own life port was dark.

She must have unplugged the lava lamp.

Ali turned a corner and Esther and Tunde were hanging in front of her. Hanging? Suspended from near-nothing. Gently twisting in the absence of gravity, slightly out of true

- their forced-entwined bodies micro-meshed in web, the dim reflection of the service globes warping up and down the surface as if it were monochromed candy floss. The big spiders scattered.

Esther was still alive and was trying to speak.

"It's time to compare notes."

But it wasn't the girl who had spoken. Oskar bobbed out of shadow, his tone cheerful, matter-of-fact. Eyes of grey and amber.

"Yes." Ali tried to match her timbre with his, her mind reeling and re-setting itself to this new and final situation. "Excellent. Excellent idea, Oskar -"

She glanced sideways, out into space.

Romilly was there now - staring out at her across the kilometre-long vane of the spaceship. She held an electric torch and a white card scribbled with black marker. The distance was long but Ali didn't need to read the single questioning word:

OSKAR?

*

The bone ship is complete and its two pilots are ready for the Up.

The world's Oskars are now here. No biggie. #lifegoeson. In former eras, church bells might have been silenced or governments annulled for the weekend. The massed Oskars have crossed continents and now they are moments away, sliding against each other on the shingle to get closer to the two women. Their final gift. Smothering them like honey bees smother a raiding wasp. Squeezing out their oxygen and loosing them from life; folding the fossils into the restful nothing beyond the black and the stars.

One could almost say they approach with love.

But there was never love.

A PLANET CALLED RUBY

Ahmed A Khan

Once upon a time there was a planet called Ruby – and it still is. Oh, what a strange and wonderful planet it is! The only thing wrong with it at that time in the recent past was that four people – including me - were going to die on it. Or so it seemed to me.

It is a self-evident truth that we survived or I would not be here, telling my story.

A lot has already been talked and written about our almost disastrous expedition but the media seems to think that I can provide a unique perspective on the events as the only woman abroad the spaceship. So here goes.

Our spaceship was named Ibn Batuta, after the famous fourteenth century explorer. There were four people on the spaceship on that trip. It was a hand-picked crew. We were chosen because each of us had expertise in more than one field and each of us was among the best in these fields. There was the silent, shy, cute, cuddly, whiskered teddy bear called Jon Ammar (Captain of the ship and navigator), the dark haired, pint sized, energetic Krishna Arokiaswamy (geologist and in charge of the telemetric instruments on board), the big, genial, blond haired, blue eyed Cornwallis Anderson (software engineer and hyper drive technician extraordinary), and myself, the ship's medical officer and xenobiologist. At that time, my name was Ruby Calebi and I was very pleased that I was going on this mission. How shall I describe myself? Let us put it this way. Just about an hour back, Jon had told me that I was beautiful.

Some people believe that women in general are very observant about the appearance of other persons, particularly their dress and shoes. If that is true, then I am an exception. I am quite unobservant in that respect, therefore, if anyone reading this account want more detailed description of us four, please look up our photographs and holographs circulating in the media.

Before we got together for that fateful trip to the pulsar on board Ibn Batuta, I didn't know Krishna and Cornwallis very well but I knew Jon Ammar from way back when we were in our pre-teens. We were next door neighbors. His parents and mine were great friends, and our families often visited each other in the evenings and weekends. Jon and I went to the same school. We were both bookworms. Given all that, is it strange that I felt myself close to Jon? At first, it was hero worship on my part. He was the strong, silent type and I found him fascinating. Moreover, he was very protective towards me and he is one reason why I was never bullied at school. Jon was two years older than me so he graduated before me and joined a university in a different city. Two years later, I joined the same university and it was no coincidence. We graduated and stepped into our professional lives without losing touch with each other. It was around that time that I started giving him subtle hints that, though I was too good for him, I wouldn't say "no" if he asked me to marry him. But either I was too subtle or he was too dense, or both. The only reaction I could discern was that his cheeks would turn slightly pink whenever I was close to him.

There I go, talking at length about that dumbbell. Let me get back to Ibn Batuta's fateful flight.

Our mission was supposed to be short, simple and exciting. It was supposed to last for two weeks. But didn't Robert Burns say something about the best laid plans of mice and men (and women).

We were to take our spaceship in the vicinity of a pulsar and go into orbit around it and remain in orbit for two weeks during which time, the telemetric instruments on board the ship would record as much data as possible about the pulsar. Then we would turn back home.

This pulsar held special attraction for the scientists back home for two reasons: one, it was emitting in the visible light frequency, which is kind of rare; two, it was astonishingly close to Earth, a mere five light days away; and three, in spite of being so close, it had not been discovered till a few months back. Where was it hiding all this time? The scientists were curious to know. Theories and hypotheses flew about like nobody's business. (A particular favorite of mine was the one that said it had recently popped out of a white hole in that region of space). This mystery still remains unsolved.

Anyway, ours was going to be a preliminary survey mission. Once we returned back home with our data, the scientists would go crazy over it and, hopefully, come up with some interesting information or speculation. The next trip of Ibn Batuta would then carry a full load of these scientists for further investigations.

It took two minutes for us to leave the atmosphere of Earth. Then began the preparations for the hyper jump which took another eight or nine minutes. Then there was the jump itself, which took practically no real time at all.

We emerged nearly twelve million miles from the pulsar and started taking our bearings. Based on observations from the earth, we already knew that this pulsar was about 19 kilometers in diameter. As far as its mass, without going into the specifics and stating so many quintillions, let me just say that it was about one and half times more than the sun.

Suddenly there was a shout from the whereabouts of the telemetric instruments panel. Krishna's highly excited voice was heard: "Captain, there is a planet orbiting the pulsar".

And what a planet it turned out to be! A planet called Ruby.

The data started pouring in. The planet was quarter the size of our moon but at least fifty times denser. It had no atmosphere and no seas. The planet was an almost perfect sphere devoid of any and all kinds of high structures. The surface of the planet seemed to be curiously smooth and glassy.

Spectroscopic analysis revealed a startling fact.

"Lady and gentlemen," announced Krishna, "most of the planet is nothing but solid diamond."

We looked at Krishna as if he had gone mad, but once we realized that he had spoken the truth, all of a sudden, we found ourselves more interested in the planet than in the pulsar itself.

"What would this discovery of a planet sized diamond do to the world economy in general and the diamond prices in particular?" That should have been our first thought but I doubt if it occurred to any one of us at that point.

Jon moved the ship closer to the planet and set it in orbit. At this distance, the planet became clearly visible on our telescope, and it was a breathtakingly majestic sight. Against the black backdrop of deep space, it seemed to give off its own light – deep, dark red.

"Captain," said Krishna in his usual, excited way, "what do you think of making a planetfall?"

"It would provide an ideal base for the study of the pulsar too," I added. I was as excited as Krishna at the prospect of landing on that hunk of diamond.

Captain Jon Ammar orbited the planet twice, chose a landing site and brought in the ship. It was a good landing. The huge ship drifted to the ground like a feather and amid the sibilant hiss of its plasma jets, settled down softly on the hard, ruby-red diamond that was a planet.

The ultra-strange landscape of barren red magnificence lay spread all around us.

"Walking on the surface of a new planet for the first time is always exciting," Jon was heard to say. I knew Jon well enough to know just how excited he must be feeling. In spite of his serious, world-weary air, the cute feller was a child at heart.

We started setting up a base. The standard pressurized dome, quite a big one, was soon erected a few hundred meters away from the ship. Most of the food, water and air supplies and other necessary movables were shifted from the ship to the dome. After all this hectic activity, we were tired and went to sleep. A day, measuring time by Earth standards, passed.

The second day, there was a discussion about the naming of the planet.

"There is a perfect name for this planet," said Jon, with a slight smile playing around the corners of his mouth. "Just consider the fact that it is diamondine, then consider its color, and finally consider our lovely medical officer, and now tell me what should this planet be called?"

"Ruby," shouted Krishna and Cornwallis together while I stared open mouthed at Jon.

Then came the hours of collecting, analyzing and manipulating data about the pulsar and the planet.

In our free time, we either played games on the ship's computer or gossiped, and, in case of Corny and Krishna, this gossiping extended to colorful discussions of each other's love affairs. At these times, Jon smiled amusedly at their talks, and I resisted impish impulses to pull his ears and tickle him and relate some saucy love affair of mine as well – made up, of course.

Through the course of the next few days, we discovered various facts about the diamondine material of Ruby.

The material was carbon but a form of carbon totally unknown till now. It was at least ten times as hard as the hardest diamond known on Earth, and it had an enormously high melting point. We tried to collect samples of the material, but we did not succeed. We had no tools which could chip off the material and we had no source of heat sufficient to melt out a part of it. We felt a sense of wonder and awe when we tried to speculate about the incredible forces, stresses and strains under which a material such as this must have formed.

Under the dark skies and amid the red landscape, work proceeded. We explored the surface of the planet but did not move very far from the landing site because it was not necessary. Our telemetric instruments had charted out the planet quite thoroughly while we had orbited it.

On the fourth day, disaster struck. Our dome sprung a leak and we lost more than half of our air supply before the leak could be closed.

Jon decided that because of the loss of air, we would wind up our mission a week earlier than our schedule and would take off for Earth.

Came the next day, the day of our take off. Cornwallis was performing the routine check of the ship's hyper drive systems when his face paled.

"What's the matter?" asked Jon, alarmed at the expression on his face.

"The hyper drive is down," said Cornwallis.

"What?" roared Jon. He held his head in his hands. It was an unprecedented event.

Those were the days when ships did not carry a spare drive.

Jon finally raised his head. "Let's get going with the repairs," he said.

Cornwallis started to say something, then stopped himself, shrugged his shoulders and left.

He was gone for about an hour.

"Need any help?" Jon shouted.

"No," Cornwallis shouted back.

Another hour passed before Cornwallis returned, shoulders drooped.

"Beyond repairs," he whispered.

"Send SOS to earth," Jon said.

Cornwallis drooped further. "Tried. The communication system is down too."

"Sabotage?" That was the first thought all of us had but it was Krishna who gave it voice. We now know that it was not. It was just a string to mishaps.

That night, (figuratively speaking of course, since night on the planet was the time when everyone went to bed), none of us could sleep. We simply huddled close together, either fidgeting or simply staring out into space.

Next day, Jon called a formal meeting of the crew. The item on the agenda was: What should we do now?

Jon was perfectly calm and collected as he summarized our predicament.

The standard procedure in a distress situation is to beam SOS messages and hope for some nearby ship to pick up the signals and come to the rescue. The problem was that we had only about seven days of air supply left, and the chances of a ship being in the vicinity to pick up our distress signal within this time frame were infinitesimal.

Our mission was supposed to last two weeks, as I have stated earlier. Of those two weeks, five days had passed. Nine days were still left, and so no one on Earth would be bothered about us until it was too late for us.

So what do we do now? That was the question of the day.

"There is only one thing to do," Cornwallis said. "We have to find a signal source much stronger than the distress beacons we have, strong enough to reach the earth."

"Yeah, like what?" said Krishna sarcastically.

It was then that something clicked in my mind.

"Wait, I have an idea," I said.

"What?" Everybody fixed their eyes on me and suddenly I was extremely self-conscious. Slowly, haltingly, I tried to convey my idea to them.

"We do have a force shield on our ship, don't we?"

"Of course," said Cornwallis. “It is standard equipment.”

"And how much can the field be expanded?"

"It could have an effective radius of about twenty kilometres," Cornwallis replied.

"Enough to blanket the radiation from the pulsar if the ship was close to it?"

"Yes, but…"

"The pulsar must be under constant observation from Earth, right?"

"Yes, but what are you getting at?" asked Krishna impatiently.

And I told them.

"You are crazy," declared Corny.

"Absolutely rockers," agreed Krishna.

Jon suddenly got up from where he was sitting, pulled me off my feet, swung me in a long arc and shouted "You are wonderful." Was this my shy, silent, teddy bear? I wondered dazedly as I dug my fingers into his forearms and hung on for dear life.

"You mean there is something in her idea?" asked Krishna.

"There is a lot in her idea," he said, and gave me another jubilant swing. It looked like it was hard to stop him once he got going at anything. Not that I complained.

I saw hope dawning on the faces of Cornwallis and Krishna. Then the three of them joined their heads and went into discussions over the technical aspects of my suggestion, and for three hours I couldn't get any of them even to acknowledge my existence, the beasts.

The imminence and closeness of death seems to do strange things to people. Just before the next sleep period, I watched the faces of Krishna and Cornwallis and saw there a seesaw of hope and despair. But still they talked, they joked.

Jon was more silent, more brooding than I had ever seen him before. His chin resting on the palm of his right hand, he would stare at the ground for a long while. Then he would raise his head and look at me. Then he would once again stare at the ground.

This went on for quite some time. Then suddenly he got up from where he was sitting, took me in his arms, and crushed me to him.

"Ruby," he whispered."Yes?"

"Ruby."

"Yes?"

"Will you marry me?"

The intensity of his voice startled me more than the question. I tried to speak but I found I had lost my voice.

"Will you marry me?" he asked again.

"Yes," I said in a small voice and buried my face in his chest.

"Now."

"Now?" Once again he had managed to startle me.

"Yes, now."

"How?"

"We will say our own marriage vows."

Then, on a strange planet under strange skies, in the cabin of a spaceship, Cornwallis and Krishna witnessed a strange marriage and, after throwing numerous ribald comments after us, left the ship and made their way to the dome. I watched their faces as they were leaving and wondered at the unpredictability of the human nature. Our marriage seemed to have done something good to them. The seesaw of hope and despair was gone from their faces and they were once again the same old Corny and Krishna, full of life and zest.

Once Corny and Krishna had left, Jon got up and closed the door of the cabin....

.... And the threat of death made the pleasure just that much more intense.

The next figurative morning, when I opened the ship's door and looked out at the red splendour of the planet called Ruby, I felt that this planet had been created for the express purpose of acting as the venue for my marriage to Jon.

Soon, the day's work started in earnest and proceeded with swiftness.

The force shield was connected to the ship's computer which was then programmed to switch the device on and off at appropriate times.

The course of the ship was plotted and fed into the computer. Then the ship was switched to autopilot.

All of us disembarked from the ship. All the necessary things that could be transferred from the ship to the dome were transferred. Jon then, with what was analogous to a pat on the rump of a horse after the removal of its saddle and reins, started the ship's engines by remote control and sent it hurtling through space toward the neutron star. It would take some time for the ship to reach the pulsar and then to come close enough to the pulsar to be destroyed by the stress of its gravitational pull. Hopefully, that time would be enough for what we had planned to accomplish.

Now all we had to do was to wait and pray.

*

Five days later, on Earth, in one of the many observatories where the strange pulsar was being monitored, an astronomer jerked upright in her seat, rubbed her eyes twice and looked at the latest readings from the neutron star.

The radio pulses from the neutron star were no longer regular. Astounded, she noted the pattern of the pulses as they came in now. She pondered over the pattern and suddenly realized what it meant.

The other people at the observatory momentarily thought that she had lost her marbles when she shouted on all communication channels:

"The pulsar is sending SOS signals."

SENTIENCE

S.Gepp

The four people seated in the small room fell silent as Commander Oliver Haskins entered. He was the only one wearing a uniform – the standard dull blue of the Earth Corporation Exploration Corps. He stood behind a metal desk and nodded at the small gathering.

"Thank-you," he said. "And welcome, Team Alpha, to your final briefing. Tomorrow morning at oh-seven-hundred, Earth standard time, you will be leaving us to set foot on a virgin world. This is something that very few have done before you."

A ripple of happiness ran through the room.

"As you are aware, preliminary surface scans have been completed. I hope you have all read the briefing notes sent to your PMCCs. It is important that you understand that your mission is one of First Contact Protocols and all that entails. Now, while we would ideally like to spend a few more days scanning the surface and especially the waters, the incident at the asteroid belt has put us behind schedule. However, based on the scans done so far, our risk analysis states that, so long as you follow First Contact Protocols, this should go off without a hitch."

He waved his hand over the desk and a pale blue keyboard made of light appeared before him. He tapped at it and between the desk and the crew a large sphere appeared, rotating slowly. Slowly more details appeared over it – a wide band around its centre, like a girdle, and an apparent splotch on top. Both these grew many lumps and ridges, indicating mountains and hills and valleys and lakes, and the edges became more defined and detailed – the whole topographical landscape. "This is the planet, as our scans have delineated," the commander said. A red dot appeared above one of the southern edges of the central band. "We are in geostationary orbit right here."

"So much water," mused Captain Samuel Hobbes.

"Yes, so much water," smiled the commander. "This could be the greatest resource the Corporation has discovered." He touched the floating keyboard and a stream of data appeared before the image. "As was detailed in the briefing notes, a day is twenty Earth hours and twenty-five minutes. The yellow star is ten per cent larger than Sol, and so the average temperature is greater on the surface than you may be used to. Magnetic and geographic north are situated in the same region, meaning standard compasses will function. You may not be aware that this planet sits right on the edge of the Cinderella Zone for this star, so its discovery has been something of a miracle, especially as its size matches that of Mars."

"Does it have a moon at all?" Dr Tien Ng asked.

"No, no satellites. The gravitational force is eighty-six per cent that of Earth at sea level, and it has a sea level atmospheric pressure of point seven two of Earth." The data stream stopped. "Now, that was all in your notes. This next is the newest information." The patch at the top of the sphere glowed. "This is an area of some apparent volcanic activity."

"Dormant or active?" Dr Ng asked.

"We believe active, but have yet to detect any seismic disturbances." Now the central band glowed. "This area, though, is geologically stable. Its width ranges from approximately nineteen to twenty-nine hundred kilometres and it completely encircles the globe, separating the waters of the two hemispheres." He paused and tapped a few more times so that the image zoomed in closer to the central strip. "This is only the second mono-ecological system we have encountered on atmosphere-rich satellites. As such, I can tell you that the entire land mass is some sort of swamp forest."

The four of them murmured amongst themselves. "So, there are life-forms?" Dr Helena Bascombe asked.

"Oh yes. But all of our surface scans have found only vegetation. As to other life-forms, the scans appear inconclusive. The sheer abundance of vegetation makes it difficult to tell, but there is also a marked lack of movement. However, we have not had time to scan the waters," the commander explained.

"So, there could be animals, real xenobiology?" Dr Bascombe was clearly excited by the prospect.

"Yes, possibly." The four of them just stared at him with open mouths. All knew how rare it was to find any non-terrestrial creature. "And the atmosphere certainly gives indication that it may be so. We received the details from the drone sent to the surface before we lost contact with it. It appears the atmosphere is made up of thirty-three per cent oxygen and fifty-five per cent nitrogen."

"Very different from Earth," Dr Ng muttered.

"Even more so," the commander said. "Five per cent carbon dioxide and five per cent pure water. Quite high for both. The final two per cent is made up of trace elements – inert gases predominantly – and unidentifiables. As such, you must wear face masks, but full body pressure suits will not be necessary."

"So, we are to follow the two First Contact Protocols, and that is all," clarified Samuel. "Gather soil and vegetation samples and look for traces of non-plant life."

"Actually, you will have a third task. We cannot leave the drone on the surface. That must also be retrieved." He tapped the keyboard and the image disappeared. He sat on the edge of the desk and folded his arms across his chest. "If this place is just plant-life, then we'll probably mine it dry. The southern waters are what we seek. Those to the north have a pH of between five and six, so we will not touch that zone. However, our activities will leave this world an acidic wasteland. If we do find animal sentience, then we will be forced to be more careful. Otherwise samples of the plants will be taken by botanists over many decades until all have been catalogued, and over the centuries this place will be destroyed utterly, mined dry for its water." He paused. "As occurred on the fifth planet of the Tau Epsilon system."

"So, the second protocol is the most important?" the final crew member, Lieutenant Lidia Delsanto, asked carefully.

The commander looked at all of them. "You did not hear that from me," he said slowly. "Dismissed."

*

The sleek craft glided down, headed for a vacant patch of mud extremely close to the pre-programmed co-ordinates. It descended slowly, firing its down jets carefully and came to rest with barely a jolt. A ramp descended from the side with a slight hiss and after a brief delay the door of the airlock popped open. The four of them walked slowly down and stood on the muddy ground, taking it all in. To the south stretched an apparently endless sea, while north of them the plant-life formed a seemingly impenetrable barrier. Despite the fact it felt like they were in a steam room, with the heat from the sun and the high moisture in the air, not even their full face masks could hide their broad grins.

"Wow," Lidia whispered.

"It's your first time on a new world, isn't it?"" Helena asked quietly.

"Oh yeah," Lidia whispered.

"Well, take it in, take it all in," Samuel said. "It's not everyone who gets a chance to do this."

Dr Ng nodded his agreement. "This is certainly much more pleasant than that rock in the Centauri system."

"Yeah. That was a hole, wasn't it?" Samuel replied with a shake of his head.

"But the ice mines on that place are making a substantial amount for the Corporation," Dr Ng added. "And, with any luck, the water here will do the same."

"What's first?" Helena asked suddenly.

"The drone," Samuel replied. "Have you got a fix on it, Grig?"

"Please hold," came the voice of the shuttle craft's on-board computer. The vocal tones had been made deliberately mechanical so that the personnel had no doubts they were talking to an inanimate object. Too many incidents of anthropomorphisation in the early stages of autonomous computer systems had seen to that. After a long pause, the voice returned. "The readings are erratic. However, it appears that it is located north twenty degrees east, approximately fifty-five metres beyond this craft." Another pause. "Seventy-seven per cent accuracy."

"Tien, the drone is your department. What do you want to do?" Samuel asked.

"Grig, any signs of life-forms?" Dr Ng asked.

"Please hold." A pause and the two men exchanged curious glances. Then: "The only life signs come from the botanical inhabitants."

"Scan again," Helena said suddenly. She looked across at the other two, who nodded at her; this was her area of expertise and neither would dare contradict her.

"Botanical signs only." There was no emotion or judgement in the mechanical voice.

"All carbon-based?" she asked.

"In the immediate vicinity all are carbon-based."

"Heat signatures?"

"Negative."

Helena paused and sighed. "Maybe I should go with you, Dr Ng," she suggested.

He smiled at her. “I just want to look at the moment. When I work out how to move it, then I’ll have help.” He looked in the direction Grig had indicated. “And it’s only fifty-five metres. I’ll be fine.” With those words he disappeared from view as he slipped between two large trees.

The other three watched him go, listening to the rustle of vegetation against his body until it faded.

Helena looked all around. “Do you hear that?” she asked with a hushed voice.

“Hear what?” I can’t hear anything,” Lidia answered.

“Exactly. There’s no noises apart from us. No wind, nothing. Just us.” She indicated the vast sea. “No waves. And no tide lines on the shore. This place is completely still.”

“But there’s got to be something here, doesn’t there?” Lidia asked.

“Of course,” Samuel said. “Where do the gases in the atmosphere come from?”

Helena shook her head. “This feels strange,” she mumbled.

“Just different,” Samuel countered. He looked around once more and grimaced a little. “But yeah, I agree. It is strange.” All three of them now gazed at their surrounds nervously. The beauty of the placed felt suddenly muted.

“I’ve found the drone,” Dr Ng’s voice said through their ear-pieces, breaking into their trance-like states. “It looks completely rusted out. It’s been here for – what? – two days and it looks like it’s been here for a few years. Is this moisture in the air acidic like the northern ocean? Grig?”

“No. The pH of the atmospheric water content is seven point five.”

The others waited for the doctor’s reply. “Tien?” Samuel asked eventually. There was no response. “Grig, what is Dr Ng’s location?”

"Dr Tien Ng no longer appears on the scans," was the emotionless response.

"What?" Samuel hissed. "We've lost Tien?"

"His vital signs no longer appear on the scanners. There is no heat signature. His locator is not sending out a signal. Dr Ng no longer registers."

"What's happened to him?" Lidia asked, unable to hide the panic in her voice.

"Maybe he's fallen into a deep fissure in the ground, covered by the vegetation or something?" Samuel suggested.

"The scanners would not indicate such an occurrence," Grig's voice stated.

"Are there any heat signatures at all?" Helena asked.

"Negative." Pause. "His locator has sent out a signal. He is near the drone. His communication system appears to be non-functional. The on-body scanners are not functioning correctly."

She looked at Samuel. "I'll go then." She pulled out the baton at her hip and switched it on, an arc of electricity flashing between two small pieces of wire at its tip. "I'll keep up constant talk." She pointed at a thin tree at the edge of the dirt patch. "If you two can cut that one down for me while I go, that would help. It'll be a good example for analysis. And then we can get the hell out of here."

"Well, you just keep on talking," Samuel said as he unbuckled the laser knife from his own belt. He flicked it on and the blue glow of the guide light flashed along the edge of the blade.

"I'm walking through trees," Helena said, disappearing as Samuel and Lidia approached the sapling. "They are thick and difficult to pass by. The ground is very soft underfoot. It is covered in what looks like moss, only with occasional sproutings of large leaves. There are no flowers. I can also see growths on the trunks of many of the trees that appear to be separate plant forms."

Samuel drew the knife once across the trunk.

"That was strange," Helena went on. "The trees just moved, but I didn't feel any wind. It happened to all of them at once. Definitely strange. Hold on, I can see the drone. Wow, Dr Ng was right. It looks rusted through. Hey, Tien, is that you? He appears to be sitting, leaning against the drone."

"Be careful," Samuel said, then drew the knife again, cutting deep into the pulpy wood as Lidia grasped it above the cut.

"I will," she replied. "I am approaching the drone now."

"No, wait there. We'll finish this and be with you," Samuel said suddenly.

But even as he spoke, Helena's voice sounded. "The trees are moving again. Definitely moving. Tien, can you hear me? I don't think he's well. His face mask is fogged over, like he's had a leak. That may explain the communicator issues."

"Helena, stay where you are!" Samuel yelled as, with barely a sound, the tree fell into Lidia's grasp. They both looked around as the surrounding vegetation bowed to a breeze they could not feel.

"Tien, it's me, Helena. Are you… What is… No, it can't…"

Silence once more filled the air.

"Helena. Helena! Helena, respond! Samuel screamed, but there was nothing, just the unnerving silence. "Grig, can you detect her?" Again, no answer. "Grig?"

A popping sound came through their ear-pieces, and the mechanical voice said, "Infiltra…" then more silence.

Complete and utter silence.

"What's happening?" Lidia muttered.

Samuel helped her place the tree on the ground, his eyes fixed on the shuttle craft. Lidia looked in the same direction and gasped. A patch of what could only be corrosion seemed to have formed around the door. "I don't know," he replied as he approached the craft. He touched the damaged spot and ran his hand over the front of the craft, then moved out of Lidia's view as he walked behind the vessel.

She stood where she was for a long time. Not a sound reached her. All she could hear was her breath behind the face mask and the blood pounding through her ears in an even louder crescendo of terror.

"Samuel?" she finally managed. "Samuel? Captain Hobbes?"

Nothing. Just the empty stillness of this planet of plants.

"Helena? Tien? Grig? Anyone?"

She spun and looked all around, at the trees, at the shuttle craft, at the endless sea with the glow of the yellow sun glaring from its still surface.

She gazed down and saw Samuel's laser knife beside the tree they had felled. She lifted it nervously and held it in front of her, the blue guide light sitting there like her only remaining friend.

She heard the plants move and swung the knife as she turned quickly around.

Nothing was there. She turned back to the craft and saw that the corrosion had taken hold over a lot of its surface. That was not right.

A face appeared through the foliage.

Lidia managed to smile. "Helena," she breathed. "Am I glad to see you." She moved to the edge of the forest and stopped. "Why aren't you wearing your face mask?" she asked suddenly.

The trees once more moved all around her.

She tried to take a step backwards, but could not move. She looked down. The moss had wrapped around her foot. She opened her mouth to scream.

All that came out was a slow and thin exhalation of air.

A branch from one of the trees moved in front of her face. The leaves moulded themselves around the face mask and forced themselves inside, covering her mouth and nose. She felt all air leaving her in a continuous stream, as though being sucked out. She tried to fight, but all her energy was gone.

Everything was gone.

And silence and stillness was all that was left.

*

"We'll send down a second shuttle," Commander Haskins sighed.

"But we still don't know what happened to them," Dr Jacobs said, shaking her head. "We couldn't hear any of their internal communications after they landed. The interference was too high, and, no, my people cannot find a cause for that."

Haskins nodded; he already knew, but that didn't mean he understood. "The visuals of the ship show a lot of wear and corrosion." He paused. "There's no signs of any corpses, though. And the drone is virtually just a shell. It's as though we left everything there for years."

"There is no acid in the air, we know that. Spectrometry is showing nothing of the sort."

"What about the sea? Anything coming from that?" Haskins tried.

"We can't tell. But at the moment that does seem the most likely scenario." The doctor sighed. "Helena was my best xenobiologist and no-one had more experience on new satellites than Dr Ng. I can't believe we've lost them."

"There's still a chance they're okay," Haskins offered. "We may have just lost communications. They may be safe inside the craft and are awaiting rescue."

Dr Jacobs did not respond. They both knew the unfortunate truth.

"We'll send the second shuttle down on the other side of the drone. They can drop an incendiary first to clear the trees before they land. Shouldn't be an issue. Scans from the first shuttle and the drone have shown absolutely no non-vegetation life-forms," Haskin said.

"But that includes our people as well," Dr Jacobs muttered.

"I do understand that, and there may indeed be other life-forms down there."

The doctor stood. "Just make sure they wear suits, though. The deterioration of our equipment shows there is probably something in the air," she added.

"Of course. Get in, find out what happened to the others, then get out. Hopefully all they'll have to contend with will be the plants." He smiled a little. "Thank God it is just the plants. They're easy to deal with. No sentience."

Dr Jacobs smiled a little and nodded her agreement as she repeated, "Just the plants."

BLACK YONDER

Bryn Fortey

They had entered an orbit deemed safe enough to study the inner planet, a fire-ball world that apparently consisted of a single volcanic core that erupted by means of a multitude of flaws that peppered the burning globe. What had not been realized was that the planet was about to trigger the next stage of its eventual destruction; a surge of increased volcanic activity and temperatures that flew off the scale, well beyond safety levels, catching them all unprepared. The outer shell melted while the inner layer buckled, and crewmen died.

On an uneventful exploration of what lay beyond civilized space, on a quiet trip into the Black Yonder, the ERT (Emergency Response Team) helped out wherever needed and everybody would be grateful that their expertise had not been called upon. But not on this trip, and Commander Terr San Bao became immediately aware that this was a Damage Limitation situation. The ship was lost and soon everyone still on board would be dead.

His built-in computer systems were evaluating every possibility, but San Bao knew that this melting hulk had to be abandoned with all speed. His Oxen – powerful, steady, dependable – were already clearing a route to the Exit Bay where Life-Raft Spacers were waiting, but they would have to lift off soon before the heat rendered them inoperable as well. The Commander's number two, Sergeant E'Tain, was herding as many living crew members as could be found.

Just in time, the three Life-Rafts lifted clear and zoomed away from the raging planet, escaping just moments before the Mother Ship disintegrated into globules of molten metal, falling into the inferno below. The three vessels assumed orbits at the outer limits of the system they had been investigating, transmitting their position and situation on all wave lengths prior to settling all personnel into induced hibernation.

Two Standard Years passed before rescue arrived and the survivors were returned to the safety of civilized space.

*

Though they retained the attitudes of their origins, established procedure dictated that those who sailed the uncharted hazards of Black Yonder should be physically genderless. A breed apart, though breeding was no longer possible, dedicated to the ideals of exploration and discovery. Even Zips had to comply.

San Bao recuperated at his villa, within easy reach of the training ground where Sergeant E'Tain was already drilling recruits who hoped to replace the team members lost during the mayhem of their last voyage. Three Oxen, a Horse and a Tiger had perished, positions that needed to be filled. The Sergeant herself being a Border Collie.

Though not impossible, it was very rare for someone from the General Population to achieve a position of importance. The Ruling Class ruled and provided the leaders. It was the way of things, planet by planet, throughout the Harmonization. At the bottom, carrying out tasks even the GP felt beneath them, were the Zips, descended from humans whose brains had been unzipped to incorporate specific animal characteristics. A combination of such abilities, directed by a computer enhanced human leader, performed well in ERT situations.

"Is there anything else you need, Terr?" asked Lydia, his wife.

The villa was his, though he saw it only between voyages. For Lydia it was home and she had shaped it to her own personality. He often felt like an awkward guest, not wanting to outstay his welcome. Or was that the call of space, forever playing at the edge of his mind?

"No, I'm fine thanks," he replied. "Please withdraw if you have arrangements."

"Nothing that couldn't be cancelled, if you would rather..."

Their marriage had been arranged, of course, and they had met but briefly before the ceremony. It had been while he awaited the finalization of his commission, so was prior to the surgical necessities of a deep space career. They had coupled enthusiastically and often, knowing it would shortly become impossible, and when the time came Lydia had insisted upon having the procedure too. Some partners did, some didn't.

Love hadn't grown for them, the way it sometimes did; a fondness, yes, in a sort of brother-sister symbiosis, but not true dependency. What, he sometimes wondered, had prompted Lydia into a celibate relationship with a husband she rarely saw? She seemed content enough, on the surface at least, but what did he really know about her inner motivations? Such introspection remained rare on his part though. Mostly he rested, while home, waiting until a tingle became an itch, then uncontrollably so, and the call of Black Yonder had to be answered.

"Ah, husband...I see you are studying bids again."

His team was highly respected and there were always offers for their services.

"My sergeant tells me the new recruits are up to standard. It's time to ship out again."

"I had hoped you might have stayed with me a little longer, given the unfortunate circumstances of your last voyage."

"I'm a Deep-Spacer, Lydia! They didn't give me improved metal parts for nothing. I'm driven to go, not because of what I leave, but because of what is waiting. New suns! New worlds! You knew when you married me, where my career lay. You know it now."

Lydia bowed her head. "Your travel bag is packed and ready, Terr."

He smiled and nodded. It always was.

*

The spirit of exploration could never be dimmed because the end would never be reached. Deep-space voyages might investigate and report on new systems, drawing them into the ever-expanding Harmonization, pushing forward the boundaries of civilization, but the Black Yonder was always ahead of them. The pull of the unknown could not be denied and a certain type of man – and, indeed, lesser-man – found the prospect irresistible.

Proudly displayed in the Great Hall of the Space Academy San Bao had attended, were the words: "Man wants to know, and when he ceases to, he is no longer a man." (FRIDTJOF NANSEN). Who Nansen was, or even what planet he hailed from, was forever lost in the mists of time, coming from before the Interplanetary Wars that had preceded the emergence of the Harmonization. Men like San Bao, wanted to know.

Each outward voyage was given specific coordinates to prevent pointless overlaps. The expeditions were not in competition. Their only rewards lay in being out there: first-footing new planets, adding flesh to skeletal charts. The days of the Privateers, exploring space for profit, were long gone.

Zips were almost totally humanoid in appearance, with just three purple lines going from front to back on their hairless heads marking them for what they were; inherited from the ancestors who had originally undergone the surgical implant of specific animal traits. Oxen, for example, were powerfully built and muscular.

Most of the planets they surveyed might one day be plundered for natural resources but would be of no other use. Some showed potential for changing and adapting to make them suitable for human life. A very few needed little or no work for immediate colonization. Some had life forms: docile at times, antagonistic at others, but none of it intelligent. In all the worlds that made up the Harmonization, mankind had not yet found its equal.

Each new planet would first be studied from orbit. When ready, the ERT would land, setting up defensive positions and establishing a base camp before the scientific teams came down. However benign a world might appear, sometimes the unexpected would rear its head.

In his role as Commander, San Bao considered himself fortunate to have a Sergeant like E'Tain. Ever alert, her energy and tenacity sparked a workaholic attitude, and her intelligence meant she didn't have to come to him to confirm every tiny little decision. He sometimes had to remind himself that she was Zip, and therefore not fully Human. In home-world society they would have been poles apart. Only in military and space situations were the two strands able to participate with any degree of intermingling; though even then, on the strict understanding that one remained inferior to the other.

The surgical zipping procedure had been outlawed several generations back, but still their numbers increased. They reproduced like...well, like animals. There had been recent talk of an enforced sterilization program and San Bao guessed that something along those lines would have to be implemented sooner or later. His sergeant though, was as good at her job as he could wish for, lesser-human or not.

*

On a number of occasions both had reasons to be grateful for the other's quick response to the unexpected. There had been the time they had been escorting a survey team who wanted to map a mountainous region of a hot and sweltering giant planet that seemed to be predominately jungle. Their two

Trackers had been continually on edge, claiming they could sense a life-force nearby, but there were no signs of the planet bearing sentient life; not until the mountain range suddenly shook itself and stood.

Identified later as the largest living entity ever known. A huge, monstrous, harmless creature, unless it stood on you; but all San Bao and the rest knew at the time was that their vehicle had summersaulted down the side of whatever it was that had moved.

He did a quick check once they were stationary; there were bumps and bruises aplenty but the only serious hurt was one surveyor with a broken arm, which was promptly immobilized. The vehicle though, was a write-off.

Then: "My globe!" exclaimed E'Tain. "It's cracked!"

The atmosphere on this planet was not able to support human life, thus the necessity to wear globes. San Bao knew, without having to consult his internal computers, his sergeant would be dead as soon as her air supply hissed through the crack to be replaced by the planetary version. Acting automatically and without thought, he grabbed E'Tain and pressed the damaged section of her globe against his chest, covering the crack while snapping quick orders. The medical supplies were plundered and an incapacitating compound readied for immediate application to the relevant part as soon as he released the globe from his grip. This in turn was protected by self-adhering pads, though restricting her vision, but which kept her alive during their hike back to base camp.

It was only later that Commander San Bao faced the fact that he had broken a universal taboo by having physical contact with a lesser-human. Zips were considered untouchable. It was an unwritten law that he had always accepted without having ever really thought about, and he was surprised to find that he did not consider himself unclean for having overstepped what society considered proper behaviour. Should he have stepped back and let his sergeant die? He thought not.

Those Emergency Response Team members present would have kept it to themselves, but the surveyors had also witnessed his actions and one of them would be sure to report it. San Bao, anyway, was always prepared to accept his responsibilities as an officer, and sought an immediate interview with the ship's Captain.

"It's a long held custom, but not a statute book law," decided the experienced Deep Spacer, "more strictly observed within the civilised worlds of the Harmonization. Under the circumstances, as presented, I think it can be ignored on this occasion. What happens in Black Yonder, stays in Black Yonder. Of more concern is the fact that the globe cracked at all. Those things are supposed to be indestructible!"

And there were times, in turn, when E'Tain helped him out of tricky situations; their abilities slotting to the benefit of both.

*

Some Commanders moved up to eventually Captain their own Spaceships, but not San Bao. The men in overall control were rarely able to explore the worlds they discovered, and on some footfall excursions they didn't even leave the ship. San Bao had found a position that suited him, as head of an Emergency Response Team.

E'Tain had been with him from the very beginning, though initially as a very junior team member, but she had shone from day one. His first sergeant had been a veteran Bloodhound, fully experienced and a good pick for a new Commander, and when the Bloodhound retired E'Tain was promoted to the position. Now, with San Bao himself having just passed two hundred Standard Years, they were the veterans, though any thoughts of retirement were quickly pushed to one side.

So it was that they landed on a small inhospitable ball of ice. Of no interest as far as permanent habitation was concerned, but was however chock-a-block with a mishmash of natural deposits. Sufficiently so to make it a prime target for exploitation, and the Tech Boys were rubbing their hands with glee. San Bao's team was on escort duty as the full extent of what was on offer was measured and recorded.

Sub-zero temperatures, howling winds, ever changing surface conditions as lower level ice sheets clashed and slid over and into each other. San Bao knew they could have figured it all out from orbit, but no: Science Level personnel always looked to make Footfall discoveries, even on a hellhole planet like this.

The Commander remained inside the portable exploration laboratory, along with the driver and three Technicians, while members of his ERT were functioning as outriders on individual transporters. Conditions made it a slow-moving convoy, as expected. The change, when it came, was something not seen before.

First the ground shook, the sheets of ice bucking and twisting beneath them. The laboratory was thrown onto its side. Then ice boulders, bigger than a man, rained down all around. Some struck the front of the vehicle, where the driver, still struggling to free himself from his seat, perished under the onslaught. San Bao hoped that only a limited number of his outriders would have been hit.

Next, as the boulders eased off, the ice beneath the stranded lab cracked open into an ever widening and lengthening fissure that the vehicle tumbled into, shuddering to a destructive halt as it struck a ledge, maybe a hundred metres down, and stayed there. Only San Bao survived the fall, the three Technicians being mangled and crushed within the twisted metal of the machine, but his injuries were severe. His left leg and hand had both been completely severed and his right leg was smashed beyond saving. Only the blood freezing at the stumps prevented him bleeding to death. With a struggle he managed to tourniquet his amputations prior to resealing his protective suit; though when he surveyed his position, it all seemed rather pointless.

His radio had been crackling all the while and now he readjusted it. "Commander? Where are you?" came E'Tain's voice. "Have you survived?"

"Skylah, I have a problem," he replied. Why, for the first time ever, he used his sergeant's Christian name, San Bao didn't know. Maybe, realizing the likely outcome of his situation, he needed a show of comradeship. Or maybe it was just a meaningless slip. "The others are dead and I am badly injured," he continued. "Return to base immediately. This planet has to be evacuated."

"Not without you, sir. We have you spotted now. You were lucky with the ledge! The crack looks bottomless. We can lower a harness to you and pull you up."

"One leg gone, the other useless, and a hand gone too; I couldn't even get out from the wreckage, and would struggle to put on a harness anyway. Obey orders, sergeant: return to base. I am beyond saving."

Skylah E'Tain had never disobeyed an order during all her years of service, but this current situation was different. A number of outriders had died or were hurt during the boulder bombardment and she would lead the survivors back to base, but their Commander would not be left. "I will be lowered down and get you into the harness. Then, after you've been pulled up, the harness can be lowered again for me."

"It's too far!" he exclaimed.

"A hundred metres? We did more than that in training."

“But...”

“Too late for buts,” she said, interrupting him. “I’m on my way, sir”

Neither of them had any thoughts about human/non-human taboos as she manhandled his broken body away from the wrecked laboratory and onto the ledge proper, where she could place him into the harness and radio the order for him to be lifted.

Slowly, hand over hand, the team at the top pulled their Commander to safety. “Quickly, drop it back down for the sergeant,” he said, once free of the harness himself, but while they were doing so a massive rumbling echoed around and the two walls of the fissure started to move towards each other. The deadly, inevitable outcome was obvious to all.

“Why?” shouted a distraught San Bao, shaking his solitary fist at the gods of this hellhole planet. “Why?” he whispered into the radio.

“Because I love you,” replied Skylah E’Tain, “and I would do it again.”

Then the sides slammed together, and it was as if the crack had never existed.

*

Back on his home world, they patched San Bao’s broken body as expertly as possible. His new legs and hand functioned well, though never with quite the fluency of their originals. He accepted retirement since he knew there were no alternatives, and opted to have his bodily computer parts removed. What could he use them for now? To calculate the exact moment of his death? Best to let that creep up, unannounced.

Lydia, his wife, of whom he was fond, was happy to care for him and to share his retirement years. She was wise enough to know that when he left their villa to sit and look up at the night time sky, he was best left alone. No Deep Spacer ever got Black Yonder completely out of his system.

During such moments, secretive thoughts of Skylah E'Tain would often surface; the Zip who had given her life to save his. If her last words had been to express devotion to him, he could have understood, because that would have been acceptable as devotion to the uniform and his position as Commander. Maybe she had meant devotion, but she had used the word love. It was unthinkable, of course, love between a human and non-human, even the genderless Deep Space varieties.

"Don't stay too late, Terr," Lydia would say, not wanting him to be chilled, and he would nod agreement, but at regular intervals the night sky would draw him out. Stars, like magnets, holding his gaze, and the call of Black Yonder would echo through his mind.

Terr San Bao would relive his years of voyaging and exploration. He would remember his Teams, and especially the sergeant who had died in his place: Skylah E'Tain, a Border Collie Zip, who's Christian name he had only ever used once.

"Of course I didn't love her," he would mutter to himself. "A human, love a Zip? Never!"

But as he looked at the stars, a tear would sometimes trickle down his face.

PETRICHOR
Mike Adamson

I was at 70, 000 feet, on my way into Basecamp 12, when the screaming began.

There is a moment when the hairs stand up on your neck, and the timbre of horror in the human voice, beyond horror - the sudden realization of impending and horrific death provokes that reaction in me.

I stabbed the radio contact, momentarily blocking out the appalling sound on the open channel. "Basecamp 12 from Icarus, do you copy? Marty, it's Jack, what's happening? Tell me!" I unkeyed and the screaming filled the air once more.

Ahead, stormclouds were a sullen, blackish blanket across Penthesilia's western continent and its attendant ocean as I came down from the transfer station in equatorial orbit. The long late afternoon horizon was a bright arc below the two moons, Ister and Herodotus. I would be on the ground at 12 in twenty minutes with a load of supplies, but now my blood ran cold and I knew the station crew would be listening.

"12, what's happening? Tell me!"

Again screaming, but this time I made out a few words. Spores was the one which came clearest. Burning, blinding - the rock, the stones - didn't know, thought they were just -

At this point the voice on the open channel faded and I was left with a racing heart, listening to white noise. My first impulse was to tie onto ground video but my hand was shaking as it traced across the panel at my side - what would I see? The feed from a couple of static cameras, covering the compound outside the inflatable habitats of the basecamp, were on permanent broadcast to the station, and I picked up a low-res feed from the omnidirectional mast.

Nothing seemed odd at first, then my eyes adjusted for the grainy image and I realised it seemed to be snowing.... A soft blanket of something pale, almost reflective, was settling over every surface. I saw shapes I did not recognize, jumbled lumps where I was sure only bare rock should be, but the habitats, the vehicles and stores, seemed untouched.

I punched the com select. "Surveyor Station, are you getting the visual?"

"Affirmative, Icarus. Be advised, we have a maximum priority alert going into effect."

"Do you want me to abort landing?" Softly asked, the question was by the book though my heart was ambivalent. The need to find out what was happening to my friends warred with the instinct for self preservation, and I am proud to say it won.

The reply took a few moments. "That's negative, Icarus. Command says continue in, circle 12 and send us back all the data you can." The station com officer unkeyed for a moment, then came back. "Command says get into your hardsuit - now."

I was happy to oblige. The shuttle was running in full autopilot mode so I slid the pilot's seat back from the instruments, turned and eased out from under the long plasteel canopy. I made my way by handholds through a short corridor into the crew support area and flicked on the lights in the suiting bay.

All shuttles carried three standard suits: signal orange beasts of laminated titanium-plastic alloy and a dozen other exotic materials, able to withstand extreme environments. I voice-printed to authorize Suit 1 to come online, and the machine's LEDs and pilot lights came on. The suit parted at a waist joint; the upper half lifted clear on a hydraulic hoist and I climbed into the lower, my heart thudding painfully as I thought about what lay ahead. The computer would not allow me to make a mistake in procedure, and in a way I was sorry we had such an overburden of safety features: I would have been happier to have the demand of getting things exactly correct to occupy my ragged thoughts as the ship ate up the hundreds of miles to destination.

The top came down gently. I worked my arms into the sleeves and relaxed as the halves lined up, locked together with a contact of pressure dowels and gaskets, and I breathed the cool air in the helmet. At a voice command the suit disengaged from the support systems. I stepped back up to the cockpit, hearing the whir of servos as the machine carried its own mass.

The seat reconfigured for the bulk and I tucked in at the controls again. We were nine minutes out and the video feed showed the snowing effect continuing unabated. The scene was dark, gloomy and inescapably alien. I shook my head, sick at heart, feeling that hope for my friends of the Penthesilia expedition was fading by the moment.

"Surveyor, I'm suited up and on approach. I'll be into the weather in a few minutes. It's thick down there, we can expect heavy static conditions."

"Understood, Icarus. Gently does it - if conditions are too hairy, get out of there. But if you can give us a look at what's happening…."

"I know. It'll be invaluable." My voice was a whisper, my throat dry. I drew on the drink tube by my lips, tasted the flat, recycled water of spaceflight.

Radar and lidar painted the atmosphere ahead, gave me my entry point, and I let the shuttle bore into the storm belt. Visibility dropped sharply. I picked up IFR to run the next four minutes, velocity down to below mach one and engines ticking over comfortably. Turbulence bounced me around and lightning filled the clouds with purple ferocity. I came out of the cloud base over the Ayrie Plateau of the Magadan Mountains to a soul-stirring image of flicker-filled clouds backing an awesome expanse of dark rock and stunted trees, where streams now ran in spate.

What could have happened? The thought hammered my mind without pause. We had been here for months, cataloguing the biota, geography and geology of this inviting world; it was deep in the Middle Stars and - one would have hoped - ripe for colonization at some point. Planetary survey was the bread and butter of no few spacefarers and scientists as the 24th century neared its end, but it seemed space never lost its ability to surprise, sometimes painfully.

I brought the scan platform online and directed the mutlispectral cameras onto the base as I orbited a mile out. The computers registered data as the instruments picked up fluctuations from baseline conditions. Data went automatically up to Surveyor; the specialists would be poring over it already.

With two orbits completed, I saw nothing moving on the direct video feed. "Surveyor, I'm turning downwind for a pass over 12."

"Roger, Icarus, no lower than 300 metres

"Understood." I brought the sharp nose around, felt her jostled in the storm winds over the plateau and pulled speed back to just above stall, flaps and slats deployed to give the instruments their maximum recording time. As I went over I saw the entire upland now taking on that frosty gleam, as if snow, not rain, was coming from those clouds. Wipers flicked back and forth across the canopy but I was flying more by instruments than VFR and ignored the angry sky ahead as I realized the radio band was vacant. Not even an open key, just…nothing.

Whatever had happened was fast. The event seemed to be over, and I pulled back up into a racetrack pattern, five miles on a side, to wait on the word from orbit. My engines were running smoothly; fuel was not an issue with air compaction thermal propulsion - I could climb back into orbit without refueling. But leaving answered no questions. I rested my hands in my lap as the autopilot flew the pattern and I tried to control my impatience.

"Come on, Surveyor," I called at last, "I want to get down there. If there's anyone alive they need help now."

"Icarus," came the reply a moment later, "science team is conferring, wait one."

"One is about all the patience I have," I whispered, knowing it was at least half bravado. My gut told me all fourteen members of the landing party were dead, but I needed to know it. If anyone was alive, I could not abandon them to whatever had happened. I drummed heavily-gloved fingers on the seat arms and counted my breaths.

"Icarus, command authorizes you to touch down, using maximum biohazard procedures." I knew what that meant. The airlock was designed for sterilization.

"On my way," I reported softly as I took control back from the autopilot and entered a landing cycle. Flaps, slats, deploy gear, engines vectored for VTOL…I came down out of the angry sky toward the clear area we used as a pad, a hundred yards from the collection of habitats. My downwash blasted water and whatever the pale substance was in concentric waves. The gear touched and took hold, and the craft went through a normal shutdown to hot-standby. I could be back in the air in one minute if need be.

Now the silence closed around me. Only the rub of the wipers on the canopy broke the stillness as rain continued to patter and infrequent thunder backed a desolate scene. I slapped my harness release and shoved the seat back. "Surveyor, I'm going out. Stay on my suit cam."

I was hyper-aware of my breathing in the closeness of the helmet as I stepped into the external access lock. The inner door hissed shut, seals inflated and warning lights on the bulkhead steadied to tell me the interior was hermetically sealed. The moment I cracked the hatch, the lock was contaminated.

How many times had I landed here? Stepping out into the muggy, upland air of this promising new terrestrial planet was always like coming home. Bouncing ever so slightly in the 0.92 Earth-normal gravity was a delight, and the effort to understand the local life systems had so far been an intense scientific pleasure.

But all this ended with the screaming. I stepped down the metal companionway which had extended from beneath the lock and hesitated before setting a massive boot to the muddy ground. I waited, heard thunder in the distance over the helmet speakers, and rain ran in rivulets down my faceplate. I listened to drops sizzle and steam on the hull, red-hot from its hypersonic passage of the atmosphere.

Get it over with, part of me counselled. I walked with the springy stride of the suit servos, splashing through mud toward the compound. The season had changed quite abruptly; this was the heaviest rain we had encountered so far.

At the compound I knelt to inspect the snowy stuff which flowed sluggishly in the watery runnels. It seemed faintly glassy, as if composed of masses of tiny spheres, and I blinked to activate a helmet sensor. Macro magnification projected into my field of vision from the helmet cam, and the stuff in my glove jumped into sharp relief.

"Are you getting this?" I asked softly.

"Affirmative," was the whisper from orbit.

The glassy spheres were minute but definitely real. I flicked them from my glove and moved on to make an exhaustive search. The power shed was across the compound, near the base of the com mast, and I looked into it first - the thermoelectric generator was still purring softly to itself, undisturbed. The habitat buildings would have been open at this time of day, and I looked into each - the mess, stores section, lab, two bunkhouses. There was no one in any of them; the whole complex seemed deserted, and Surveyor urged me to keep moving, document as much as possible with my camera and above all not linger.

The control room was the last I entered, though perhaps it should have been the first. At the communications console was the team member who had made the final, awful call, though I could not tell who it was. I swallowed hard and made myself look, record the sight from all angles while keeping my distance.

The body slumped over the work surface had almost ceased to be recognizable. The glassy material had bonded to the flesh and seemed to be dissolving it - hair was gone, eyes, mouth, all hollowed out already; fingers were withered to claws, the bones showing. It was as if decomposition was accelerated ten thousand times - which was probably a fair approximation. I'm scientist enough to know I was seeing a process of digestion occurring. The matter of the body was being converted to raw materials for the use of something else. Before my gaze, a piece of flesh disengaged from the shoulder and fell to the floor on a string of slimy mucus, and I fought back the urge to gag.

Now I understood those shapeless lumps out on the plateau. If I counted them, I was sure I would find thirteen.

I rose, turned a slow circuit and noted that fruit in a dish on a table was also liquefying. All organic matter. Metal and plastic were untouched. I stepped outside once again, made my way to the edge of the compound and stared across the rough field of rock. My curiosity was piqued enough for me to ignore cautions from Surveyor, and head for the scrubby, broad-leafed local trees. Yes…they were dying too. The process was one of mass-conversion, something was annihilating the biota at all levels. There were no mobile life forms here, I realized - nothing that flew or crept or burrowed; only vegetation - and humans ignorant of the danger.

Nearby, a stunted tree collapsed as its roots gave way, and the mass lay like a sodden death shroud. The digestive process was rapid; my impression was, much of the mass would have dissolved in a matter of hours. But what gathered the resulting broth of nutrients?

The answer was at once so simple I could have laughed, and so horrific I felt a wave of giddiness sweep over me. The clue came when I knelt to examine the fallen tree, and found bare rock puckered and cratered with a million apertures, as if the familiar ores had been converted to pumice.

Macro examination revealed the glassy spherules emitting from those pores, flowing away by the trillion even now - spat forth on gassy bursts to coat every structure, carried far and wide by the storm wind to begin the conversion of vast tracts of the biosphere to…slurry.

I straightened and breathed deeply, disinclined to pre-guess the scientific results yet knowing instinctively what they would be. This was a case of fleas believing they understood the dog. As I walked back to the welcoming red dart of the shuttle waiting in the rain, I went over my thoughts with Surveyor.

"It's the mountains," I whispered. "You saw the pores. The rock is alive. The mountains are alive. Like coral reefs spawning on Earth - the right full moon of the year triggers them to release eggs and sperm into the ocean. Here…probably the rain. The right rain at the right time strikes the ground and signals the mountains to spawn. They release seeds that'll mature as the next layer of rock, and enzymes to digest every organic thing they touch to feed the process." I was speaking as if half in shock, walking without feeling the ground beneath me. "What could make more sense? Everything liquefies, it flows back to the earth - into the pores, feeds the living mountains." I was speculating, letting myself run on in the disorientation of the moment. "Then sunlight breaks down the remaining enzymes, the rains sweep it all away into new mud and soil.... Seeds blow in and the forest regenerates. In five years, in ten, the cycle repeats. The animals knew. They were gone days ago."

I seemed to wake from the dream when my hand touched the shuttle hull and I realized my face was wet with tears which had flowed unconsciously.

"We just got in its way," I whispered. "Nobody's fault, we were…in the wrong place. Wrong place."

"Icarus," was the call, and when I did not respond at once the voice was firmer. "Jack, do you read?"

"Here."

"Get aboard, go through a sterilization sequence. You can't afford to bring one spore up with you."

"Understood," I added, still more than a little blank. I stepped onto the platform which had run out before the lock. I spread my arms and turned slowly as jets of scalding steam scoured the surface of the suit. When I was cascading boiling water I stepped into the lock proper and sent the hatch across. "Computer, flame lock," I said softly.

A moment later the airlock filled with intense jets of pale flame enveloping my suit. I let the burn run ten seconds - no conceivable biological molecule could withstand so much.

Refrigerated air blasted from vents to strip heat out of the chamber and I wept softly as I waited. I had the vague impression I would not be fit for duty for quite some time. Losing your companions is, thankfully, a rare event in space exploration, and I might be forgiven the consequences.

Most of all, I regretted the mark it would leave on my psyche. The moment when rain comes after a long drought, and that smell rises from the parched ground - petrichor, it is called, the "ichor of the stone." I had always loved it. It brought a sense of immediacy, and that the living world was greater than ourselves.

But no matter what planet I was on, I would never again smell rain striking dry ground without thinking of this hellish place, without remembering the screams, and our terrible disillusionment with the existence of the Land Reefs of Penthesilia.

SYMPHONY

Douglas Smith

FAST FORWARD: Third Movement, Danse Macabre (Staccato)

They had named the planet Aurora, for the beauty that danced above them in its ever dark skies. At least, it had seemed beautiful at the time. Now Gar Franck wasn't so sure.

Gar huddled on the floor, shielding his two-year-old son, Anton, from the panicked colonists stampeding past them in the newly-constructed pod link.

"Damn you, Franck ! When will you make it stop?" a man cried from across the corridor. A woman lay in the man's arms, convulsing as her seizure peaked. She was dying, but to Gar's numbed mind her moans harmonized with the screams of the mob into a musical score for his private nightmare.

Anton sat on the floor, a broken comm-unit held before his blank face. The child let it drop to strike the metal surface with a dissonant clang. More people fled by. The child ignored them. With morbid fascination, Gar watched Anton repeat the scene. Pick up the comm-unit, let it drop. Pick it up, drop it. Again. Each clang as it struck the floor was more chilling to Gar than any cry from the dying.

This attack had blown the colony power grid. The only light now came through the crysteel roof. Gar looked up. The aurora blazed and writhed in the night sky, a parody of the chaos below. Greens, reds and purples shimmered strobe-like over the corridor, turning each person's frenzied flight into a macabre dance.

"God no!" the man cried. The woman stiffened then fell limp. "No!" The man pulled her to him, sobbing.

The rainbow lights of the aurora dimmed and the flickering slowed. The screaming died. Gar stood and looked around, dazed. People were shaking their heads, helping up ones who had fallen, poking at bodies. The man still sat holding the dead woman, his eyes hard on Gar. Other colonists stared at Gar too.

Gar swallowed. Picking up Anton, he walked past accusing faces toward their dorm pod. Anton squirmed in his arms. The child didn't like to be touched, let alone held.

Someone whispered as he passed. "How will he talk to this thing when he can't even talk with his own son." Gar pulled Anton closer, smothering his sobbing in the child's sleeve.

REWIND: First Movement, Prelude (Agitato)

Six months ago. Anton was eighteen months old. Their ship, The Last Chance, had just dropped out of the worm-hole, leaving a poisoned Earth and the plague behind. Earlier probes through this hole had identified a G2 star with planets within range.

The plague had forced the Last Chance to launch before completion of its biosphere. The ship was only partly self-sustaining. They had only a year left to find a new home. It wasn't called the Last Chance for nothing.

Gar lay exhausted on the wall bed of the small ship cabin that he, Clara and Anton shared. Clara's latest holographic sculpture spun suspended before him - shifting geometric shapes in greens, reds and purples. Vivaldi filled the room, wiping words from his head like rain washing graffiti from a wall. Gar lived with words all day. He'd had enough of words.

The jump had flooded MedCon with hyper-space shock cases. Gar was logging eighteen hour days translating between colonists and doctors. Fluency in ten languages and a name in computerized speech translation had won him his berth as Communications Officer. With over six thousand refugees from all over Earth, both human and automated translators were invaluable.

Gar rubbed his eyes. Overtime was at least an escape from the routine of translating the captain's messages to the crew and passengers. And from the growing tensions of his family life.

He checked the time. Clara worked as a laser and photonics specialist in TechLab. Her shift should be over by now.

Anton sat on the plastek floor, flapping his hands, staring. At what Gar could not say and a fear grew in him each day that Anton did not know either. Gar got down in front of the child. "Hey, big guy. What're you doing?" Anton looked right past him.

"He stared like that for twenty minutes today." Gar turned. Clara stood at the door, her lip trembling. "I measured it."

"Clara..." Gar felt himself tighten up.

"These spells just seem to blend together now."

"Maybe it's the jump," he said, not believing it himself.

"He was like this before the jump, Gar."

"He's just slow developing. How was your shift?"

"Most children are speaking by a year," she said.

"He walked on time, right?" Gar turned up the music a bit, not looking at her. "I just did a translation. They've found the system. We'll be there in four months."

"He never looks up when we speak, Gar."

"We'll have his hearing tested again."

"He won't let me hold him." Her voice broke and Gar turned back to her. She was leaning against the wall, her arms wrapped around herself, sobbing. "I can't hold my own child, Gar."

Gar swallowed. He walked over and took her in his arms.

Clara pushed away from him. "I want Ky to look at him."

Ky Jasper was MedCon Leader. "He's too busy," Gar mumbled.

"He owes you for all the overtime. Talk to him."

Gar looked at Anton. The child sat with his hands over his ears, rocking back and forth. The Vivaldi, calm and soothing in the background, gave the scene a surreal feeling.

"He's disappearing, Gar. Disappearing into his own world."

Gar closed his eyes to shut out both the scene and his tears. He nodded. "I'll ask him tomorrow."

First Movement: Finale (Largo)

In the ship's darkened MedLab, a hologram of Anton's brain spun glowing and green, areas of red flashing within it. Gar stood stunned beside Ky Jasper and Clara. The imaging unit beeped musical tones as Ky outlined a red area in purple.

"...repetitive mannerisms and actions. Autistics are neurologically overconnected, as in this area of the cortex that handles hearing. Their senses are so acute they can overload. A touch is painful. Speech scrambles. Soft sounds are like explosions. One overloaded sense can shutdown the other four."

"So he covers his ears. And won't let us hold him." Clara spoke in a monotone, face blank. "Why won't he talk?"

Gar shook his head. This wasn't happening.

Ky sighed. "Autistics are blind to other minds. Anton doesn't know we're fellow beings with thoughts and feelings. To him, we're just things, moving through his world at random."

"Is there a cure?" Gar asked. Clara's sobs and the beeping of the imaging unit played like a discordant sound-track to the scene. Ky turned to him, his face half in darkness, half in green from the hologram. He shook his head.

Second Movement: Main Theme (Accelerando)

They were lucky, the captain had said on reaching the system and finding a habitable planet. Breathable atmosphere, 0.95 Earth gravity. Hotter than Earth, but a polar temperate zone held a suitable land mass. The axial tilt meant they'd be in night for the first 2.4 Earth years, but that was a small issue. Besides, the polar zones offered spectacular auroral activity.

Lucky, the captain had said. Still reeling from the news of Anton, Gar hadn't felt very lucky at the time. Now no one did.

On first seeing the aurora on orbital displays, Gar had felt a dread he couldn't reconcile with its beauty. He had assumed he was subconsciously linking its colors to those of Anton's MedLab hologram. Now he wasn't sure. Now people were dying.

Walking through the main colony dome, Gar noted without surprise that all ceiling panels had been opaqued to block any view of the sky. He cranked up Mozart in his translation headset and tried to relax as he neared the newly-built dorm pod.

The construction of the colony on the planet had gone well in the beginning. Gar had made planet-fall with the first group. To translate between engineers and work crews, he had said. Both he and Clara knew he was avoiding the situation with Anton.

Clara had accepted the diagnosis quickly. During the trip to the planet, she had buried herself in researching autism and working with Anton. Gar just couldn't. So he hid in his work.

At their dorm unit, Gar hesitated then stepped inside. Clara sat with Anton, one of her light sculptures hovering before them. Anton rocked back and forth, eyes on the floor.

"Is that a new sculpture?" he said, forcing a smile.

She looked at him and his smile died. "Old one. New colors." Gar noted the absence of greens, reds and purples. "Autistics think visually. Words are too abstract," she said. "I hoped the shapes and colors might prompt a reaction."

Gar noticed she wasn't in uniform. "Did your shift change?"

"The captain needs to see you about an announcement. He asked me to brief you." She spoke a command. The hologram disappeared and a MedLab report appeared on a wall screen.

Clara led a photonics team analyzing the aurora. Gar had no idea how her work had been going. They didn't talk much lately. He scanned the report. "...high amplitude gamma waves in the brain, resulting in massive and prolonged epileptic seizures. Most victims are adult females. Attacks match peaks in aurora activity. Shielding attempts have failed."

"So it is the aurora," he said, as he finished.

"This thing isn't an aurora." She didn't look at him.

"What do you mean?"

"This planet's magnetosphere is too weak." She stared at Anton. "So are the solar flare levels. Besides, the timing of the attacks doesn't even match the solar wind cycle."

"Then what's causing the aurora? Or whatever it is?"

Clara reached out and stroked Anton's hair. The child began shaking his head violently and she stopped. "We think we are."

Gar felt a chill. "What?"

"The aurora was stable until our planet-fall. It's grown steadily since. We think our arrival prompted the attacks and our continued presence is causing their escalation."

"Attacks?" He wished she'd look at him.

"It's not a natural phenomenon. The electron flow doesn't even follow the planet's magnetic field. It appears to go where it wants to, and it seems to want to be over our settlement."

"But why?"

Clara finally looked at him. "We believe we're dealing with a sentience, Gar. An alien intelligence. The Captain wants to try to communicate. He's asking you to lead that team."

FAST FORWARD: Fourth Movement, Nocturne (Allegro)

Gar leaned against the wall of the main colony dome, staring at the fire raging above. Out here he was at least alone in his misery. No one else could stand the sight of the sky any more. Gar preferred it to the accusing stares of his fellow colonists.

All their attempts to communicate had failed. His team had used ideas from the ancient SETI project, transmitting universal mathematical concepts. For six Earth weeks, they had broadcast over the full range of EM frequencies detected in the aurora.

If any message had been received, it created no visible effect. The deaths continued. The aurora still burned the heavens, and he could no more tell what message it held than what was in his own son's head. Standing, he started to walk.

She sat slumped against a boulder crying, Anton in front of her. The child had his back to her, rocking gently. Gar sat down and pulled her to him before she realized he was there.

She pushed away at first but then collapsed against him. Her sobs stopped, and they held each other for a long while.

"Do you know why I came out here?" she asked finally.

He paused. "You hoped the aurora might reach Anton."

"In a way," she said. Gar had never seen her face so sad.

"Well, it's quite the light sculpture," he said.

"Gar, I came here... so this thing would kill our son."

The words ran around his head as he tried to pull some meaning from them. "Clara..."

"Practically every victim's been a woman," she said.

"That doesn't..." He stopped. He understood.

"What will happen to him then? You won't..." She turned away, not finishing. He sat there, his face burning, realizing what she had been living with, and living with alone.

"I'm sorry," he whispered.

"Promise me you'd take care of him, that you'd love him."

"I promise," he said. They made love then, there on the ground, Anton as oblivious to their passion as he was to the monster rampaging above. After, they lay gazing at the aurora.

"I realize now how Anton must feel," Gar said.

"What do you mean?"

"Blind to other minds. We've been blind to this thing. Now we're shouting, 'Hey look, we're alive' and it doesn't hear us."

She looked at Anton. "Maybe he's shouting too." Clara stared at the sky. "Words, mathematical symbols are too concrete, too cerebral for this thing. We need something more abstract. Something with emotion. I can feel it."

"'Music is born of emotion.'"

"That sounds like a quotation."

"Confucius. Music can express ideas, subtleties, and emotions that words can't. The language areas in the brain show activity when we listen to music. Too bad the sky has no ears."

Clara smiled. "You and your music. That's what first attracted me to you, when we met after the launch."

"Really?"

She nodded. "The first crew briefing. You had Bach playing in the room. I remember the colors - all golds and reds."

"Music helps to... wait a minute. Colors?"

She looked embarrassed. "I'm a synesthete. Sounds make me see colors. That's why I always have music playing when I work on my light sculptures. Inspiration."

"Synesthesia. You've never told me about this."

"I once worked in a laser lab with another synesthete. With her, light prompted sounds, even tastes and smells. It was so distracting for her that she had to quit her career. So when I applied for a berth on the ship, I kept quiet about it."

"No need to be ashamed. Lots of creative types have been synesthetes. Scriabin even built a 'color organ' for Prometheus: Poems of Fire..." He stopped and stared at the sky.

"Too bad my synesthesia isn't like that. I could tell you what kind of music the sky is playing..." She stopped too.

They looked at each other.

"We could use colors for different pitches," he said.

"You mean, correlate the spectrum of EM frequencies displayed by the aurora with sound frequencies of the music."

"That's what I said."

"Rhythm can just stay the same. Brightness for volume."

"What about orchestration? The timbre of each instrument?"

"Holographic images. Different shapes for each instrument."

"Your sculptures ! We could adjust sizes too."

"Small shapes for high notes, larger for the bass range."

"And add more shapes for more volume as well," he said.

"What about harmony? Melody?"

"Tough one. Don't know what colors or shapes go together."

"You'll figure it out." She stood and picked up a wriggling Anton, giving him a hug. "Come on. We've got work to do."

Fourth Movement: Finale (Crescendo)

Gathered under the sea of swirling light, the entire colony seemed to hold its breath as Gar spoke the command. Lasers flared into life, and Schubert's 8th Symphony danced in cubes and stars and dodecahedrons of rainbow colors across the sky. Gar had always thought the Unfinished was music for the end of the world. A fitting epitaph for the colony if they failed.

A computer controlled the shapes, colors and other aspects of the display, monitoring the aurora and repeating patterns that prompted lower EMR levels. "Audience feedback," Clara called it.

The music of the lights played. The colors and shapes of the music kept changing and the colony kept waiting. Ten minutes. Fifteen.

The aurora seemed to slow, to drop in intensity. A murmur swept through the crowd, and Gar's heartbeat quickened.

Someone screamed.

Gar spun around. A woman trembled on the ground. Another fell. Then a man. More dropped. Gar's ears buzzed and his head throbbed. "Gar!" Clara fell to the ground, hands stretched toward him, twitching. Anton still just sat, staring at the sky.

Gar moved to help Clara. Pain flamed in his head and he fell. The air seemed thicker, misty. Then he understood.

The aurora had dropped from the sky. It enveloped them, a swirling cloud of colored sparks and flashes. Electric shocks stung his skin. Saliva trickled from Clara's mouth. The comm-unit to control the display lay before him. He forced his hand forward. The screaming grew louder as he clawed the unit to him.

His lips began to form the command to kill the light music when he saw Anton. The child still sat but his eyes...

Gar felt a thrill of joy as for the first time Anton's eyes focused on something in this world. Clara's sculptures danced in the sky to Gar's music and their child followed every pirouette.

Twisting his head, he saw that Clara was watching too, the happiness in her face shining through the pain.

Whether it was the sculptures or the music or the aurora, Gar neither knew nor cared. He let the comm-unit slip from his fingers. This scene would play itself out.

He reached out to clasp Clara's hand, wondering with a strange calm if they would survive. Together they lay in the dirt of that alien world and watched their son turn to look at them - and smile.

THE HEAD OF THE DRAGON STAR

Russell Hemmell

They stared at the 3D map hovering above the holodeck, showing all the stars in their motion toward the galactic centre together with their courts of planets and moons. The rendition was incredibly accurate and fascinating to observe, but the message it conveyed was grim nonetheless. A message that had never changed since they had left the Solar System: no habitable worlds to settle down.

And things had just got worse.

"It has been years, and we still look at the same scene," Stanley said.

"Not really. Stars are different," Lena replied with a shrug.

"And useless all the same," he said, turning his back to the holodeck. "We're reaching the point of no return." He rubbed his eyes, before looking at her again. "I don't know what Erin would have done. She's no longer with us; but we're here, and we'll have to make a decision."

"We don't have to decide now," Lena said. "We've been on board since how long – fifteen, no, sixteen years. You can allow us, and yourselves, a few months of soul-searching exercise."

"There's probably less soul-searching than you imagine. Decisions are often extraordinary simple, even when they're difficult," Val said quietly.

Both looked at Val. He's always like that, Stanley thought, seldom assertive, never vocal, straight to the point. Dead calm even now, as we were not juggling between life and death.

Without a word, Stanley left the main deck.

*

The ceiling of his cabin offered another fine view-titanium and graphene in a fascinating pattern that looked almost artistic. This is the way we the Moonwalkers are, Stanley thought, always searching for beauty even in the most unlikely places. Lena moaned softly and turned toward him, caressing his face. He noticed her expression. She understood the enormous strain he was under, as much as she knew there was nothing she could do to help, apart from offering him tenderness. He had become the Ship Commander after Erin's death, and that meant the burden of the ultimate decision was on his shoulders' only.

Except for the fact that I've not applied for this role. I'm an astrobiologist, that's all I am.

"You need to relax, Stan."

"It's not just us. We're going to make the call for almost 500k people on board with us."

"They made their choice when signing in for this adventure. They knew it."

"They've not chosen to die."

"They've not chosen to live either. Otherwise they won't be now in the cryo compartment, waiting to be thawed whenever we find Earth 2.0."

"We're searching for more than that," he said in a low voice, looking outside. "Otherwise, I wouldn't have been here either."

He saw Lena shake her head. She didn't share his political views, and he could easily imagine why. A Moonwalker like him, she had lived in too many colonies when serving in the intersystem military corps for her to understand the importance of what they were trying to achieve with this mission. Stanley suspected Lena was simply bored of living in the Solar System and in need of new challenges. To her, jumping from the Miranda Rupe with only a transparent, winged exoskeleton and risking her life in what could turn into a one-way trip were probably two things of the same kind and meaning.

"I'll call a meeting. This can't be a one-person decision," he said.

"You're fooling yourself. It's going to be your decision at the end of the day, and yours only."

"Don't be so goddamn gung-ho special forces, Lena," he replied. "This is not the military. And Moonwalkers are democratic to the hilt."

"Democracy and starships don't play well together. Philosophy apart, you're the leader here, and we will go by whatever you decide."

"Erin was the mind behind the whole operation and our leader – not me."

"Warm up to the idea. You are now."

*

He left Lena asleep and went out. Time to check the garden area and see how the latest grafts were developing. In the nightmarish seven weeks since Erin had died, his beloved plants were the only thing that gave him any sort of peace.

He was on his way to the Green Hexagon, when a view of SILUS -where the propulsion system, antimatter rockets included, was located - caught his attention. There were blinking lights in an uneven pattern, a good hint that somebody was working even at that late hour.

Val Helken was there, eyes fixed on the complex mainframe that maintained the ship's rockets. Val looked younger than his forty-five years, Stanley thought. If it was true that the whole crew was young looking - the interstellar travel had kept all of them in an admirable shape indeed - Val didn't seem to have aged a day since, not even thirty, he had embarked on that journey.

With him were Lena, Carmen – the physician - and Erin – when she was still alive – Val was one of the permanent, off-storage members of the CHOLCHIS. All the rest of the crew – the 31 ship operators in various roles, plus four nuclear technicians, six physicians and sevenpilots. A total of 53 people– were subjected to shifts of three months off, one month on in active duties. This was meant to keep the overall consumption at an optimal minimum for sustainability and correct rate of resource regeneration. We've not yet selected who will take Erin's place, Stanley reminded himself, a task we'd better get started with. It's not wise to remain below the magic number of permanent five for too long. You never know what can happen.

He sat near the engineer, observing, in silence, the series of equations appearing on the virtual desk. "How did you decide to join this mission, Val?" He asked. "You were not from the Moon in the first place. And this was our private crazy initiative, stress on crazy. The Moon colonies are buzzing with lunatics – you remember the joke that went around."

Val smiled that dry smile that Stanley had learnt to recognise in those years. "It's not correct, Stanley. I'm a Moonwalker like you; I was born in Mare Imbrium, in what was the first of the colonies established on the Satellite."

"Only because of the jus soli. And it was by accident; your parents were not."

"Who told you that?"

For once, Stanley noticed surprise in Val's green eyes.

"Erin. You knew her well, I reckon." He added, not sure how to phrase the concept. The rumour that Erin and Val had been lovers since long before the mission had never died, no matter if Erin had always denied it.

Val didn't offer any comment.

"She told me one of them was from the Titan's Orbital, sent to the Moon for a common science initiative," Stanley continued.

"My mother," Val said, without looking at him.

"And your father?"

"It's a long story."

"We have time."

"Not really," Val replied. "We have a decision to make."

"As I said this morning, we'll need to find a way to discuss it with the others. We have to face the hard fact that we're not going to reach any suitable system for life here, which means our time is running out. Either we come back or we go… to re-join the human settlements already established. The ones with the Guests, I mean."

"I thought the whole point of this endeavour was to do something alone, not with Them," Val said. "At least on that, you and Erin were on the same page."

"Ours has always been a minority opinion."

"I know. Still, we might have other options, Captain."

"What do you mean?"

"So far we've just cruised. Using our ramjet propulsion, scooping up our hydrogen to sustain our trip," he said. "Our problem has been that, in order to keep our options open, we've never gone to proximity of any star, and we've only surveyed them from a distance. We might have missed the exomoons, or even small planets that our sensors were not sophisticated enough to detect."

"But there was a reason for that, and I still maintain Erin's strategy was correct. We don't have enough antimatter to get us closer to systems. We can only do it once, for the right target – and misjudging it's a risk we can't take."

"Sure," Val said. "Thing is, I think we have a target this time."

"What are you saying, Val?" Stanley looked at him with curiosity.

"Come with me to the other unit. I want to show you something."

They moved to the propulsion sector's lab, where the engineer switched on the holodeck and a series of 3D images of space in their neighbourhood popped up in front of their eyes, showing stars and nebulae in delicate colours.

"You see those clouds on the screen?" Val pointed at a blue and green nebula on their left. "This is what remains of a supernova of a couple of million years ago."

"Yes?"

"Behind there's a star called Eltanim. It's a system you might want to consider."

Stanley glanced at the nebula and then at the engineer, not sure he understood correctly. "It's a star known since the Earth's early history: a red giant. Whatever habitable planet over there has been burnt long ago –not that any has ever been detected," he said.

"Yes. It was too far away from the Earth, and there was no real interest on top of that." Val quickly tapped on the holodisplay's input keys, magnifying the shapes just behind the nebula, barely visible but still detectable. "And you're right if you consider it in terms of the Solar System. But think about a different scenario: frozen, rocky planets that would have thawed now that the star is no longer in its main sequence – changing completely the HD zone of Eltanim's system."

"Theoretically yes, but…"

"It's more than just theory, and it's what seemed to have happened here. Here is what I've mapped – you see these signatures? They're planets. Some are life-compatible, Stanley -I deem at least two of them. Two super-Earth, one of them with about eight Earth-masses and two point seven-one times the radius, for what I could compute from here. This means surface gravity would be just slightly higher than one Earthian g, so perfect for habitability. I can't analyse the exomoons from where we are now, but there are at least thirty of them around the three gas giants. They might also be suitable for life- maybe in a domed landscape, in a stage-two colonisation." He zoomed on the star -its orange hue visible even in that small scale. "I think we should go. If there's anything suitable in this space sector is there – or at least, it's the only one that gives us more than just hopes."

"Well, it's interesting, but not feasible. If we use our antimatter reserve to get there, we won't be able to land. I am not an expert like you, of course but…" Stanley shook his head, "…for what I can see from here, it will take us too much acceleration to be able to reach Eltanim within our lifetime and won't remain enough to stop and make our insertion into orbit of whatever planet might be suitable. We knew since the beginning when we choose this specific direction; we knew that we couldn't make any detour. We've just hoped to be lucky, which it has not been the case."

"Not completely accurate, Captain." Val looked at him. "In these years I have worked on our reserves of antimatter. I've found another, simpler way to synthesise it on board. It's not a huge lot, but enough to give us suitable acceleration and still get us into orbit once near a suitable system."

Stanley remained speechless for a couple of moments.

"You have done this?"

"Yes."

"Why haven't you told anybody?" He said, then stopping and staring at him. "Erin knew it."

Val nodded again. "She knew, of course. We made this decision together after the first couple of years, when she realised we might have needed extra power since inhabitable systems failed to materialise. The idea was to keep cruising until our reserves of antimatter were substantial enough to reach a system not straight on our path."

"That was a risk."

"Everything is a risk in outer space."

"This was riskier than others. I can't imagine anything more dangerous than messing with antimatter – let alone in the confined space of a vessel. I would have liked to be informed."

"This was for the Commander's Eyes Only. Yours, Stanley."

They remained in silence, looking at the shapes on the holodeck.

"Tell me something, Val," Stanely said, quietly. "How did you manage to synthesise antimatter here, without those huge facilities that perform this outrageously expensive and painstakingly time-consuming task on the ground?"

"I've devised a new method. Something with greater performance than the one they currently use in the Solar System."

Stanley observed him. The man was announcing something worth three Orion prizes for physics with the demeanour of somebody that fries hamburger on a different iron plate. "If this is true, it's the most advanced technology ever used for ship propulsion system."

The engineered smiled. "Half-true. People that left for colonising Aeglem many centuries ago used something even more advanced."

"Our ancestors from planet Earth. Yes, sure – but they had, how can we put it, substantial help from the Guests. Without their technology and the ship design they provided we wouldn't have now any settlement in this small corner of our Galaxy."

"We can still learn from their example," Val said. "It's what we've decided to do after all– this is why we're here."

"Except that this is a human-only enterprise, with a ship built and staffed by Moon-born and bred people. I maintain it's quite different," Stanley replied. "It has taken – how long, fifty years? - to put together the small antimatter reserves for this mission. And now, just few years after leaving the Moon, you come out with something that beats to dust anything humans have been achieved so far, and on a ship equipped with limited facilities and virtually no supplies."

"Again, not correct. The beamed core antimatter rocket only needed minor adjustment, and I already had, of course, the magnetic nozzle and the beam machinery to focus the particles. I decided to use the reaction of electrons and positrons instead of protons and antiprotons, since it's the only one that immediately converts into 100% energy. And I broke down hydrogen atoms, the same our ramjets collect for the conventional propulsion system of the COLCHIS, which results in less by-product of dangerous elementary particles. As you see, it was not that complicated."

"Sure. On a spaceship, with no other people to help you," Stanley remarked.

"My bots and the AIs do the lab work more accurately than any assistant."

"Because you coded them."

"Yes."

"And this gets us back to stage one. You," he said. "Who are you, Val?"

"The same one you've known for fifteen years."

"Which I realise now I don't know at all."

Val shrugged. "I can see you're not comfortable with this. Erin had figured it out, which is why she decided to keep it quiet. What are you worried about – that I made mistakes in my calculations and kill us all?"

"No. I'm sure everything is more than accurate. You might even be right about Eltanim, and our chances to get there. But I'm not going anywhere if you don't answer this question now." He came nearer to the engineer, staring at him straight in the eyes. "Are you one of Them, Val -one of those puzzling aliens that after so many centuries we still fail to understand and are not even sure what they look like?"

The other looked at him, his regard as calm and detached as usual. “No.”

“I don’t believe you.”

“I’m telling you the truth.”

“In this case, tell me something I can possibly live with. Why are you capable of scientific achievement no other could claim in our world?”

Val smiled. “My father has been there. On Aeglem – even though only a few were still on that planet when he arrived. The majority had already left for systems farther away, like Iota Spicae. But he lived for twenty years with the people that still inhabited Aeglem before he came back to the Solar System. He learnt the Guests’ Way, their technology and their scientific rigour. He loved Them, I think.”

“And he transmitted this knowledge to you,” Stanley concluded for him.

Val nodded.

“Where is he now?”

“He left again. He found out he couldn’t live any longer in a human-only environment. I’m not sure where he headed to, only that he asked to be cryoed. I imagine he’s travelled somewhere farther than Aeglem.

“Have you ever wanted to follow him and see with your eyes things your father was talking about?”

Val was silent for a while. “Yes. Obviously. Then I’ve decided otherwise.”

“Why - fear you wouldn’t like it?”

“No. Fear of liking it too much and never leave.”

They turned to look again at Eltanim, at its binary stars and the tiny, almost invisible dots of its planets. They stayed there, each of them lost in thoughts.

*

The alarm rang loud for half a minute, before all the three joined Stanley on the command deck.

"Are we going into a collision, Captain?" Carmen asked, yawning out loud.

"Nothing of the sort."

"Anything wrong on the ship itself?"

"No."

"So why are you in such a haste?" Lena said. "You could have waited for the end of the night shift."

"What we have to discuss can't wait for a minute longer," Stanley replied. "We can't go on this way. Either we zero-in on one system or we turn back to the Moon while can."

"Stan, another possibility has always been open to us, and it is to reach out for the ones that have left before," Lena said. "I know you don't want to, like Erin, but it's better - anything is better - than coming back defeated to base."

"But we won't," Stanley said. "Thanks to Val, we've found a fourth alternative. We will do exactly what we've avoided doing until now, shoot for a system." He operated the holodeck commands, displaying Eltanim and its system in all the possible magnification allowed by the CHOLCHIS's sensors. "Here. The Head of the Dragon. The place we're going to make a new start for mankind."

Lena stared at him with wide-open eyes. "You can't be serious, Stan. There's nothing out there."

"Nothing close, for sure. But Val found life-compatible planets, and gave us enough antimatter to get there."

Carmen looked at Val with a nervous smile. "I knew that was going to be bad. What else wakes you up in the night?"

Stanley tried to touch Lena's arm, but she moved away. "You're going to get all of us killed," she said, biting her lips.

Stanley realised he had never seen her so stressed. Maybe all those adrenaline-seeking stunts were a mask, it occurred to him. This one is real. "What did you think, Lena? That we would have eventually followed Them and our ancestors in an adventure we have no control over?"

"Better than following one who has no idea where he's leading this ship." She glanced at Val then back to Stanley. "You can't trust him, Stan. He's not one of us, and you know it."

"Yes -that is exactly why I'm going to trust him."

"You've no right to decide for us," she replied.

"I remember somebody saying the opposite just yesterday." Stanley smiled. "You also rightly said we had already chosen not to live. Well, we're certainly going to not live the way we've done so far - that is my promise to you all right now." He turned to the engineer that had remained silent during the whole discussion. "Val, proceed. This time we get somewhere, or we die."

There were no other words, and everybody left the deck to get the sequence started.

The beaming particles surrounding the vector area began to accelerate and collide - in a process that was going produce the most amazing, man-made burst of energy of all times. Strapped to the COLCHIS's command chair, Stanley felt peace for the first time.

ELEGY FROM THE LOST COLONIES

Colleen Anderson

Sing to me of distant mud baths
where swim the cresting hornbacks
One warm memory will buoy me
before journey's final freeze

Remember that eternity, yesterday?
Seductive vapors swept low
You and I, like entwined vines
were sure the land was ours

And the hornbacks, ah the hornbacks,
with long-tested frozen smiles
shone like gems from hissing pools
trilling counterpoint in wallowing joy

Hornbacks floated in steaming mud
and shook exultant, rainbow crests
The swollen cankerous, sky
increased its dredging rain

And we were happy, for a time
to ride the bucking world
We ignored tempered warnings
and tried to cool mud, tame geysers

The world disgorged, spit us out
while hornbacks coasted storms
ridged leather balls rolling along
They alone flowed mud-way veins

Then the pumphouse hiccupped death
homes collapsed in seismic shudders
Habitats dwindled, still we strove
to see the hornback way

Among the ruins of a world's steaming fury
I fear my journey begins to frost
So let the hornback take my bones
to warm in their life mud.

THE WAY STATIONER

Tim Jeffreys

On nights when the wind was still, Amelia liked to take one of the sling chairs from the reading room outside and watch the stars. She would carry a glass of lemonade with her, or home-made ginger beer, or just water if her supplies were low. Mister would come too; sometimes curling up in her lap, sometimes wondering to the edge of the light cast from the tungsten lamps above the entrance and peering forward into the silent dark. Because the sun, never quite dipped below the purple-coloured hills along the eastern horizon, the night sky above Kayin, was always a spilled paintbox of colour; a solarised sunset. Every night it changed and every night it never failed to impress her. Sometimes she gasped with delight as she stepped out into the cool evening. Other times she was so overcome her eyes welled with tears.

Now and then, as she sat gazing at the heavens, Amelia would think about Earth—the planet her visitors always referred to as home, no matter where it was they were headed next.

"The stars look different here," they would say. Or they would stare in confusion at Kayin's twin moons and shake their heads.

"Why has this planet got two moons?" the children would ask. "Why aren't they round like the one back home?"

With a shrug and a smile, Amelia would answer: "That's just the way it is." Or she would tell them the names of the moons—Uri and Dorcas—and watch their eyes widen.

The visitor ships always departed soon after they arrived. The occupants were making new homes out in the far reaches of the galaxy, new homes with a new set of wonders. Kayin was just a stop along their way. A way station, they called it. Its soil had been deemed too acidic for agriculture; it's winds at times too relentless for human beings to tolerate. No one mentioned the breath-taking beauty of Kayin's sky at night. Instead, for more than a hundred years, they had stored fuel and foodstuffs here, in the huge station complex where Amelia lived most of the time alone. Amelia sometimes tried to imagine these other planets her visitors said they were headed too, but mostly she thought about Earth. She pictured in her mind Earth's cities, its oceans, it deserts, its green meadows. Polluted, the visitors said when she asked them about it. Dangerous. Overcrowded. Concepts she found it hard to imagine.

One night as she half-dozed in her sling-chair watching the sky, she saw what she thought was a shooting star. Visitor children had told her that on seeing a shooting star, you had to make a wish. This she was about to do, when she realised it was not a shooting star at all but a small, approaching spacecraft. It was forty five days until new visitors were expected; and, besides, this craft could not have carried more than three or four passengers. The craft tore out of the heavens and through the sky, streaming smoke and fire, then came down somewhere in the west beyond the dunes. There was a single hollow boom when the ship came to ground, at which a startled Mister scampered from the dark and disappeared through the complex doors. Amelia stood from her chair and stared into the darkness as silence settled again. Tomorrow she would take one of the pulsepods into the west and check the crash site for survivors.

"You can stay right here, Mister," she said, when the cat poked his head out from the complex doors.

*

The spacecraft had disintegrated on impact. There was nothing left except a line of scorched wreckage across the sand on the far side of the dunes. Thinking it possible someone had ejected before the crash, Amelia took a pair of binoculars from the pulsepod's saddlebag, climbed to the crest of a dune and scanned the surroundings.

Almost at once, she saw the dun-coloured parachute splayed out across the sand a kilometre or so away. She could not see a body, though it was clear something was attached and preventing the parachute from tumbling away in the wind. Returning to the pulsepod, she struck a course northwest where the dunes gave way to cracked, boggy lowlands.

On nearing the parachute, she saw that there was indeed a seat attached. And in the seat, a body. She drew the pulsepod to a halt. She thought of turning back, but she made herself check the pulsepod's display screen to see how much charge remained. She'd seen the dead and dying before, of course, on the visitor ships; but she herself had never had to deal with them. If the pulsepod's charge was low, she could use that as an excuse not to investigate further. But the pod had a third of its charge remaining, as she knew it would, more than enough to get her back to the complex. She wondered what it was she feared. Was it the idea of having to handle a dead body, or was it more the thought that this person might still be alive? Knowing she would not rest unless she found out one way or the other, she continued on until she drew the pulsepod up alongside the billowing parachute. Dismounting and taking a serrated blade from the saddlebag, she approached the body. First she attempted to disconnect the parachute from the seat, as it's billowing and buffeting hindered her. Unable to do this she simply cut it free and let the wind take it. She felt a twinge of guilt doing this. On Kayis, nothing was ever discarded. She relied on the visitor ships to bring her everything she needed, and the things that were already here had always to be repaired and recycled. But there was nothing else for it. The wind was so strong that she could not have reigned in the parachute alone.

Next she removed the helmet from the body, revealing the face of a man. His eyes were closed. His brown hair and short whiskers were threaded with grey. He wore a flightsuit, dull-orange in colour. Blood caked his nostrils, and there was a bloodied scrape across his forehead.

Dead, Amelia thought. Now what do I do with him?

To be certain, she pressed two fingers to his exposed neck and was surprised to find a pulse. Now she had no choice but to take him back with her to the complex. She'd not been counting on company for another forty four days.

*

She made it back before nightfall. Mister sat by the open doors, waiting for her. He came down the ramp to sniff and mew at the unconscious man as Amelia struggled to get him inside.

"Surprise guest," Amelia said to the cat. With her hands hooked under the man's armpits, she managed to drag him up the ramp and inside. By the time she laid him down in a visitor room, she was exhausted and slumped down in a chair opposite the bed. Mister slinked into the room and sat down by Amelia's feet, gazing up at her in query.

"I know you were hoping for a few more weeks of peace and quiet," she said to the cat. "But I couldn't just leave him out there now, could I?"

Mister turned his head to the side, his unblinking eyes fixed on Amelia's face.

"Don't you look at me like that," she said, then shooed him away as she got to her feet. Crouching over the prone man, she took off his boots before carefully removing his flightsuit, then checking for further injuries on his body although she found none that were obvious. She left the room for a few moments then returned carrying a bowl of warm water and a facecloth, by which time the man was rolling his head from side to side on the pillows and moaning under his breath. At the first touch of the wet cloth to his skin, his eyes sprang open and he stared at Amelia with such intensity that she drew away.

"What…? Where…?" he said, flicking his gaze around the room.

"You're on Kayin," Amelia told him. "Your ship crashed. Don't you remember?"

"Kayin? What the hell is Kayin?"

"The way station to the planets on the outer rim."

The man groaned and turned his face to the wall.

After a moment's hesitation, Amelia crouched beside the bed again and dabbed the cloth once more to his forehead.

"What shall I call you?" she said.

"Major Thomas Hamnett."

"I'll just call you Thomas, if you don't mind. Or Tom. Does anyone call you Tom?"

After a short silence in which he only gazed at her in incomprehension, he said: "My wife used to."

"Your wife? Where is she?"

"Dead. They're all dead. My sons too."

"I'm very sorry."

He turned his face from the wall and met her eyes. "We thought it was going to be so different out here than it had been on Earth. We thought it was going to be a new beginning. We vowed not to make the same mistakes. But it turned out just the same. War and greed. Brother killing brother. Fighting over scraps of land on planets covered over in ice, planets with boiling seas." Then he closed his eyes and under his breath said, "Madness."

*

Once Tom was on his feet again, it wasn't long before a quizzical expression fixed itself upon his face. As Amelia went about her day – much of her time being spent in the communications room checking on information from ships making their way to Kayin; or down in the underground store completing inventories – she would occasionally find Tom stood by the main doors, gazing out across the landscape; or he would appear in a doorway looking confused, as if he'd been searching for something else entirely. Amelia could see from his face that he had a lot of questions, but he didn't know where to begin. She went about her tasks, letting him formulate these questions in his own time.

"You were alone here before I came?" he said at last, eight days after his arrival. Amelia had been in one of the kitchens preparing a meal when Tom had surprised her by entering.

"Not alone," she said, smiling and nodding towards Mister, who sat in the corner of the room watching the two of them.

"I mean people. Where are all the people?"

"There's a ship coming from Earth in forty days. A cruiser. It's called The Strident. There are three hundred people on board. They'll be staying here for a few weeks to recuperate then heading for their new home in the outer rim."

"A few weeks? How often do these ships land here?"

"I get two or three ships a year usually. Also, supply ships land here from time to time. But there won't be one of those passing for another—"

"And the rest of the time you're alone apart from a cat? There's not a single other person on this entire rock? How can they expect that of you? They should station more people here."

"No one else wants to be stationed here."

"But you do?"

"Yes."

He was silent a moment. Amelia listened to the wind running around the complex's outer walls. She knew that Tom heard it too. "But how can you stand it?"

"I like it here on Kayis. I like the peace and quiet."

"But that doesn't make any sense!"

"It does to me. This is home. I'm happy here. And the sky at night is so beautiful. Have you noticed?"

"How can you be happy, all alone here day after day? A young woman like you, with your whole life ahead of you? You can't be the only person living on a planet like this! You need companionship. It's human nature. What if something happened to you? What if you fell sick? Who's going to come to your aid?"

Amelia thought a moment as she chopped a red pepper then tossed it into a frying pan.

"It's true that everything sustaining my life here comes from Earth. Without the supply ships life would be impossible on Kayis. If one day, the supplies stop coming and I had to leave, that would make me very sad. Yes."

"But don't you miss Earth?" Tom said.

"How could I? I never knew it."

"We all miss home."

Amelia turned her head and met his eyes. "Do you?"

"Yes, I miss it. I missed it from the day I left. People think they can make a new life out here on some other planet, but everything's so different and...bewildering. It's true what they say: there's no place like home."

Amelia smiled, returning her attention to chopping vegetables. "What do you miss?"

Tom drew a deep breath. "For one, I miss the ocean – swimming in the ocean. And I miss the mountains. And I miss that we had a name for every one of them. Can you believe that on those planets in the outer rim, there are men fighting wars over who some hump of rock should be named after?"

"I suppose I could believe that," Amelia said. "There are no mountains here, just hills. And hills don't seem to need naming. There are no oceans either. Most of Kayin's water is deep underground."

"I would give my right arm for one more swim in the ocean," Tom said.

Amelia flicked her gaze to him again. He had sat down at one of the tables. He had his chin resting in one hand and his eyes were glazed and fixed on the opposite wall.

"You never told me where you were going that day your ship crashed."

"Away," Tom said after a pause. "Just away."

"What were you looking for?"

"Looking for? Nothing. Just escape."

"And you found Kayis. You found me."

"By accident."

"What will you do?" she said. "Will you go with The Strident? Back to the outer rim? Try to start over again?"

He shifted his eyes to hers. "I think we should both go."

Amelia laughed. "I belong on Kayis."

"No one belongs here."

"I do. And so does Mister."

"Why do you say that?"

Amelia was silent a moment as she stirred the contents of the frying pan. Then she glanced over her shoulder at the cat. Mister had remained in the same spot in front of a heating vent, gazing back at her. He raised his head as if she'd asked him a question. "Because we were born here."

*

That night Amelia awoke to loud knocking on the door of her cabin. Getting groggily to her feet, she instructed on a light and went to the door. Mister prowled in her wake, looking just as sleepy and disgruntled.

Tom stood in the corridor outside her cabin. His expression appeared distraught.

"What is it?" she said, blinking at him. "What's wrong?"

"What's wrong?" he said. "Don't you hear it?"

"Hear—?"

Realising what he meant, she laughed.
“The wind’s got up.”
“How could you not notice? It sounds like it’s going to tear this whole place apart. The walls are shuddering.”
“We’re quite safe,” she said. “Do you want to come in?”
“I…I don’t want to disturb you.”
“No, it’s fine. Really. Come in for a little while. Until it dies down.”
After hesitating a moment, Tom stepped forward inside her cabin and she closed the door. He glanced at what she was wearing.
“Were you sleeping? How could anyone sleep with that racket going on?”
She smiled to herself. “I must be used to it.”
“That’s impossible.”
“Sit down. Would you like a drink?”
Tom sat down in one of two chairs facing each other whilst she prepared lemonade.
“Haven’t you anything stronger?” Tom said.
“Not here. I’d have to go down into the stores.”
Tom grumbled and took the glass she offered. He sipped at his drink, his head turned to one side, listening; whilst she sat in the opposite chair and watched him. The fear and wonderment written on his face as he listened to the wind battering against the outside walls amused her. She wanted to tell him how when the winds got up, it comforted her. She loved to lie awake sometimes and listen to the storm. She knew that inside the complex nothing could touch her, nothing could disturb her; and this gave her an inner tranquillity. Thinking this, she was surprised to realise how much she enjoyed having Tom here, sharing this moment. She liked the fact that he could be so still and quiet, that he didn’t feel the need to talk. This pleasure in his company she could barely admit to herself, and would certainly never have

voiced out loud. She went on watching his face reacting to the sounds from outside. The moment was broken when he shifted his gaze, caught her looking, and finally did speak.

"Listen," he said, in a reverential whisper. "I've never heard a storm like it. It's frightening. How could anybody possibly want to live their life in a place like this?"

*

Amelia thought it might help Tom better understand her life on Kayis if she showed him the canyon. Each taking a pulsepod, they drove for an hour northeast until they reached the ledge from where they could look down into a ravine. Amelia often brought her visitors here, and they were always awed by the depth of the precipice, the vast shapes that had been cut from the sides of the mountain, the gradations of colour in the rockface. She led Tom down into the valley where they were shielded from the wind, and where she often walked alone, finding paths amongst the formations of rock. She had always found it a peaceful place to visit. When she went there, she often felt like she was communing with Kayis itself. She could tell from Tom's expression that he saw it differently. Through his eyes, she saw the valley as alien and eerie; the rock formations suggestive of threatening forms and figures.

They had been walking only a short while, when Tom stopped to drink from his water bottle.

"How is it you came to be born here?" he said.

"After my parents left Earth, my mother became pregnant. They hoped to reach the outer rim before I arrived, but by the time they got to Kayis I had decided to come along, one month early."

"And you stayed here together – all three of you?"

"Only for a little while. They were still determined to reach the outer rim. When I was still a baby they took me to a planet called Cassandra. You know it?"

Tom nodded.

"It's not a bad place. Cold. My parents were happy, but I don't think I ever really felt at home. I kept thinking about Kayis, this place they told me about. where I'd been born. I had to wait until I was twenty-two before I could come back. I heard they needed people to man the way station, so I applied. As soon as I arrived here, I knew. I knew this was where I belonged. As soon as the sun set and I saw those skies. There were others here before, but no one ever stays very long. Except me. I've been here twelve years now." She met his eyes and smiled. "Isn't it strange that we still calculate our age in Earth years? A year on Kayis has only one hundred and fifty eight days. Plus, the days are shorter here – only eighteen hours. In Kayis years, I'm an old woman already."

"And me an even older man." Tom laughed under his breath. It was the first time Amelia had seen him express amusement. Lines appeared around his eyes, making her think he must have done a lot of laughing once. "Aboriginal," he said, "that's what you are. You're Kayis' one and only aboriginal."

Amelia had never considered this. She thought about it for a moment. "I suppose you're right."

"And your parents are still on Cassandra?"

Amelia lowered her gaze. "No. They're gone now. They were killed shortly before I came here. A terrorist bomb."

"Terrorists?"

"From the north of Cassandra. The early settlers. They wanted independence. There was always resentment towards those who came later."

She glanced up at Tom, but he had turned his head to the side. His eyes were far away.

"Same old story, wherever you go."

"Not here," Amelia said. "Not on Kayis."

Tom switched his eyes back to hers. "Not yet."

She frowned. Then, half turning, she pointed ahead into the valley. "Come this way. There's something I want to show you."

She led him onwards until they reached an opening in the side of the rockface. It led into a cave, at the centre of which a small pool of groundwater had formed. Sunlight entered the cave through an opening above, falling in a wide beam into the pool and throwing a blue sheen across the water.

Tom took a sharp intake of breath and walked to the edge of the pool.

"Like glass," he said, gazing into the pool. "Just as clear as glass." Amelia smiled. She'd never shown any of her visitors the pool before. It was, she felt, her secret to keep. A kind of sacred place, that only – as Tom had it – aboriginals should know about.

She could not think why she had decided to show the pool to Tom. Was she making him an honorary citizen of Kayis? Was she trying to convince him to make a home here alongside her?

"You can swim," she said. "I do it all the time. It's not the ocean but it's the nearest thing you'll find on Kayis."

Tom watched in silence as Amelia stripped down to her underwear then leapt into the pool. The water was cold and bracing. It had a purity which could be felt. Amelia dived then surfaced again.

"Coming in?" she said to Tom, her teeth chattering.

But Tom only sighed, turned, and walked out of the cave.

"Not right. It's not right," she could hear him muttering to himself somewhere outside.

*

Later, back at the complex, when they were eating dinner, she asked him: "What's not right?"

He raised his eyes to hers and sighed. "That a young woman like you should be stuck here alone on this rock. There are men out there who would love…who would…you could marry someone. Have children. Have a family. Why would you choose to stay here all alone? Do you really want to grow old all by yourself on Kayis?"

Amelia allowed herself a small smile. "Yes, I do. I'm aboriginal, remember?"

"This planet isn't even designed for human habitation."

Amelia shrugged. "Nevertheless, its home."

Tom huffed. "Is that so important to you? To have a home?"

She looked into his face for a moment, seeing something in him, below the surface, like a lost little boy. "You said yourself you missed Earth from the moment you left."

"But that's different."

"How is it different?"

"Earth is home to all of us really. It's where we started out, as a race. It's a place that was made for us, designed for us. Or rather we were designed for it. It's where we belong. The home planet. No one would choose Kayis over Earth. Even Cassandra would be better than this rock."

Stung, Amelia dropped her gaze from his.

"Cassandra never felt like home to me."

"And Kayis does?"

"It does," she said, lifting her head and smiling again.

"But on Cassandra you could have friends, even a family if you wanted one."

"And have them sacrificed to some cause or other," she said. Seeing his expression darken, she quickly added, "I'm sorry. I forgot…"

Tom set down his knife and fork then stood.

"If you were my daughter…"

"I'm too old to be your daughter."

He raised his voice a little. "If you were my daughter, I wouldn't let you do this. You're not living, you're hiding. That's what you're doing. You're hiding yourself away from life." Then he bowed his head and walked out of the canteen.

*

Tom was civil but distant from that day onwards. One day he told her that he had decided to leave with The Strident, and Amelia – though she nodded and told him she understood – was surprised at the dull sense of loss which settled on her chest.

"What's happening to us, Mister?" she said that night when she lay on the bed, the cat purring contentedly beside her. After she turned out the lights, she listened to the wind howling beyond the complex walls and in that moment it was the loneliest sound she could imagine. Her sense of bereavement swelled. She even shed a few tears onto her pillow, then sniffed and wiped her eyes, thinking herself a fool.

*

When The Strident arrived, she was immediately so busy with the visitors and the supplies they brought that she barely thought about Tom. Though she was used to the bemusement with which the visitors viewed Kayis, especially the children, now she noticed something in their expressions she had never acknowledged before. As they departed The Strident and looked at Kayis for the first time, she saw the disillusionment in their faces. She would notice it again when she saw them looking out of the complex windows, or out through the main doors.

What the hell is this place? she imagined them thinking. It's just a rock. An uninhabitable rock. Who would ever want to live here?

And when they spoke about Earth she felt, more and more often, a cold anger which she struggled not to let show.

If everything's so wonderful there! she would imagine herself telling them. Why did you spoil it? You had a home and you destroyed it. Now you're going to do the exact same thing to the planets in the outer rim. Lay concrete over green meadows and poison the seas. Well I'm glad you think Kayis is just a rock. I'm glad you'd never think of making a home here, if that means you'll leave it alone and not ruin it!

Tom sought her out the day before The Strident was due to leave. He was smartly dressed and clean-shaven, preparing himself for his return to the outer rim. She blinked at his appearance. He looked younger, his eyes bright, the grey in his hair not so noticeable. She found herself thinking that there could not be too many years between them.

He took hold of one of her hands.

"Won't you reconsider?" he said. "Thinking of you here all alone. It tears me up."

"It shouldn't," she said. "I'm happy here. I've told you often enough. Kayis is home to me."

"You know you can make your home anywhere, anywhere you go. It's not the place, the planet, it's what you make it."

Looking him in the eye, Amelia shook her head.

"You could stay," she said, "if you wanted to."

"No," he said. "Not here. Not this place."

She frowned. She could think of nothing else to say.

His grip on her hand tightened for a moment. "Be well," he said. Then he was walking away. As she watched, her lips worked, but she could not find words.

*

Four days after The Strident departed, Amelia was sitting outside the complex in her sling chair looking at the stars with Mister close by, when she saw a streak of light in the sky. Clutching at the binoculars she now wore around her neck, she brought them to her eyes.

"Just a shooting star, Mister," she said after a moment, lowering the binoculars. "Well, what did you think it was, huh?"

Mister shifted his head to one side and blinked.

"Still…" she said. "It means I get to make a wish."

She spoke the wish under her breath, then wondered why, since there was no one but the cat to hear. Then she settled back in her chair, looking at the stars again, waiting to see if her wish would come true.

THE LAST TRANSPORT

Frank Coffman

No ship had come since 4082.
An old man now, he knew no more would come.
For many years, he'd wondered what he'd do
When his time came—on his, now loneliest, home.

Only the few and hardy had survived
Since Ares[2] shot that frazzling EM burst.
For thirteen generations they had lived
As primitives. But what had been the worst

Was having that wealth of wisdom locked in text,
Each epoch striving to regain its power,
Rekindle with slow science for the next
To come—the world they'd lost in that dark hour.

So many had died of hardship, from disease,
From rampant crime, one small-scale civil war,
Before the remnants found a state of peace
And pushed on toward the goals they'd had before.

And—finally—they'd crept
back to that place.
The lights came back—
technology reborn.
The old tools once again
could etch the face
Of that harsh world,
forbidding and forlorn.

They had surprised
themselves, that tiny band.
At last the terraforming was
all done.
He'd found a companion,
taken her hand.
They'd had three sons under
the triple sun.

They'd tried again to make
contact with Earth
And (now three generations)
had waited for reply;[3]
Scanned for that mythic place
of ancestral birth,
And found—Alas! a void in
that distant sky.

The Earth was gone! Their
world alone remained.
This home of theirs—was
now all that was left
Of what that Blue Sphere's
beings had attained.

They were the remnant. Now,
at the last, bereft.

But they had persevered, this
New Earth theirs,
Bought with the tens of
thousand deaths before,
And all the blood and toil
won for their heirs
A hopeful home....
The
plague struck in 7004.

Some native pestilence had
stirred awake
With their transforming of
this foreign place,
This giant rock that they had
dared to take,
This grain of dust in the
enormity of space.

Death had spread swiftly, and
the massed
Thousands who had survived
on their new world
Shrunk to the very few quick
death had passed—
Immune to the plague that
Fate or Fortune hurled.

Soon they discovered the
ironic cost
Paid for immunity: Sterility
Beset the young and virile
who weren't lost.
No more of humankind
would ever be.

The outpost signals held no
hope—then stopped.
His wife and sons were gone,
his kith and friends.
"Don't let me be the last,"
he'd often hoped,
But hoped in vain, "So this is
how it ends?"

"Ah well, perhaps it's best?
We'll leave this place
An Eden in this wondrous
universe.
And we would very likely fall
from Grace
As we've always done
before—and still rehearse."

"Perhaps a Paradise no longer
trod by Man
Will finally our greatest
offering be.
Leaving our mark is maybe
all we can
Hope to bequeath to Time
and Infinity."

His last strength used to
climb the gentle slope
That overlooked a landscape
red and vast,
Fixing his mind on that last
soothing hope,
Leaned back against a tree—
and breathed his last.

Below, the fauna played, the
flora thrived.
Under three suns, 'neath
constant twilight lit,
The last man on that brave,
new world had lived
And died. And it seemed that
it was fit.

. . . . .

Just then—in that sky that
never knew the night—
One glistening golden speck
in the welkin's dome.
Larger and larger in its
arching flight:
The last transport from Earth
had finally come.

NOTES:

[1] Gliese 667 Cc is the third planet (c), orbiting star C in the triple star system Gliese 667. Orbiting its sun every 28.155 Earth days (1 3/8 days short of a lunar cycle on Earth)— hence the great number of years (7309.9 GYH is approximately 563 earth years).

2 Astronomers know that the planet is a "superterran," being rocky and earthlike with water and atmosphere, but almost five times larger than Earth in diameter. The colonists named its red dwarf sun [Gliese 667 C] *Ares*, after the Greek god of war, and being very close to the planet (though a dwarf), the star appears more than three times larger than Earth's sun does to us. Tidally locked, like Mercury in Earth's solar system or Earth's moon, the planet always presents the same face to the sun, thus leaving a light side of very hot to mild (130°f avg. to 40°f avg.) and a dark side ranging from cold to extremely cold (30°f avg. to -325°f avg.). The pioneers on Gliese 667 Cc set up their colonies and camps in what they came to call "The Twilight Zone," within the bands of temperate climate on the light side, "The Lightland," and some few rough outposts into "The Nightland" where frigid to arctic temperatures prevailed.

3 The star system of Gliese 667 C is 22 light years from Earth. Thus, it takes a minimum of 44 Earth years for a signal to reach from one to the other AND be answered.

SKIN SUIT

Mark Towse

I don't belong here.

Every lunchtime at school, instead of kicking a soccer ball around, spitting up walls, or lying about how many titties I have touched, I sit on the bench near the playground, staring up at the sky with absolute wonder. I tolerate the other kids and envy how comfortable they are in their skin. They chase each other around, and they fight and laugh and entertain themselves with banality. It's not that I feel superior, just different.

My fascination with space began in the summer of 1986 after watching the Star Trek re-runs, William Shatner as Captain Kirk was my hero, and I longed to be a space explorer, "To boldly go," well, you know the rest. My parents often joked that when the show was on, they could have been walking around with axes in their heads, and I wouldn't have noticed. I challenged them on that. I can see things without looking sometimes.

Before the show started, I greased my hair back with brill cream and wore my orange T-shirt, and from the moment the music started, I was entranced, wondering where the crew and I would be going and who we might meet. I was the extra crew member you didn't know existed, funnier than Scotty and bolder and even suaver than Kirk. I was Donovan, chief explorer; I never carried a weapon and just relied on my wit and coolness to get out of sticky situations.

I still wear the brill cream daily as the sweet floral scent often encourages one of my daytime adventures. I'm not sure when they first started; as far as I can remember, I've always been a dreamer. I feel them coming on. It's hard to explain, but it's as though I am slipping into a different existence—the images that filter through my mind are so vivid they feel like memories rather than fantasies. When I am lost in these galaxies, I can smell the air, feel each gust of wind, and am witness to the dust storms that terrorise the surface of countless moons and planets. I have a name for each of them, but it isn't something I can speak—it's just a sound that plays in my head. Throughout these experiences, my adrenaline surges to such an extent that I feel that I might explode—sometimes it gets too much, and I end up on the classroom floor, quivering and frothing at the mouth. In the background, I hear the other kids laughing and the teacher cursing, but eventually, the smell of paper and chalk filters through my nostrils like a dose of smelling salts, and I'm back. The pleasure drains from my body quickly, and I am left feeling empty once again and with a sick feeling in my stomach.

*

I don't find the work at school challenging or exciting; it is dull, and I hunger for more. I want to know everything. But more than that, I want the truth.

The other kids think I'm a nerd and regularly bully me. I asked them once why my intellect induced such hatred—they gave me an extra pounding that day. Nobody knows that I am subjected to this as my body is incapable of bruising. I feel physical pain, but I can block that out. The emotional pain is alienating, though. The only consolation I have is that I know it's all a front—a mask they wear, and a demonstration of bravado. Each time someone punches me, I get a glimpse of their lives, and I never feel anger—only pity.

I often eat lunch on my own, but sometimes a girl called Jessica comes to sit next to me. She is also fascinated with space. She is brighter than most of the other kids and gets similar treatment from her friends. I like talking to her, and I know she gets teased for talking to me, but she still does, though, and I admire her for that. She wants to be an astronaut when she grows up. I don't think Jessica is as smart as she thinks, but I'm not going to tell her that as she might not come over anymore.

Jessica's Mum died of cancer a few years ago, and her Dad struggled with subsequent alcohol addiction. She lives with her Auntie now but says she would do anything to have her Mum back. She says she often feels alone, and on reflection, I think that's why we have always been drawn together—a couple of outcasts trying to find our place. We accidentally touched once, and for a moment, the connection felt good, but the subsequent pain that ripped through my body almost made me pass out. Sometimes I get these premonitions—it's why I try and avoid physical contact—but I saw the tubes sticking out of her and people gathered around her bed. The cancer is already in her—but how could I possibly know that? And am I supposed to tell her?

My parents have always worried about me; once they took me to see a therapist that claimed to understand the workings of a child's mind. She sat me on an expensive-looking chair and smiled and frowned simultaneously. She then asked me to talk through some of the experiences. I told her everything, and the words came out quickly as I relived my voyages, and she smiled and nodded throughout. The excitement must have been apparent as I often saw my spittle spray ahead as I thundered words out and threw my arms around wildly, graphically trying to describe vast new worlds and galaxies I encountered. In the end, I threw myself in the chair with exhaustion, and I remember she gave me a handful of jellybeans. As we made contact, it was as though I could read her thoughts; "Thank God, it's the last session."; "I need to pick up some wine tonight on the way home."; "This kid is off the charts."

If it wasn't for the jellybeans, it would have been a waste of time.

The upshot is my parents want me to live in the real world; they want me to be present and to behave like the other children. I want to please them—I really do—and I am trying to be more mediocre at school and attempting to fit in, and I have even started to watch how the other children interact with their parents. But when I try and duplicate their actions, it only plays out as an awkward charade. They are nice people and deserve happiness, but I feel incapable of giving them what they need. I look at my mum and see the sadness in her eyes, and I want to console her, to tell her everything is going to be okay, but I can't as I don't think it is. I call them my parents, but I know that not to be true. I have seen—through the flashbacks when we touch— that she is not my birth mother. I have so many questions, but I don't want to upset her as I know she loves me with all her heart.

When I cry in the solace of my room, it's then that I feel a connection to something, as though the energy released is being picked up and reciprocated. My body starts to feel different, wired, and the hairs on the back of my neck stand to attention. When I stop crying, I lose the sensation immediately. I often try and force tears, just to have that feeling again, but I guess the energy must be on an exact frequency just like the way my Dad tunes up the old transistor radios that he collects. I do like the music they play. Sometimes we sit in the shed together, and I drink pop, and he opens a beer, and we listen without speaking. I suppose he thinks we are bonding, and out of all the forced situations and interactions we have, our time listening to the radio is when I do feel closest to him.

Today has been such a hot and dry day, not a cloud around, and the sky outside is still so clear—a spectacular light show of vast proportions. As I lay here looking at the stars through my open bedroom window, I feel even more lonely—the familiar lump in my throat is back, and my eyes are beginning to glisten. And immediately, there is that feeling of connection once again, but it somehow feels stronger right now—as though the signal is clear. Something is different tonight. I can hear faint music playing in my head. Not like the stuff Dad listens to—something else that is both familiar and strange—and magnificently beautiful. I throw my legs out of bed and slowly begin to walk towards the window. As I get close, the wind outside suddenly picks up, and I see leaves and branches outside caught in some sort of vacuum, swirling with tornado-like aggression. I can feel a pull now—as though the vortex is trying to pull me through the window—it's so strong. I am starting to feel dizzy. Legs like jelly, I slump into my Captain's seat—a wooden dining chair covered in LED's, held on by manky old bubble-gum. The seat begins to move—toppling forward—and suddenly, I am thrust through the window. Now, I am in the vortex, being propelled upwards at ferocious speed as though in the world's fastest elevator. I feel as though my stomach is floating in my chest as the Earth beneath me gets smaller and smaller and then finally vanishes out of sight.

It takes me on an incredible journey through stars and galaxies, planets of gas and rock—some that I recognise, others that I don't. I am disoriented, confused—amazed—and I begin to laugh—and it echoes through space as though my voice is traveling light years ahead. It's a strange sound to hear, and the raw and uncontrived cackle takes me by surprise. I laugh until there are tears in my eyes, and the connection is powerful now. I am beginning to reach a new level of happiness that I can only describe as euphoric.

When I wipe the tears of laughter away, I see the ship—a gigantic spherical mass of twisted metal and colour—a floating work of art. I notice one of the cannon shaped structures start to home in on me—it emits a laser-like tractor beam that cuts the black void of space in half and locks on to a bubble of air around me. I feel a sharp jolt, and then—

*

Where am I?

My eyes are shut tight, but I see everything. I'm not scared, though.

I know immediately that this is where I belong. I just know.

I step off the silver table and watch as the translucent shapes float around the room with ethereal ease, manifesting into familiar shapes—birds, dogs, humans—and I know they are trying to make me feel at ease. My body starts to sing with pleasure in a way that feels familiar, but certainly not human—actually singing, emitting an impossible melody of beautifully strange sounds. The shapes around being to reciprocate the noise, and we are soon in complete harmony.

One-by-one they begin to pass through my body and emerge from the other side disguised with my human mould. The warmth that I feel from them is completely at odds with the silver and clinical neutrality of the ship.

One of the human shapes drifts towards me, stopping only a few inches away from my face. It feels like an important moment as silence falls, and as the circle begins to close in.

The face begins to take on human form, but it is one with a far too perfect arrangement of bland and symmetrical features—it has nothing distinguishing—and the skin is smooth and synthetic looking. I feel, though, immeasurable affinity to the form in front of me.

"I—I—I come in peace," I say and smile.

Instinctively I raise my hand in the shape of a Vulcan salute in a Spock like gesture.

The counterfeit human in front of me lifts its hand and duplicates the symbolic gesture; it hangs there for a few seconds before falling back to its side. The shape begins to cry then; even producing water from the corner of its newly formed eyes and mopping it up with the left hand as any human would. I feel that overwhelming connection again—it's getting stronger all the time.

And immediately, I know.

My hand suddenly starts to lose its molecular structure and begins to swim around in front of me; the skin that used to cover it now floating to the ground. I am beginning to feel free—normal. Energy surges through me that brings a new level of alertness—as though I can feel and hear every single molecule in the air. More of my skin falls to the floor as I begin to take on the translucent greyness of the shapes around me. I start to tune into the emotion of the forms and they sing with obvious pleasure and fill me with a sense of companionship and love that I have never felt before—even from my parents. My drab grey starts to fill with warmer colours, and now I am radiating fiery shades of red and orange like the lava lamp that sits on my bedside table at home.

Home?

The other shapes accompany me and begin to glide across the room with such grace and kaleidoscopic beauty. I hear the other music start to play quietly in the background—the songs from the shed—and the static output of what could only be Dad's transistor radio. The shapes begin to dance in front of me then, putting on a show, and I sense pleasure as they couple up—their colours syncing—until the whole room is alive with shades of blue, green and red, and other colours that don't have an earth name. They begin to part then, providing a path for me, and I take that as my cue. The last of the skin falls to the floor, and I cannot do the feeling of euphoria justice as I lift from the ground and soar, escaping the confines of the human body.

I stretch, I shrink, I morph into the form of a dinosaur, a tank, a bird, and there are no limitations; and I laugh—another uncontrollable child-like giggle that comes out as the most beautiful sound I have ever heard, a heavenly and comforting series of notes that vibrate through my entire body.

The others join in, and I feel the pleasure of each one of them bursting inside me, a collective high that supersedes any previous emotion felt.

Intermittently, I start to pick up little bits of the language. I can't put together any sentences though, just odd words that loosely translate as Earth, life, war, peace, and death.

One of the shapes drifts towards me and reaches out in what I can only describe as a mental embrace. A strong sensation sweeps over me, one I can only describe as—love. We lock together, and memories start to come back, ones that I have difficulty putting into words and ones that do not constitute typical human experiences, but still ones of times gone, of love, of family—and belonging.

Mother.

The rush of such a wide range of emotions in such a short space of time is difficult to describe, but I at once feel happy, sad, and vulnerable.

The translation is rough, but she tells me that she watches over me when she can, that when I cry in my room, she is connecting with me, albeit it on a distant frequency. When the transistor radio in the shed plays, they collectively embrace and create a frequency strong enough for the music to filter through the ship, and they dance, and her heart sings as she knows I am at peace.

In as close to human language as I can describe, she tells me she didn't have any part in this, and it was all done against her will—that I was the chosen one and taken from her after only three earth years. They tell her that she should be grateful for my experiences and the knowledge that I will bring back, but she isn't—she just wants my return. I tell her that I love her, that I always have—and deep down that I knew I belonged elsewhere.

I still have so many questions, but all I want to do is make up for lost time and bathe in the golden orb we are creating.

But suddenly, the music stops, and the bright colours begin to fade—the room is once again cold and neutral. I hear a noise behind me—and without turning, I see the doors slide open. The language from the two approaching shapes is urgent and aggressive. Something is getting between Mother and me—the embrace is slipping—and the subsequent pain is intense and violent.

Mother is thrown to the other side of the ship, and her scream pierces the air. In complete contrast to the previous soft harmonies, it is a discordant and incomprehensible shrill that fills me with anger. Years of pain and rage surge through me in one cataclysmic wave, and my body erupts in an inaudible sonic wave that sends the two new shapes flying in the opposite direction. Taking my chance, I try and reconnect with her, but she is still hurting and too weak. More shapes swarm the room from all directions, beginning to form a physical and mental barrier between us, and I feel as though I am losing her. A battle of wills ensues as we fight to establish our connection, and mine is strong—bottled over all this time—but just as we are getting close and about to re-join, we are ripped away from each other by a much greater power. There is an invisible but insurmountable wall between us now, and even though I can still see her, she might as well be light-years away. I watch helplessly as they physically escort her through the doors, and as her colour dwindles. She emits a parting sounds that is haunting and fills me with sadness. My remaining family is silent, their colours already faded back to grey.

As the sliding door opens, another shape emerges, unmistakably the leader—and no doubt the one that pulled us apart. I watch as the others split into two lines and let her through. She positions in front of me, and I try and fight it, but she's far too strong and easily locks with my mind. I know all too well what is happening—she is collating everything I have learned since my time on Earth. And now she is done.

Desperately, I begin to morph and stretch myself as thinly as I can, wrapping around as many objects as possible. I try to lock back in with my family members, but the leaders' embrace is strong and unbreakable. I scream again, but this time it has no effect; my powers negated this time. There is a ripple of intense light and an accompanying high-pitched cry that is over-powering—and in the blink of a human eye, I am back; head spinning, and translucent fingers wrapped around the chair's wooden arm.

Slowly, but surely, the human skin claustrophobically begins to generate itself around my form, as the word "Mother" leaves my once again human-like mouth, and as a tear runs down my human-like cheek

THE CREW

MIKE ADAMSON

Mike Adamson won a Silver-level Honourable Mention in the Writers of the Future contest for third quarter, 2016. His work has appeared in in *4Star Stories*, *Outposts of Beyond* and *Heroic Fantasy Quarterly* plus the anthologies *Temporal Fractures*, *Future Visions #3* and *After the Orange*.

COLLEEN ANDERSON

Colleen Anderson is a Canadian author writing fiction and poetry and has had over 170 poems published in such venues as *Grievous Angel, Polu Texni, The Future Fire, HWA Poetry Showcase* and many others. She is a member of HWA and SFPA and has performed her work before audiences in the US, UK and Canada and has placed in the Balticon, Rannu, Crucible and Wax poetry competitions. Currently she is working on two poetry collections. Colleen also enjoys editing and co-edited Canadian anthologies *Playground of Lost Toys* (Aurora nominated) and *Tesseracts 17,* and her solo anthology *Alice Unbound: Beyond Wonderland,* was published in 2018. *A Body of Work* was recently published by Black Shuck Books, UK. Living in Vancouver, Colleen keeps an eye out for mold monsters and mermaids, and will be guest of honour in 2020 at the Creative Ink Festival. www.colleenanderson.wordpress.com

ALLEN ASHLEY

Allen Ashley is a British Fantasy Award winner who works as a creative writing tutor. His groups include the advanced science fiction and fantasy group Clockhouse London Writers http://clockhouselondonwriters.wordpress.com/ Recent publications include stories in the anthologies *Once Upon A Parsec* (NewCon Press) and *The Thread of the Infinite* (Snow Books). Moonfarers are pointed towards Allen's anthology *The Once and Future Moon* (Eibonvale Press) http://www.eibonvalepress.co.uk/books/books_Futuremoon.htm

FRANK COFFMAN

Frank Coffman is a retired college English and Creative Writing professor. He has published poetry and fiction in various magazines and anthologies. His poetry collections include *The Coven's Hornbook & Other Poems*, *Black Flames & Gleaming Shadows*, and *Khayyám's Rubáiyát*.

RAY DALEY

Bio:- Ray Daley was born in Coventry & still lives there. He served 6 yrs in the RAF as a clerk & spent most of his time in a Hobbit hole in High Wycombe. He is a published poet & has been writing stories since he was 10. His current dream is to eventually finish the Hitch Hikers fanfic novel he's been writing since 1986.
https://raymondwriteswrongs.wordpress.com/

SARAH DOYLE

Sarah Doyle is the Pre-Raphaelite Society's Poet-in-Residence, and co-author of *Dreaming Spheres: Poems of the Solar System* (PS Publishing, 2014). She is widely placed and published, winning the Wolverhampton Literature Festival (WoLF) poetry competition and Holland Park Press's Brexit in Poetry 2019, and being runner-up in the Keats-Shelley Poetry Prize 2019. She was highly commended in the Ginkgo Prize for Ecopoetry and in the Forward Prizes for Poetry 2018. Sarah is co-editor of *Humanagerie*, a 2018 anthology from Eibonvale Press, which was shortlisted for a British Fantasy Award. She holds an MA in Creative Writing from Royal Holloway College, University of London, and is currently researching a PhD in meteorological poetry at Birmingham City University. Sarah tweets as @PoetSarahDoyle and her website can be found at sarahdoyle.co.uk.

SOPHIE ESSEX

Sophie Essex is a softcore bunny, poet, and editor. Her work currently focuses on correlations between sex and power dynamics in insects mapped onto the human condition. Published works include her pamphlet, *Objects of Desire* (2015, Pyramid Editions) and the collection *Some Pink Star* (2019, Eibonvale Press) in addition to several magazine appearances. She also runs Salò Press together with a monthly open-mic poetry night, Volta.

BRYN FORTEY

Bryn Fortey is a veteran writer from South Wales whose short stories and poetry has been well published over the years. The Alchemy Press has published two collections of his work: *Merry-Go-Round* (2014) and *Compromising the Truth* (2018).

S GEPP

S.Gepp is an Australian who has been writing for a number of years in the horror, fantasy, sci-fi and humour genres. Tertiary educated, former acrobat and professional wrestler, a father of two and well past 40 years old, with more than 100 writing credits to his name, he hopes to be a real writer when he grows up.

TERRY GRIMWOOD

College lecturer, actor (ham), occasional Director (drama queen), harmonica player and writer, Terry Grimwood is the proud owner of the**EXAGGERATED**press and author of a number of novels, novella, plays and short fiction. He is also co-author of a series of engineering text books for Pearson Educational Press. His latest novella, *Joe*, is available from Demain press and his collection *There Is A Way To Live Forever* from Black Shuck.

RUSSELL HEMMELL

Russell Hemmell is a statistician and social scientist from the U.K, passionate about astrophysics and speculative fiction. Recent publications in *Aurealis*, *New Myths*, *The Grievous Angel*, and others. Find her online at her blog earthianhivemind.net and on Twitter @SPBianchini."

TIM JEFFREYS

I am UK-based and write mainly speculative fiction. My short stories have been published in various anthologies and magazines including *Nightscript*, *Weirdbook* and *Sanitarium Magazine.*

AHMED A KHAN

I am a Canadian writer, originally from India. My works have appeared in various venues like *Boston Review*, *Murderous Intent*, *Plan-B*, *Strange Horizons*, *Interzone*, *Anotherealm*, *Riddled With Arrows*. My stories have been translated into German, Finnish, Greek, Croatian and Urdu. I have social media presence at twitter.com/ahmedakhan and www.facebook.com/ahmed.a.khan.140.

TIM NICKELS

Full-time reader and part-time writer, Tim lives and works in Dorset.

DAVID RIX

David Rix is an author, editor and artist from London's East End, where the canals, railways and wild areas of street art and alt culture have been a major inspiration. His published books include the novelettes *A Suite in Four Windows* and *Brown is the New Black*, the novella/story collection *Feather*, which was shortlisted for the Edge Hill prize, and the novel *A Blast of Hunters*. He also runs Eibonvale Press, which focuses on unusual new writing in the area of Slipstream, Speculative Fiction and Horror. He has been designing the covers of Eibonvale Press books since the press was founded in 2004.

DOUGLAS SMITH

Douglas Smith **is** a multi-award-winning Canadian author described by Library Journal as "one of Canada's most original writers of speculative fiction." His fiction has been published in twenty-six languages and thirty-four countries, including *Amazing Stories*, *InterZone*, *Weird Tales*, *Baen's Universe*, *On Spec*, and *Cicada*. His books include the novel *The Wolf at the End of the World*, the collections *Chimerascope* and *Impossibilia*, and the writer's guide *Playing the Short Game: How to Market & Sell Short Fiction*. Doug is a three-time winner of Canada's Aurora Award and has been a finalist for the John W. Campbell Award, CBC's Bookies Award, Canada's juried Sunburst Award, and France's juried Prix Masterton and Prix Bob Morane. His website is: www.smithwriter.com and he tweets at twitter.com/smithwritr

J. J. STEINFELD

Canadian fiction writer, poet, and playwright J. J. Steinfeld lives on Prince Edward Island, where he is patiently waiting for Godot's arrival and a phone call from Kafka. While waiting, he has published 19 books, including *Would You Hide Me?* (Stories, Gaspereau Press, 2003), *Identity Dreams and Memory Sounds* (Poetry, Ekstasis Editions, 2014), *Madhouses in Heaven, Castles in Hell* (Stories, Ekstasis Editions, 2015), *An Unauthorized Biography of Being* (Stories, Ekstasis Editions, 2016), *Absurdity, Woe Is Me, Glory Be* (Poetry, Guernica Editions, 2017), and *A Visit to the Kafka Café* (Poetry, Ekstasis Editions, 2018). His short stories and poems have appeared in numerous anthologies and periodicals internationally, and over 50 of his one-act plays and a handful of full-length plays have been performed in North America.

MARK TOWSE

Mark Towse is an Englishman living in Australia. He would sell his soul to the devil or anyone buying if it meant he could write full-time. Alas, he left it very late to begin this journey, penning his first story since primary school at the ripe old age of 45. When he isn't writing, Mark can normally be heard mumbling maniacally to himself in various locations of the house, trying desperately to avoid DIY and gardening jobs. All Things That Matter Press has just released his first collection of horror, *Face The Music* - available via Amazon, Barnes & Noble, Dymocks, etc.

Other books from
theEXAGGERATEDpress

DARK BATTLEFIELDS ed Terry Grimwood
THE DARK HEART OF PEEPING TOM ed Terry Grimwood
THE EXAGGERATED MAN by Terry Grimwood
THE MONSTER BOOK FOR GIRLS ed Terry Grimwood
OPEN WATERS by David Gullen
SLOW MOTION WARS by Andrew Hook and Allen Ashley
THE JUST NOT SO STORIES by Rhys Hughes
BUSY BLOOD by Stuart Hughes and D. F. Lewis
DREAM CITY BLUES ed Mark Howard Jones
BROWN IS THE NEW BLACK by David Rix
APOIDEA by Douglas Thompson
THE SLEEP CORPORATION by Douglas Thompson
THE TERROR AND THE TORTOISESHELL by John Travis
THE MAGONIA STONE by Markus Wolfson

https://exaggeratedpress.weebly.com/

Wordland 1: Twilight
Wordand 2: Hi Honey, I'm Home
Wordand 3: What They Saw in the Sky
Wordland 4: Whited Sepulchres
Wordland 5: True Love
Wordland 6: Black is the New Black
Wordland 7: Mountebanks

https://wordlandhome.weebly.com/index.html

Lightning Source UK Ltd.
Milton Keynes UK
UKHW022257080321
380016UK00006B/1267